Out of the Silence

A Dramatic Retelling of the First Christmas

God is with us!

Patti Hill

Out of the Silence

A Dramatic Retelling of the First Christmas

PATTI HILL

A 25-Day Advent Reader

GARDEN WALL PRESS
COLORADO

Out of the Silence

Cover Design/Photography: Rebecca McKenna
Images: View of Bethlehem (chromolitho), Philip Richard Morris (1838-1902)
        Bridgeman Art Library
Interior Design: Sharon K. Souza

ISBN:

This book is a work of fiction, except when it is not. Scripture is quoted as being spoken by the characters. All other dialogue is a product of the author's imagination. The timeline and events of the Christmas story as reported in the Gospels of Matthew and Luke has been followed with only minor adjustments for clarity. Extrabiblical characters are also a product of the author's imagination.

To my family—
by blood and marriage,
near and too, too far away.
I love you!

Table of Contents

Introduction

Long before there was such a thing as a Bible, the eyewitness accounts of Jesus' life, death, and resurrection ignited faith. The stories were told and retold in all of the known world, reaching Rome within ten years of Jesus' death and resurrection and thereby disturbing the workings of the empire.

Around 60 to 80 AD, Matthew and Luke noticed the eyewitnesses to Jesus' life weren't getting any younger. Perhaps they feared the story—and the hope the story inspired—would perish when the eyewitnesses died. And so they penned the stories of Jesus' life in two documents referred to as *The Gospel of Matthew* and *The Gospel of Luke*.

Luke was not one of the twelve apostles, but he became a believer in Jesus through the eyewitness testimony of Paul, a man who went from Christian-slayer to church-builder after his encounter with the risen Jesus. By the time Luke wrote his account, Paul had paid dearly for his switch in allegiance by being flogged and stoned. Maybe Luke saw the frailty of his mentor and decided the time had come to record what Paul and the others had seen. It's likely that Luke interviewed an aged Mary for the Christmas portion of his gospel, since so much of the story is told from her point of view.

Matthew was a despised tax collector and collaborator with the Romans. Nevertheless, Jesus remarkably invited him to follow along as one of the original twelve eyewitnesses. Surely Matthew felt the gathering of years in his bones and saw a need to record what he'd seen before he died. He wrote with care about Jesus' birth to help his fellow Jews see that Jesus' family tree and fulfilled prophecies qualified him to be the Messiah. In the end, the time and care Luke and Matthew put into their stories is why we stop to celebrate Jesus' entrance into humanity every year at Christmas.

When Luke and Matthew sat down to write, they wrote without worrying if their readers understood the nuances of Hebrew culture, whether they were familiar with the political turmoil under which Israel lived with the Romans, or if they knew the geography of Palestine. Because of this, Matthew's and Luke's accounts leave out details that would bring the story into sharper focus for modern readers. Not because they were careless with those important points, but because in their minds:

It went without saying the Jews had been waiting for God to speak after 400 long years. *It went without saying* what it meant to be betrothed. *It went without saying* Joseph had to quietly divorce Mary when they had never lived together. And *it went without saying* why a baby would be laid in a manger, or why Magi from another country would be drawn to worship the newborn king of the Jews.

My hope and purpose in writing *Out of the Silence* is to transport 21st century readers back to the very first Christmas, which actually happened over the course of three years, from Elizabeth's surprising pregnancy to the visit from the Magi. To the best of my abilities, I have included those things that *went without saying* in Luke's and Matthew's accounts, not because the authors did a half-hearted job, but because they could not have fathomed readers separated from their stories by twenty centuries.

I should warn you that *Out of the Silence* may challenge some of your long-held ideas about the Christmas story. The story has been embellished over the centuries, and those adornments have become accepted facts.

The story of the Magi is a good example. The account in the *Gospel of Matthew* never mentions camels, or the number of Magi, or that the wise men came from three different countries, nor are we given their names. These details were added much later, not to the official text but in extrabiblical texts.

You should also know that worthy scholars differ on the details of the Christmas story. For instance, some say the Magi were Persian, and some argue convincingly they were Nabataeans. Some believe the shepherds were of a special Levitical order that supplied lambs for temple sacrifices, meaning these men were highly honored. Others believe quite the opposite. The shepherd's occupation set them apart as they were seen as less pious and certainly less clean. I came across these differing opinions at almost every step through the story. When a decision had to be made about who to believe, I embraced what seemed most plausible. Having said that, I'm fallible. And this *is* historical fiction.

The danger writers of historical fiction face is trying to pack too much of their research into the story. Then the reader feels like they're sitting in a lecture hall rather than reading something for pleasure. I apologize ahead of time if I've done that. To help me wield a disciplined pen, I've included chapter notes to define terms, add more insight, or plead my case for including one thing or another. You can enjoy *Out of the Silence* without reading the chapter notes, but they're at the back of the book in case your curiosity wakes you in the middle of the night.

The story of Jesus' birth is a Jewish story, lived by people who practiced their faith in the Promised Land, Israel. They took the Law—the rules given by God through Moses—very seriously, and that dedication showed in how they lived. For instance, the Sabbath was set aside as a holy day of rest, and no one worked that day, not even donkeys. Also, the faithful traveled to the temple for three feasts a year, some walking over a hundred miles each way. Their Jewishness wasn't something they wore casually. That's why I've used the Hebrew names of all of the familiar characters of the first Christmas. Mary is Miryam; Joseph is Yosef; Jesus is Yeshua, and so on. My hope is that using their Hebrew names will give them a fresh start in your imaginations. If you have a question about who's who, there is a glossary of Hebrew names in the back of the book.

Rules, of course, were made to be broken. I let the Old Testament (all those who came before the birth of Christ) keep the Greek form of their names, like Abraham, Isaac, and Jacob. This should lessen your flipping to the glossary quite a bit. If two characters share a name, I reverted back to the Greek form for one character. As a further kindness to my readers, I've left place names as they are found in modern translations of the Bible

How to use this book: Since the very beginning of our lives together, my husband and I have tried to keep the first Christmas central to our celebration of Jesus' birth. We have failed miserably some years and enjoyed a modest success in others. We've especially profited from reading a portion of the Christmas story each day of December. That's why *Out of the Silence* is organized in twenty-four daily readings with a Christmas prayer for day/chapter twenty-five. The story will keep you in the events of the first Christmas all through December. *Out of the Silence* can also be read as a novel anytime of the year. The choice is yours.

My hope for you, my reader, is that experiencing Christmas within the context of culture and history will spark a refreshed or new faith in you. I hope, too, you will see how God partnered with very ordinary people in long-ago Palestine. That collaboration has impacted the course of history and society to the present day. The Father still invites us to join him in reaching the world with His love.

The birth of Jesus is not the headwater of our story with God. We're entering the story downriver, so to speak. Centuries of time have already swept by, but now something new and glorious is about to happen. At this point in the story, God takes the humble form of a babe to grow and walk among the people he created and loved. He crossed the divide between the eternal and the temporal to show us what God is like and to draw us into an everlasting love relationship. Christmas is like our first date with God, full of potential. Enjoy the read.

Chapter One

A Silent World

Elisheba woke with a start. No hint of day brightened the room. All was black. What had woken her?

She listened for the rooster belonging to Azriel the baker. No doubt he had awakened her, yet again. That bird knew nothing of the rhythms of day and night. If the rooster had crowed, he was silent now, but Elisheba was wide awake. To prepare for the coming day, she listed what still needed to be done before Zekharyah left for Jerusalem and his week of duty at the temple.

Her first task was to breathe life into the oven's embers to bake bread. The walk wasn't long to Jerusalem from their village of Ein Karem, only four miles, but Zekharyah walked slower than he used to, and fresh loaves of bread, along with some goat cheese and figs, would give him the energy for the last climb into the great city. She would also brew a strong tea of willow bark against the pain in his knees.

Before she rose from the pallet, she reached over to touch Zekharyah, as was her habit over the many years of their marriage, but the linens lay cool under her touch.

She rose quickly, fumbling into her cloak in the darkness, and tiptoed past the sleeping animals, careful not to wake them, for she wasn't ready to answer their boorish demands for breakfast. She rushed into the courtyard, where the moon washed its silvery light over all that awaited her hands—the quern, the water jar, the loom. She had expected to find Zekharyah stoking the embers in the oven, but only the hens roosted nearby.

Her gaze rose to the roof. He had not troubled those stairs for many months, such was the aching of his joints. She gathered the hem of her tunic and climbed. When her vision adjusted to the darkness, she found Zekharyah wrapped in a linen cloak against the refreshing coolness of the summer morning, looking toward Jerusalem. Always looking toward Jerusalem.

She whispered a silent prayer of gratitude. "What troubles you, my love?"

He started at the sound of her voice, but he opened his arms to her. "Must a man be troubled to rise before dawn and take in the great expanse of HaShem's heaven?"

She leaned into his chest. "Perhaps not any other man I might name. But this man, this man whom I have slept beside for more than forty years prefers a warm pallet above all else, even HaShem's heaven. So tell me, my love, what troubles you? Is it the journey? Are your knees hurting you?"

He kissed her forehead and sat on the parapet, drawing her to sit with him. "The journey is not as easy as it used to be, that is true. But I travel with HaShem and with men I have known all my life. What robber would be foolish enough to come against fifty priests? And if my knees finally fail me, I will be surrounded by all the help I would need. That young Eitan is an ox."

She would not let him distract her. "You've heard, then, of unrest in the city?"

"No more than usual, not like feast days when Herod fills the streets with his army and wonders why the people pick fights. I don't expect trouble like that, not with his army back in Caesarea."

"The benediction then? My words, too, hide from me these days. Do you worry you will forget the blessing?"

"Woman, *you* are forgetting I am only a humble servant. It is Kayafa who burns the incense. It is his honor to send the people's prayers to Adonai, not mine, and then to pray the benediction."

"He is often—" Elisheba paused to measure her words. "He is often indisposed, is he not? You have told me. And so, you must be ready, Zekharyah. The lot could fall to you, as it surely must. And then the highest honor will be yours. You will stand alone in the Holy Place. You alone will watch as the prayers of the people rise to Adonai. You alone will stand before the people and proclaim the benediction."

"It is as you say, but you can put your worries to rest." He tapped his temples. "The words are etched inside my skull. Along with my father and his father before him, I have rehearsed the words of blessing until they come as naturally as breathing. I might forget my name, but I will never forget the benediction."

Elisheba rose, put her hands to Zekharyah's shoulders, still erect and purposeful. "I will pray for you as I always do, Zekharyah. HaShem is faithful. Whatever called you to leave the pallet and climb up those stairs is not too big for Adonai's capable hands. Now, if I don't get to the business of baking bread, you will be very hungry by the time you enter the city gates."

〜

ELISHEBA DISAPPEARED NOISELESSLY DOWN the stairs. Before Zekharyah could return to his thoughts, she reappeared, her face shaded from the moon's light by the awning. "My love, if you should—beyond all odds—find yourself alone in the Holy Place, would you…? Or rather, could you? What I mean to ask is this: Would it be allowable, prudent and within the order of what is right, to pray…?"

How many times had he prayed for a son? Was the first time at their betrothal? He had watched and waited for what seemed like an eternity for Elisheba to drink the covenantal cup. Did he pray as he waited? When she met his eyes after she drank? When had he last prayed for a son? Had a day ever gone by when he hadn't breathed a prayer to Adonai for an heir? No. There had never been a day like that.

"If I am chosen to burn the incense, I will pray as you desire, my love."

"Perhaps I'm being crazy, but what is faith if not to hope for what is good from Adonai's hand and that which will glorify him? After all, he touched Sarah, and she was well past the age for bearing babies, as I am. And there is Hannah and, of course, Rachel. It's not as if we are asking for something that has never happened before. HaShem rewards our faith, does he not?"

"As you say, HaShem is faithful."

Elisheba touched her fingers to her lips and descended the stairs.

Zekharyah would never understand why a godly woman like Elisheba was left to carry the shame of barrenness. She'd borne the taunts of women—those with clutches of children at their heels—who played at guessing Elisheba's secret sin, the very sin that had closed her womb. There was no such sin and no curse on Elisheba. There was not a woman in all of Israel who loved or served Adonai more righteously than she. Not one. With all that pressed at Zekharyah, the least of his worries and the source of his greatest joy, was Elisheba. Yes, he would pray as she desired. He would pray for a son, although his faith could not rival hers.

He drew his cloak tighter and sat back to wait for the day. Elisheba should not have been surprised to find him stewing over what lay ahead. Of late, the days leading up to his service set his heart to a consuming longing and a crushing grief. He worked at hiding his darkened mood, but such subterfuge proved impossible with her. He would try harder.

Just then a cock crowed. Zekharyah looked to the east. Indeed, the sky had brightened to sapphire at the horizon. Soon, his Abijah brothers would gather at the well for the trek to Jerusalem and the week of service ahead.

But to what end? Faithfulness beyond a few stalwarts was tough to find, even among his brother priests. Some performed their duties, but only with a begrudging sense of duty and a great deal of grumbling. And who could blame them? A steady stream of oppressors had prospered at the expense of Israel, and evil had not been brought to justice.

The same old questions pummeled him: *Have you finally abandoned us, Lord? Are we cast adrift? Do you wash your hands of us?*

At the temple. In the market. Around the well. The people sounded like the malcontents at the time of Malachi. When the prophet laid down his pen, heaven went silent. Surely, the time had long passed for the proud to enter the oven of the Lord to be burned to stubble. Surely, the time was now for the Sun of Righteousness to bring healing on his wings.

After all this, LORD, must you still refuse to help us? Will you continue to be silent and punish us?[1]

Only the grueling fulfillment of Daniel's prophecies had filled the years of Adonai's silence. First Babylon and then the Medes and Persians, until King Cyrus released Adonai's people to Jerusalem to rebuild the temple. The nation escaped the savage advance of Alexander the Great—the goat

---

[1] Isaiah 64:12 (NLT).

from the west—but only until his successors in Syria and Egypt made Palestine a meat grinder of conflict. And worse, the Greeks tainted Hebrew tradition and drew many from the might of Adonai.

And now the Romans. What began as an alliance, an answer to a call for help against the relentless press of Syria, led to yet another abomination. The security of Jerusalem was sold to Rome. And now a descendant of Esau, an Edomite, sat as king over Judea. Herod. A man of unquenchable bloodthirst and ambition.

And all through this, Adonai was silent. No prophet was sent. Never had his voice been more desired or needed.

The sun punched the sky, and fingers of light reached toward Jerusalem. Zekharyah turned toward the temple and prayed, "Hear, O Israel: The Lord our God, the Lord is one."[2]

Zekharyah's sorrow caught in his throat. The air stirred, and the richness of Elisheba's garden scented the air with life. Her song reached him, the one she sang as she kneaded the dough. But it was an owl's call from the nearby olive grove that matched his despair and longing.

"Hear, O Israel: The Lord our God, the Lord is one," he started again. "God of Abraham, Isaac, and Jacob, hear my prayer. I speak to you plainly as a man weighted by the sorrow of your people and by the shame that has imprisoned many in apostasy. We are faint with longing to be your people in our own land. We have shared your bounty for too long."

Zekharyah rose but stopped at the top of the stairs to look heavenward. "We have no hope but you. Do not forget us. Do not disinherit us. We are your prized possession, as you said through your prophet Malachi. No one can reclaim Israel but the One, the Messiah."

His prayer troubled him, and his throat closed around what words remained in him. And yet, his pining also reminded him of King David's prayers. The king spoke to Adonai with uncompromised honesty and desire. Shouldn't he do the same?

He started down the stairs. "I will remember the Laws of Moses. They are written on my heart. I meditate on them day and night. And as David prayed, 'Remember your word to your servant, for you have given me hope.' Forgive my impertinence, Lord, but it is a terrible thing to live without the sound of your voice washing over us."

---

[2] Deuteronomy 6:4 (NIV).

Elisheba held his pack out to him, and he threaded his arms through the straps. Forehead to forehead, they exchanged a silent farewell.

As Zekharyah neared the well, he paused at the sound of the voices of his Abijah brothers, laughing and talking. He closed his eyes. "Finally, Lord, I ask this of you: Remember your promise through Malachi and send Elijah the prophet back to us. We will listen. I will listen. And we will follow. Out of your great mercy, fill the silence with your message—if it be wrath or love. We cannot bear the silence for one more day. Lord have mercy. Your servant grows faint."

Chapter Two

In the Temple

Zekharyah rolled his shoulders against the knot tightening in his back. The day had started twelve hours earlier at cock crow, when he and a number of his priestly brothers inspected every corner and rafter of the temple by torchlight, purified themselves in the bracing waters of the *mikveh*, and donned their white linen robes. By the third hour when the gates were opened for the faithful to worship, all was pure and in order.

That afternoon, he stood among his Abijah brothers in the Chamber of Hewn Stones, where they had gathered for the last drawing of lots for the day. He couldn't help but turn his thoughts to the journey home in a few days. Elisheba would bake a sweet morsel of honey and grain that she milled as fine as powder. Zekharyah's stomach gurgled in anticipation.

The eager faces of his younger priest brothers surrounded him. A lifetime of chances lay before them to draw the lot to burn the incense. On the other hand, the possibility he would stand in that great chamber the next spring for *Purim* was in doubt. He was getting older. Perhaps this was his last day of service in the temple. His eyes stung with tears, even as his knees ached from all the standing.

Zekharyah dipped his head in shame. Ambition had no place in temple service. The honor alone was to be born of Aaron and to serve Adonai and his people. *Forgive me, Lord.*

The High Priest led the men in prayer and pronounced Adonai's blessing. Zekharyah stood with those who had never burned the incense—some with lush, dark beards of youth and some with a cascade of gray flowing over their chests. Only these untried priests were eligible for the honor. The High Priest offered the urn of lots, and each man thrust his hand in to grab a stone.

Lord, your will be done. May the man with the purest heart send the prayers of our people to your throne this day.

Without looking to see what he drew, Zekharyah held the stone in his fist over his heart. *I am not worthy, Lord, and I know it.* Baruch, his wife's nephew, nudged Zekharyah, who then opened his hand. The white stone.

His pulse pounded and his throat felt like sand. He longed to tell Elisheba that he would pray in the Holy Place for a son, but a woman would never be found in the Chamber of Hewn Stones. Still, there was no one he would rather share the moment with. He would burn the incense that very day and step as near to the presence of Adonai as he had ever been or ever would be, this side of heaven.

The priests who had drawn lots to be Zekharyah's assistants gathered around. Baruch lifted his chin to him as he withdrew and turned to walk away. Zekharyah mustered his racing thoughts and squared his shoulders. He led his assistants from the chamber into the Court of the Priests.

The prayers of the people, a chorus of men from the colonnade, and the lilting yet anguished prayers of the women, filled the air. His heart hitched for missing Elisheba, but only for a moment, for one of his assistants climbed the ramp of the sacrificial altar and gathered embers into the golden vessel. Another spooned the sacred incense into the golden censer. The time had come to enter the Holy Place, the anteroom of the Holy of Holies.

Zekharyah led his assistants up the steps of the portico. Two strapping Levites opened the doors, and he stepped in. He had been in the great chamber before as an assistant many years earlier. Still, the room with its massive gilt walls, nearly forty cubits high, overwhelmed him. The priests' steps echoed in the immense space.

Before him, the great curtain shielded the Holy of Holies—the very place where Adonai dwelt—and towered over him. Cords of purple, scarlet, blue, and fine white linen reflected all that the universe held—fire, earth, sky, and sea—all originating from the imagination of Adonai. He felt dwarfed by its beauty and repulsed by his own unworthiness. Zekharyah jumped at the sound of the *magrefah's* bold reverberations. Its deep tone announced to the people outside that the incense was about to be offered.

Zekharyah glanced over his shoulder to the still-opened doors. The Levitical choir and orchestra gathered on the steps beyond. When the incense had been burned, they would sing their hallelujahs and psalms.

He turned back to his task and walked solemnly between the golden lampstand and the table of bread, straight to the altar of incense. As he'd been instructed, he stopped just before the altar, only feet from the curtain. One assistant carefully placed the embers on the altar. Zekharyah surreptitiously wiped his palms upon his robe before taking the censer of incense from another assistant.

As he stepped closer to the altar, his brother priests bowed low and backed out of the Holy Place. When the doors closed behind him, all was silent. The worshippers in the outer courts had ceased their praying and prostrated themselves. They waited for the smoke to rise. Only then would they know that an angel had carried their prayers to the throne of Adonai.

Zekharyah spooned the incense over the glowing embers. The oils from the spices ignited briefly and then a thin column of smoke rose toward the ceiling. An uncommon sweetness filled the space, nearly masking a bitterness that lingered beneath. His people prayed for the sweet—provision, babies, marriages—and they prayed against the bitter, to be rid of the Romans. Zekharyah shuddered, knowing that doing so meant praying their sons toward an untimely death.

A movement caught his eye. To the right of the altar, a shimmer swirled the colors of the curtain. He rubbed his eyes, but the distortion grew and reflected light like the surface of water. His heart pounded behind his ribs. He thought to leave, but his feet would not move.

The shimmer expanded to a white as brilliant as clouds that held no rain. Within the whiteness, a form took shape, although he could still see the texture of the curtain behind. A shape of a man draped in fine cloth grew more and more distinct and ever brighter.

Zekharyah's knees buckled, and he fell to the floor. He buried his head in his arms against the light. But even with his eyes closed tight, the light burned red through his eyelids. When he chanced a look, the form was now as substantial as any man, yet he stood taller than anyone he knew. The being's hair shone like brass. His eyes glistened with such colors that rivaled the flowers in Elisheba's garden. His voice plowed a channel through Zekharyah's soul.

"Do not be afraid, Zekharyah. Your prayer has been heard. Your wife Elisheba will have a child. It will be a boy, and you must call him Yohanan."[3]

A son born to us? How can that be?

"He will be a joy and delight to you. His birth will make many people very glad. He will be important in the sight of Adonai. He must never drink wine or other such drinks."

No wine? A Levite then? But he will be a descendent of Aaron. Why won't he—

"He will be filled with the Holy Spirit even before he is born. He will bring back many of the people of Israel to Adonai their God."

But only prophets are filled with the Holy Spirit. This is impossible.

"And he will prepare the way for the Lord. He will have the same spirit and power that Elijah had."

The same spirit? Elijah? The man speaks in riddles!

"He will bring peace between parents and their children. He will teach people who don't obey to be wise and do what is right. In this way, he will prepare a people who are ready for the Lord."

Zekharyah felt his head for lumps. Surely he had fallen and knocked himself senseless. And yet, the man stood there, not diminished of even an ounce of glory by his crazy pronouncement. Zekharyah thought of Elisheba. How could he raise her hopes with such a message, and yet, how could he not tell her?

Zekharyah rose, planted his feet. "How can I be sure of this? I am an old man, and my wife is old—"

"I am Gavri'el."

Gavri'el? Daniel's Gavri'el? An angel of the Lord before me? Not likely.

Gavri'el paused ever so slightly, peering at Zekharyah, his arms crossed, his face grim. His displeasure sat heavily on Zekharyah.

"I serve Adonai," the angel continued. "I have been sent to speak to you and to tell you this good news. And now you will have to be silent. You will not be able to speak until after Yohanan is born because you did not believe my words. They will come true at the time Adonai has chosen."

---

[3] Luke 1:13 and continuing through Luke 1:20 as part of the dialogue between Gavri'el and Zekharyah. *Elisheba* substituted for "Elizabeth." *Yohanan* substituted for "John." *Adonai* substituted for "Lord" and "God." (NIV).

As the being had appeared, he receded to startling white and then to a mere smudge of iridescent light. Zekharyah watched the spot until the fibers of the curtain no longer danced. Worried whispers reached him from the other side of the door. He wiped the sweat from his brow and straightened his robe.

What just happened?

Never in all of the years of temple service had such a visitation taken place. But there was no more appropriate place for such an announcement. His heart fluttered in his chest, and he whispered into the vastness, tears soaked his beard. The surety of what he'd seen gripped him.

The Messiah is coming. Very soon. And my son—my son, Yohanan—will prepare the way for him, just as Malachi prophesied.

Zekharyah gathered the hem of his robe and ran for the doors. The afternoon sun paled in comparison to the angel's brightness, but still he winced at the pain of it.

The High Priest strode toward him, concern and agitation creasing his face. "Has the incense been burned in good order?"

Zekharyah marveled that the priest could be concerned about such a triviality. The Messiah, ushered into their lives by his own yet-to-be-born son, was coming very soon. He opened his mouth to tell him so, but no words came.

He swallowed and tried again. Nothing.

A murmur filled the outer court as the people inched forward. Zekharyah pulled at his beard. He gestured toward the doors, tried to imitate the strong stance and presence of Gavri´el in the Holy Place. He motioned with his hands that talking had taken place inside, and that something monumental and glorious was about to happen in their midst, but the priest and the people stared blankly at him.

Finally, the High Priest asked him, "Zekharyah, did you see something in there?"

Zekharyah nodded.

The High Priest's face paled. "Did…did you see a vision?"

Had Zekharyah seen a vision? Had he seen with his eyes or with something else. His spirit? Either way, Gavri´el had stood before him. And he pronounced the most joyous bit of news he'd ever heard: Adonai had heard his prayers. All of them.

Chapter Three

A Betrothal

*M*iryam tucked a loose curl into her braid and wiped the sweat from her forehead. She bent to pluck the weeds around the cucumber and melon plants that grew in the spring garden. Her mother relied on her to do the weeding, as Miryam was careful to only pick the thistles and not the young plants.

Miryam found the job pleasant. Her younger brothers left her alone in the garden, for fear they would be asked to do women's work. And her younger sisters napped in the shade of the fig tree while her mother worked at grinding the grain.

Miryam prayed as she worked, for the garden stirred hope in her. The plants—growing even through the nights—reflected Adonai's promise to sustain and provide. The tender vines thrived even in the harshest of winds and sun. When she reached the end of the row, she would relieve her mother at the quern. And then the two women would prepare the evening meal. Such was the rhythm of Miryam's day.

Her brothers disturbed the stillness long before they reached the yard with shouts of her name. They had begged Ima to let them go into the village of Nazareth, where they'd promised to consult the rabbi about a passage of Torah they were memorizing. There wasn't much else to attract young boys to the village, but Miryam traveled to the well to collect water morning and evening. What mischief had the boys found there, and what did they expect her to do about it?

Miryam stood and pressed a fist to her aching back as her brothers rounded the corner of the house, their faces flushed with exertion. She flung her basket of thistles onto a heap beside the cooking pit. She would use the dried stems for kindling in the morning.

"Miryam," Binyamin said, gasping, his hands to his knees.

She looked to Hevel, the youngest brother, so solemn and wise for his tender years. "Have you gotten yourselves into trouble again?"

"No, Miryam, we've been to the city gate."

She turned to Binyamin. "Aren't you supposed to be practicing your Torah recitations? You are the elder brother. How will Hevel learn, if not for you?"

Binyamin squared his shoulders. He didn't like being scolded by his sister, not even his older sister. "Miryam," he said, conveying with her name the importance of his news.

She hung her basket on the trellis and turned back to him. "I'm listening."

Binyamin's eyes glinted with mischief.

Miryam threw up her hands. "What is it? I still have grinding to do, and Ima expects help with the evening meal. Spit it out."

Binyamin feigned nonchalance. "You have seen that Yaakov's son Yosef has set a foundation next to the family's house? And since he is the third son, he must carve a place for the house out of the rock. It's really small, the courtyard is hardly worth mentioning."

"This is not news, Binyamin. I walk by his work every day on the way to the well. And I will tell you that the work is very slow indeed." Miryam had also noticed that while the house was going to be small, the foundation stones had been laid with precision, and Yosef had eked out space for the house by carving into a rock overhang rather than building around it. What she found most pleasing was that the door opened to the south. The winter sun would find its way in to warm the house. She'd spent many a quiet moment wondering for whom Yosef built such a carefully planned house.

"I believe that very, very soon, Yosef will start to work more earnestly on the house," Binyamin said.

"And now Yosef is confiding his plans to the likes of you, brother?"

"If you don't want to know what we saw and heard, that's nothing to me." He pulled at his brother's arm. "Come on, Hevel. Let's go sit in the shade. Sister does not want to hear what we have seen."

Hevel pulled away from his brother and clung to Miryam's waist. She wove her fingers into his hair and felt his breath through her tunic. Such an irresistible lamb. "Miryam," Hevel said, "we saw Abba talking to Yaakov and Yosef at the city gate."

Nazareth was small. Everyone knew everyone. Yosef was no stranger to Miryam, although they had never spoken. She saw him at synagogue. He spoke head-to-head with the visiting rabbis, rubbing his beard and nodding earnestly. She watched as he walked with his father and brothers past their house to Sepphoris, where the men worked to rebuild the city. When they reentered the village at dusk, the father and brothers walked with heavy steps, but Yosef looked as though he had another job waiting for him, and he didn't want to be late.

Yosef?

Miryam looked to Binyamin to verify Hevel's words. "This is true?"

"They've been meeting—"

"They've been meeting? And you are only now telling me?"

Miryam found her mother just as she expected, spinning the quern and singing a lullaby to her sleeping sisters. Her *savta* and *dodah,* her grandmother and aunt, sat shelling almonds. Savta looked especially smug. Did everyone but her know about Abba's talks with Yosef's father?

"Ima!" she said in complaint.

Her mother put a finger to her lips. "Are you done in the garden?"

"Yes, Ima, but there's something—"

"Did you hoe the furrows? If it rains—"

"Ima, please, Binyamin just told me that Abba has been talking to Yaakov and Yosef, at the gate, many times."

A small smile lit Ima's face. "It is as you say. Your father has spent many hours at the city gate, talking to Yaakov, hearing Yosef's plans for the future."

A movement in the lane caught Miryam's eye. Her father returned, and when his eye met hers, his grin stretched across his face. Miryam knew this day was coming, the day her father would welcome a groom's bid for her hand. She was old enough. Now in her fourteenth year, older than some brides, younger than others. She'd prepared all her life, learning to tend a household from Ima, although her weaving was still unfit for anything but rags. Her heart leapt in anticipation, but tears stung her eyes at the thought of leaving Abba and Ima. Even the thought of leaving her brothers brought an ache to her chest. Her sisters were aggravation and delight in equal measure, and so very dear. How could she leave any of them?

Abba bowed his head to Ima but came directly to Miryam. "My daughter," he said and swept errant curls back from her face. "Make yourself presentable. We have guests on the way."

Miryam looked at her hands. Dirt caked her fingernails and mud smeared her arms. The hem of her tunic was filthy. "Now?"

"Yes. Be quick."

Miryam obeyed as she had been taught, but she didn't feel ready, not for a husband and the children to follow. She still had so much to learn. She should have paid better attention, asked more questions. And she knew nothing of men.

"Daughter," her father said softly.

When Miryam turned back to him, his eyes glistened with tears, too. "I have lost many nights of sleep over who to accept for you. I worried that Ammiel would come to me about his basket-brained son, Dov. He's big and strong, but not for you, Miryam. And I dodged Ilan for weeks. He came to me in the orchard—at every time of day and night—but I always found a way to put him off before he brought up Noam, a most disagreeable young man. Wholly unsuitable for you, my daughter.

"And then Yaakov came to me about Yosef. A little older but solid as a rock, not born in Nazareth but of the line of David. He's well respected at the synagogue. He listens to the elders and sometimes challenges them with tough questions. He's always thinking. He is careful in all he does to serve HaShem and to keep the commandments. I have questioned him, and he knows of what he speaks.

"And he is a hard worker, a skilled craftsman. Nothing intimidates him. He works wonders with stone and wood. He makes a passable wage, working to rebuild Sepphoris. He has a reputation there for excellence. He will never be out of work, not with his skills. He won't ever be rich, either, but you won't starve. You will have a good future with him, Miryam.

"That's my opinion. Now, you must go and make yourself presentable. He will speak for himself soon enough."

When Miryam returned from washing and changing, her father was welcoming Yaakov into the yard. Yosef stood behind his father, eyes flitting nervously from face to face. He wasn't handsome, but he was tall for a man of Nazareth. Even nervous, he smiled easily at Abba, nodding in agreement with some observation about the pests that nibbled on her father's figs.

As shadows lengthened across the yard, the men and Ima sat around the low table under the trellis. A cool breeze stirred the trees, and bees hummed in and out of the branches of the fig tree overhead.

Miryam gathered five cups onto a tray and ladled wine into a pitcher. With her back to the door, she clasped her hands until they stopped shaking. She prayed, *Lord, help me to know.* Then she carried the tray outside to the table.

The conversation fell silent when she arrived. Her father gestured to the place beside him. Abba said, "Yosef was just going to tell us why he will make you a good husband."

Miryam filled a cup for each person at the table but left hers empty. When she sat, Yosef swallowed and began. "I have trained under my father to work with stone and wood since I was a young boy. I own all of the tools I need to build houses and to create all manner of household items. I have repaired or made yokes for most of the farmers in Nazareth, and my reputation is good among them. Mostly, I spend these days in Sepphoris. This work takes me out of Nazareth, but the work is steady, and should continue for some time." He turned his gaze to Abba. "Sir, I have saved a sum of wealth to offer as *mohar*."

"What about a home for Miryam and for your children?" her father asked.

"Yes, of course, that is an important consideration."

Miryam raised her eyes to meet Yosef's gaze. They were kind, sincere eyes. Not demanding. Not proud. Laugh lines radiated from their corners.

He smiled slightly. "I have laid the first course of stones for a foundation on the side of my father's house."

"I've never seen a truer foundation laid," Yaakov inserted, clearly the proud father. "The size of the house is limited by the rock ledge, but Yosef has used the solid rock to his advantage. The house will be the strongest one built in all of Nazareth. All of this hewing of rock has taken longer, but I have no doubt my son will finish in good time. He's a hard worker, the strongest and smartest of my sons."

"Yes, yes," Abba said. "Let the man talk, Yaakov. He has more to say about himself, I'm sure."

Yosef squirmed, looked to his father and around the table, as if someone should tell him what to say.

"Tell me," Ima said, and every eye turned to the sound of her voice. "Yosef, are you a kind man? A woman is not a man, and it takes time and wisdom for a man and woman to come to an understanding. Miryam is younger, sometimes more connected to heaven than to earth. Are you a man who will be patient with our daughter?"

Yosef caught Miryam's gaze again and held it as he spoke. "Everything that is beautiful and strong requires care. A house cannot be hurried, or the walls will not withstand storms. For a table to be perfectly balanced takes careful measuring and the precise fitting of joints. So it is in marriage, I think, as I have observed between my parents. A man and a woman must craft their lives together with care. My time making things has taught me not to ask a stone to be wood or wood to be stone."

If asked in the future by her children when she first came to love Yosef, she would say this moment, when he answered her mother's question.

"And it is known that you are a faithful servant of HaShem, that you observe the Law and encourage others to do the same. Is that not right, son?" Yaakov prodded.

"Only HaShem knows how much a man loves him, for only HaShem knows a man's heart, but I do desire to please him in all ways. I see that in Miryam, too. She is modest, as a godly woman should be, and I see her helping the poor and attending to the sick. That is what turned my heart to Miryam."

Miryam's cheeks grew hot, and she lowered her eyes to her lap. She hoped Yosef wasn't always so generous with his praise.

The men then discussed the *mohar*. Miryam wished Abba had excused her out of hearing, for such talk embarrassed her. Yosef was, indeed, willing to give a good sum to her father, an amount she knew would come back to her if Yosef could not fulfill his side of the contract. When the men agreed on an amount, her father handed the pitcher of wine to Yosef.

Miryam slid her fingers around her empty cup, knowing that whatever she chose, whether to say yes to Yosef or to turn her cup upside down in refusal, would change the course of her life forever.

The resolve of her heart surprised her. She pushed her cup to Yosef.

He poured the wine, and she put the cup to her lips and drank.

Every face around the table beamed and joined her in taking the wine. Yosef's smile grew so big that she discovered he was missing a molar on one side. But in that moment, his face was the most beautiful thing she had ever seen. Yosef finished his wine and turned his cup upside down on the table. He would drink no more wine until he came for her, in a year, but hopefully sooner.

Yosef unfurled the *ketubah* onto the table. There, for all to see and for her to treasure, were his words of consecration to her and his promise to take care of her. He rose from the table and recited from the prophet Hosea. "I will betroth you to me forever; I will betroth you in righteousness and justice, in love and compassion. I will betroth you in faithfulness, and you will acknowledge the Lord."[4]

Ima unwrapped the veil she'd embroidered for this moment, kissed it, and covered Miryam's hair.

Yosef heaved a sigh of relief. "You are set apart."

---

[4] Hosea 2:19 (NIV).

Chapter Four

A Prayer is Heard

Word of Zekharyah's odd behavior at the temple reached Ein Karem by sundown that day. For three days, the well-meaning and curious made their way to Elisheba's door.

First came Tirtzah, who feigned a mission of support for Elisheba. "Zekharyah is not himself." She leaned in to whisper, perhaps to prevent her servant girl from overhearing. "My son-in-law was at the temple when Zekharyah came stumbling out. He looked drunk, or so he says."

Her husband would never taint his temple service with drunkenness. The Law forbade priests from drinking wine during their times of service. Besides, he would never bring shame on himself and his family.

No, Zekharyah didn't serve drunk. Elisheba could not be tempted to believe otherwise. But what had caused him to stumble? That night, on her pallet, her thoughts wrestled worrisome possibilities. She had seen older people succumb quickly to sicknesses of the mind. At times they could not speak. Sometimes they could not walk or feed themselves. She vowed to meet his every need, no matter how demanding, no matter what the future held.

The next day Rivka came with her daughters and a servant who sat beside the gate with her chin to her chest. Elisheba admired the servant girl's humility in the face of other people's misfortune. On the other hand, Rivka's chin rode high as she affected piety and concern.

"Elisheba, we have no doubt there is a logical explanation for Zekharyah's lapse at the temple. He is known far and wide as a righteous man and good teacher. Certainly there must be a very good reason for him to omit the benediction, the benediction commanded by Moses himself. Perhaps it's time for Zekharyah to serve HaShem here in his home village, where these sorts of slips will not reflect badly on all of the Abijah clan."

When Rivka rose to leave, Elisheba put her hand to the servant girl's shoulder and said, "May the Lord bless you and keep you, child."

Finally, here came Penina with her husband, Natan, who paced the reception room, scowling and grumbling. Doubtless, he resented the time away from his field of lentils. Elisheba took a tray of figs and cheese from her serving girl to offer the couple. Natan filled his hands with treats but refused the cushions Elisheba offered.

He gestured his wife forward. "Speak your peace, Penina. We don't have all day."

Penina frowned. "Elisheba, the rumors from Jerusalem have reached us, even outside the village as we are. I thought you should know we are here to help in any way you need. The days ahead will be difficult. You must let us help you."

Elisheba wasn't sure what rumors Penina had heard or what sort of help she was expected to need, and she wouldn't ask for a clarification to give them credence. "Thank you. You are most kind. I will relay your offer to Zekharyah when he arrives home tomorrow."

A worried look passed between the husband and wife.

Elisheba added quickly, "But I'm sure we won't need any help. We are quite well situated. My nephew is attentive to our needs."

When word finally came that the Abijah priests had reached the outskirts of the village, Elisheba whispered a prayer of thanksgiving and sent the serving girl to the market with a long list. She didn't want to share this homecoming with prying eyes or curious ears who might take their private lives into the village. She splashed water on her face to wash away signs of worry and fatigue. Then she waited.

Zekharyah ambled into the courtyard, favoring his better knee and casting his gaze about for Elisheba. She stepped out of the shadows and into his arms. He didn't speak, but he held her and wept.

Finally, she held his face in her hands. His eyes shone brightly. His smile—she had never seen him smile so. He wasn't a gruff or disagreeable man, but this was the smile of a man who had found an unexpected treasure, not a man steeped in shame.

"Husband, I have been so worried. You must come inside, sit and drink the willow tea I've made for you. I will rub your knees with the balm that has helped before."

He didn't speak but held up his palms, to ask for patience, she surmised. He stepped away and headed for the gate. There, he gestured again, and Baruch joined them in the courtyard.

Her nephew greeted her with a kiss to her cheek.

"Shouldn't you be home with your wife and children?" she asked.

He shrugged. "I think Zekharyah is worried that you may have heard some fantastical stories in his absence, and he wants me to tell you what truly happened."

Elisheba looked back to Zekharyah. What she'd heard from the gossips was true, her husband could not speak for himself. Zekharyah clasped her hands and nodded for Baruch to speak.

Had Zekharyah succumbed to the disease of the aged? Elisheba's stomach tilted and her knees grew weak. Zekharyah caught her with his strong arms and led her to the bench they often shared in the evening.

Zekharyah nodded to Baruch again.

"Zekharyah can't speak to anyone, Elisheba. The reason will become clear when I tell you all that happened in Jerusalem."

"Is he unwell?"

"He walked at the front of the column all the way home."

Zekharyah squeezed her hand as Baruch dug through his satchel for a scroll. "Something extraordinary happened at the temple, Aunt. Zekharyah stood alone in the Holy Place—"

"It's true then?" she asked Zekharyah. "This was your time? You drew the lot?"

He nodded.

She turned to Baruch. "Tell me everything."

Before Baruch read, he explained how Zekharyah had demanded to write down what he'd seen. "You will see why what he wrote caused a stir—to say the least—among the other priests, and especially among the leaders." He cleared his throat and read from the scroll, how Zekharyah had been careful to do all that was required in a thoughtful and precise manner. And then Baruch read about the visitation from Gavri'el and what the angel told Zekharyah about their future. Baruch's cheeks reddened as he read about Elisheba giving birth to a son.

With wide eyes, Elisheba turned to Zekharyah. "Adonai heard your prayer."

Baruch handed the scroll to Zekharyah and stood. "You were right, Elisheba, I must get home to my wife," he said, backing toward the gate. "Little Malkiel is a trial for Yehudit. I'm sure she's nearly lost her mind by now." With a sly smile and a wave of the hand he left.

Elisheba leaned forward, glad to finally be alone with Zekharyah. "The whole village will know your story before sundown."

Zekharyah shrugged.

"I dare not doubt the angel's message, or we will both end up mute. But, oh my goodness, this is a surprising and wondrous turn of events."

He nodded, chuckled noiselessly.

Holding hands, they sat watching the sky blush as the sun dipped below the horizon. Elisheba wasn't sure what to say to her husband. Should she tell him all the rumors that had reached her from Jerusalem? But why? What hurt or help could the words of men or women be in this time?

Adonai had spoken to them through the angel Gavri´el, an angel who stood in the presence of God. This very angel had visited Zekharyah and told him they would have a son, a son who would prepare the way for the Messiah. The reality of those words would take time to settle into her heart. For them to take root and live, even longer.

She thought of Sarah, overhearing the angel speak with Abraham— and laughing. She now understood Sarah's lack of faith, for twenty years had passed since the phases of the moon meant anything to Elisheba. Large brown spots dotted the backs of her hands. She prayed the Lord would not make her wait as long as Sarah to become pregnant, for many years had passed between the angel's visit and Isaac's birth. Elisheba had no intentions of sending a servant girl to Zekharyah.

Lord, I surely haven't been shy about asking you for a son. But these thoughts are too big for me. I dare not try to figure out what you're doing or how you're going to do it all. I want so badly to believe the words sent through Gavri´el.

The warmth and heft of Zachariah beside her was as familiar as her own breath. His eyes reflected the glow of the sunset, and his face was soft with contentment. The peace that rolled off of him comforted her and surprised her.

I trust you, Lord, to do all that you have said. Remind me in the morning of these words of mine, and give me the faith to believe.

The air seemed different. Lighter yet full of life, a life she could not see but knew hovered nearby. With the presence came a surety that Adonai's rightness was coming to her world. She did laugh, then, but out of a sense of wonder. To be thinking and hoping for such things at this time in her life was astounding, indeed. Her son—Yohanan was to be his name—would prepare the way for the Messiah. The *Messiah.*

Zekharyah drew her closer.

"What truly does HaShem expect of us, husband? We are ordinary people. We are no Davids. We aren't anything like Moses. If a desert stream were to part before me, I would faint and be useless for anything. I believe and then I don't. I fear my heart and my faith are not strong enough to be the mother of such a great man."

Zekharyah's embrace tightened.

"I know, my sweet man, we are together as we have always been, and that is a gift. We learned to trust HaShem when disappointment nearly suffocated us. Perhaps all that is required is to continue on, trusting Adonai together, knowing that anything he asks of us, he will also give us strength to accomplish. We will live, Zekharyah, as we have always lived, and when the blessing comes, we will give all the praise and honor to HaShem."

Chapter Five

An Angel in the Orchard

*M*iryam! Mind the bread!"

Smoke billowed from the oven. Miryam rushed to rescue what remained of the loaves and tossed the blackened flat bread into the basket.

Ima sighed over the charred loaves and put her hand to Miryam's shoulder. "I understand your distraction, daughter. The walls of your home rise higher week after week. You are looking to your future with Yosef, but your father will not be happy to eat burned bread, yet again."

"Ima—" Miryam started, tears welling in her eyes. "This isn't about Yosef."

Miryam stepped into her mother's opened arms. "Oh, my dear daughter, when we stand at the beginning of something new, it's not so surprising to be addled, and a little careless."

"You don't understand—"

"But I do, daughter. I truly do." Ima crouched to scrape the char from the loaves with quick strokes of her knife. "There are things expected of a young wife, and I cannot fully prepare you. I certainly wasn't prepared. If truth be known, not one woman in all of history has been prepared to be a wife, not even Sarah." She stilled her hands, glanced over her shoulder, and lowered her voice. "There is one thing I can tell you: Men are strange creatures. The sooner you make friends with that idea, the better for you."

"I promise you, I have no worries about Yosef. He will make a good husband, and I will do my best to be a good wife."

"Then how do you explain a basketful of burned bread?"

Miryam hesitated. Her mother found her preoccupation with things of Adonai perplexing, at best. Ima wore her faith like a comfortable cloak, one that had lightened with wear and seemed weightless, while Miryam found impenetrable mysteries and wondrous treasures in the weft and warp of her faith.

"You can tell me anything," Ima prodded.

Her mother's words came so tenderly that Miryam blurted, "It's sin. I'm troubled by my sin."

"What sin? You are a sweet, pious girl. Some in our village might say you are too pious. What sort of silliness is this, and why now?"

Her mother would not tolerate a long-winded retelling of the passage that had burned Miryam's soul for days. She took a breath and practically spit her words. "On *Shabbat*. In the synagogue. The visiting rabbi read from the prophet Isaiah, a story about a man who suffered terribly. Afterward, the men debated about who this man could be."

Ima threw up her hands. "You are burning our bread because of prophets? My daughter, prophets speak in riddles. They give the men things to argue about, while the women tend the children and bake their bread."

"But who could Isaiah be talking about? A man pierced for our transgressions? A man crushed for our iniquities? How can one man's punishment bring us peace? What kind of man would he be? Perhaps he is the—"

Ima raised her palms. "Messiah? Enough of this talk. Go get your wedding embroidery. I will bake the bread. If your stitches are uneven, no one will starve and Yosef will never notice." She shook her head, smiled. "I've never seen a man so intent as Yosef on building a home for his family." Ima looked wistfully at the house she had lived in from the beginning of her marriage with Abba. "The wedding chamber your father built for me still stands, that is true, but the walls are in need of constant repair. You will have no such things to worry about, Miryam, and I'm glad for it. Yosef is a skilled builder.

"As for the other—these prophets who concern you so—this is one thing men are good for. They carry the burden of what we do not understand. They read Torah. They endlessly discuss its meanings. Women have no such luxuries. We have households to run, children to care for. It is time for you to accept your duty and put away all these thoughts. You are no longer a child. You're a woman, already a wife."

Miryam's heart clenched painfully, imagining a life without a moment to ponder the greatness of Adonai. To be so daily occupied with the needs of her husband and children that she could forget her God and not meditate on his goodness—how could this be?

Ima frowned at Miryam as she had done many times before, with a question creased into her brows. Miryam wanted to assent to her mother's vision of her future, but she could not imagine a life where Adonai was relegated to the edges of her domestic duties. Had she not tended the garden, ground the grain, and created somewhat passable cloth, all with the Lord as close as her breath? Still, there was no sense upsetting Ima, not again.

"I am sorry, Ima, for the bread."

"Go. It hasn't rained in a week, HaShem be praised. Take your needlework into the orchard and find someplace to work where I cannot see you daydreaming."

Miryam hurried into the house for her sewing and climbed up the terraced hill of fig and almond trees, now bare of leaves. She sat on a rock wall, raised her face to the gentle warmth of the sun, and whispered a prayer of thanks. The orchard sheltered her, any season of the year, but especially in the winter, when the men had more time to talk at the city gate. Before her, the Judean hills rolled across the horizon, now green from the saturating rains.

She unwrapped her needlework, careful to secure her needle in the fabric before unfurling the half-finished sash. Colorful designs already encircled the hem of her wedding tunic and bordered her veil. She would not wear them until she heard the blast of the *shofar*, because that meant Yosef's father had approved of the house he'd built for her, and the day of their marriage feast had arrived.

Miryam examined her stitches and marveled. When she'd started, the design was uneven, her stitches erratic, but the fabric and the thread had befriended her during their long hours together and now did her bidding. She'd never expected to find such joy in the tedious task. She held the sash before her, admiring her work, wondering if Yosef would admire it, too.

Or would he, also, berate her for what Ima saw as daydreaming?

Miryam's hands fell to her lap. The man that Isaiah described was not a daydream. Did Adonai watch the man, even now, as he grew from boyhood into a man, not beautiful or majestic, but a man who was to be led as a lamb to the slaughter? In that case, the man was a horrific reminder of her sin.

She had never bowed down before an idol, but she envied other girls their beauty and their houses in the village. Ribbons were often the object of her covetousness. She confessed with tears every lie that escaped her lips and vowed never to repeat the sin, but before the sun set again, another lie fell from her lips as easily as breathing. Did she truly honor her parents? Sometimes she sassed her mother when she didn't get her way. The hurt on Ima's face haunted her.

"Oh Adonai, my sin is ever before me, just like David. What help is there for me?"

The crunch of a footstep in the leaf debris startled Miryam. Surely her brothers were trying to sneak up on her. They took such delight in interrupting her work and teasing her about Yosef. She turned to the sound, ready to shoo them away. Nothing.

A flock of sparrows scavenged for their meals in the mustard, resplendent with yellow blooms. Feathery grasses swayed with the breeze. She was alone, or was she? She stood, alert. She'd climbed the hill without a staff or rod to protect herself. Did a lion stalk her? She backed to the nearest tree, ready to climb, her heart pounding wildly.

"Lord, close the mouth of the lion as you did for Daniel. I am your servant," she whispered.

"Grace to you, young woman!" [5]

Miryam spun to the voice, but only a blur of brilliant white rose before her. She climbed the lowest branches of the tree, pivoting back to the brightness. She waited, watched, her pulse thrumming in her ears.

The dazzling light took the form of a man, a very tall man with the arms of a warrior, although, thankfully, they rested at his side, not on the hilt of a sword. "As you can see, I am no lion."

Miryam took some comfort that he didn't carry a weapon as she had seen in the hands of Roman soldiers in Jerusalem. But clearly he could crush her with his hands. "Who are you?"

[5] Luke 1:28a (TPT).

The man smiled and opened his hands to her. "I'm here to tell you that the Lord is with you and so you are anointed with great favor."[6]

The Lord is with me? I'm only a silly girl, a daydreamer. I'm not worthy of great favor. But Joseph who wore the coat of many colors, the Lord was with him, and he was thrown into a well!

The man chuckled, and the sound of his laugh was like a swollen stream tumbling rocks in its course, joyful yet noble. She felt the reverberation in her chest. "There is no well in your future, I can assure you."

He knew her thoughts? But how? Miryam had watched him take form out of shapeless light. He'd appeared out of nowhere.

He is an angel.

Miryam lowered herself to the ground, clutching the sash to her stomach.

"Do not yield to your fear, Miryam, for the Lord has found delight in you and has chosen to surprise you with a wonderful gift. You will become pregnant with a baby boy, and you are to name him Yeshua."[7]

"Pregnant? But—"

"Miryam. Listen. In this moment, it's most important for you to concentrate on who your Son will be. He will be supreme and will be known as the Son of the Highest. And the Lord God will enthrone him as King on his ancestor David's throne. He will reign as King of Israel forever, and his reign will have no limit."[8]

Won't my son be Yosef's son?

"Sir, I'm very confused. Please, help me understand. I'm only a girl, trying to please HaShem in all things. I've pledged myself to Yosef. He is, even now, building our home. That means, of course, that he hasn't come for me, and we have not yet eaten our marriage supper. So you see, sir, I am most definitely a virgin."

"You are a girl with many concerns, Miryam, but Adonai has a plan. The Spirit of Holiness will fall upon you, and Ha´Elyon will spread his shadow of power over you in a cloud of glory! This is why the child born to you will be holy, and he will be called the Son of God."

---

[6] Luke 1:28b (TPT).

[7] Luke 1:30 (TPT) *Miryam* substituted for "Mary." *Yeshua* substituted for "Jesus."

[8] Luke 1:23-33 (TPT) *Ha´Elyon* substituted for "almighty God."

The Son of God, the Messiah? I am to be his mother? Miryam recalled the stories of women she'd heard read from Torah—Eve. Sarah. Rebekah. Rachel and her sister, Leah. Some suffered barrenness, but none of them, not one, had received such a visitation. None of them had been charged to be the mother of the Messiah. *Who am I compared to any of them? I am nothing more than a girl, an unremarkable girl, content with a simple life.*

The angel continued. "What's more, your aged kinswoman, Elisheba, has also become pregnant with a son. The one all believed to be barren is now in her sixth month. This should prove that not one promise from God is empty of power, for nothing is impossible with God!" [9]

Elisheba! Miryam knew her well, a kinswoman by her grandmother's sister. In truth, more a beloved aunt to her than a distant cousin. Miryam's family stayed with Elisheba and Zekharyah each *Pesach*, for they lived within walking distance to Jerusalem and the temple. Ima had prayed Adonai's comfort to rest on Elisheba in her barrenness. And now, she was with child?

Truly, Adonai is in this, for Elisheba is a righteous woman.

Miryam fell to her knees. "This is amazing! I will be a mother for the Lord! As his servant, I accept whatever he has for me. May everything you have told me come to pass." Miryam pressed her hands to her beating heart, closed her eyes, and waited for whatever the angel had for her.

A great cloud of light enclosed her, and a warmth bathed her, warming her face, her arms, her chest, and settling in her womb. She thought of the honey her father collected each fall, flowing like a ribbon of light into her—such sweetness. Her muscles softened. An irresistible joy bubbled in her chest, and most astounding of all, a peace cocooned her. She knew with great certainty that the Lord was, indeed, with her.

When she opened her eyes, the angel was gone.

As her pulse calmed, Miryam put her hand to her stomach. "Lord, is this the tender shoot you will watch grow before you? And is this the root out of dry ground?"

The only answer came from the chittering swallows diving for insects and the distant sound of her brothers arguing. In the way Miryam had of knowing things, she understood with deep certainty that HaShem would

---

[9] Luke 1:36-37 (TPT).

not ask this of her and then leave her without his help. Miryam stood and brushed grass from her tunic.

She remembered the story of Moses commissioning Joshua to lead the people into the Promised Land. Moses encouraged the new leader with this promise: "The Lord himself will go ahead of you. He will be with you. He will never leave you. He'll never desert you. So don't be afraid. Don't lose hope."[10]

She lifted her face to the sky and prayed. "And here I stand—in the Promised Land you gave to my forefathers—because of your faithfulness, Lord. You accomplished all that you pledged to Abraham. Like him, I don't know everything that lies ahead. That has never been your way. But you parted the Jordan. You crumbled the walls of Jericho. You subdued the Canaanites. You will make a way for me, for this baby, and for Yosef."

Yosef.

What of Yosef? What of their marriage? Her heart nearly stopped at this thought.

Only one word came in answer to her questions: *Elisheba.*

She, too, was pregnant by a miracle. Elisheba would know what to do. She was the wife of a priest. Surely she would understand better than Miryam what had just happened. But Elisheba lived five days' walk away. Miryam could not travel alone—the journey to Ein Karem was treacherous, filled with threats of wild animals and robbers. Besides, a woman alone would be considered a prostitute. No, she could not travel alone.

The words of the angel settled on Miryam, "Nothing is impossible with God." She gathered her sewing and headed down the hill. One way or another, she would seek Elisheba's help. That meant telling her mother what had just happened in the orchard.

"Lord, go before me as you went before your children in the wilderness."

---

[10] Deuteronomy 31:8 (NIrV).

Chapter Six

Two Mothers

ension hung over the house of Eli like a rain-soaked cloak. Abba slipped out before the sun rose each day to tend the orchard. Not waiting for Ima to prepare breakfast, he stuffed his bag with yesterday's bread and cheese and left in haste. When he stomped into the house at the end of the day, he avoided Miryam's gaze.

When the brothers entered the yard, they hushed their chidings and boasts, mindful enough of their stomachs not to disturb what passed for peace. Even the little girls knew not to chatter around Ima. Miryam abandoned her needlework for kitchen duties, hoping to ease Ima's workload, all the while praying for her father's heart to soften.

The force of his anger had diminished, but a wide chasm separated daughter from father. He would not consider sending her to Elisheba, although she'd begged on her knees for him to do so. That had been the day she came out of the orchard to tell her parents about the angel. Abba had not spoken to her since.

Three days later, Miryam returned from the well to find Ima at the loom, her hands resting on the frame, watching heavy clouds race inland from the coast. Ima turned to Miryam, studied her for a moment, then straightened her tunic and left the house. Miryam followed her to the door and watched her mother trudge up the hill to where her father worked.

Miryam put her forehead to the lintel and prayed. "My Lord, you whispered Elisheba's name to me, I am very sure. Please show your will to Abba. I put my trust in you, and I will accept your answer. Amen." She turned her thoughts to the angel, remembering his message and the peace that had flowed through her. "I am your handmaid, Lord."

℘

WHEN IMA RETURNED, HER jaw was set, and the hem of her tunic was soiled with mud. Miryam hugged herself and lowered her head to wait for her to speak. Ima sent the small girls to the yard to hunt eggs. She watched as they ran from nest to nest, filling the sling of their cloaks with their treasures.

Ima kept her eyes on the girls as she spoke. "You've upset your father—and me—very much with your story, Miryam. Savta and Dodah, I've never seen them so angry—or disappointed. What are we supposed to believe about you? About Yosef? An angel appearing to a young girl is a preposterous notion. That Elisheba is with child is too outrageous to consider. Where do you get these ideas?"

She stopped Miryam's reply with a raised hand. "I don't want to hear your answer...unless you are ready to tell me the truth."

Miryam had told her mother the truth over and over, how the angel had met her in the orchard and how the presence of Adonai had come over her. Each time her mother wore a deepening mask of hurt and regret. "I have nothing to add, Ima."

"I see." Ima drew in a breath and let it out slowly. "Miryam, have you been alone with Yosef? Have you been together as a man and his wife come together?"

"No, never."

"But you believe you're pregnant?"

"It's as I said, the Holy Spirit—"

"No! Do not say another word of this!" She sucked in ragged breaths and paced the small room, stopping before Miryam. "Listen carefully, daughter: Do you want to reconsider your answer? The honor of this family rests on what you have done. Is there a chance that you are too ashamed to tell me the truth about your behavior with Yosef, and now you are making up a story to cover your disgrace?"

"I have only seen Yosef in the synagogue. Never alone. We have done nothing to shame this family." Miryam fought to contain her emotion. "I don't understand why HaShem has chosen to fulfill his promises in this way, but he has. I am only his servant. Ima, you must believe me."

Ima threw up her hands. "Believe you? Believe that an angel visited a silly girl and planted the Messiah in her womb? *My* daughter? In *our* orchard? In Nazareth, of all places? How can I believe such a thing?" Ima covered her face with her hands. When she looked at Miryam again, tears streamed down her face. "Your story will destroy you, Miryam. And it will destroy this family. Yosef doesn't want a wife who brings disgrace on her family with wild talk. You must put this childishness aside. You must think of your future and the future of your family."

Miryam wanted to plead her cause but doing so only seemed to add anguish to her mother's distress. Besides, she wasn't sure she could squeeze words past the knot in her throat.

Ima wiped the tears from her cheeks. "Tomorrow, your father must deliver honey to the baker in Jerusalem for his Chanukkah sweets. You will travel with him. You will stay with Elisheba until we collect you at *Pesach*."

Miryam covered her fluttering heart with her hands.

"Listen to me well, girl. We are sending you to our kinswoman for one reason: You are to forget this foolishness, once and for all. It is well past time for you to take seriously what it means to be a wife. No more daydreaming. You must attend only to what is before you. And perhaps time away will remind you of what it means to be loyal to your family.

"Also, Miryam, you are not to be a burden to Elisheba. She is of an age when the demands of a woman's life become more toilsome, and she has no daughters to help her. You are to do all you can to lighten her load." Ima took a step closer. "Daughter, please, you are to say nothing of angels to anyone in her household. Do you understand?"

"Ima, you must know, I have never lied—"

"Convincing your father to take you to Elisheba wasn't easy. I suggest you keep all talk of angels to yourself during the journey to Ein Karem. I ask you again, do we understand one another?"

Miryam knew the journey to Ein Karem well, for her family traveled the Ridge Route every year for *Pesach*. If the roads remained dry, four long days of walking lay ahead of her, longer if the winter storms released their torrents. Adonai had answered her prayer. She would see Elisheba before the next *Shabbat*. Her heart longed to sing praises for the favor Adonai had shown her, but the scowl on Ima's face dissuaded her.

"Yes, I understand," she said.

"Gather your things. Your father wants to leave at first light. You will join a caravan in Sigoph, and journey on from there."

At the ladder to the loft, Miryam turned back to her mother. "HaShem is in this, Ima. We are at the beginning of something new and wonderful, I promise you."

CR

ABBA ONLY LOOKED AT Miryam when he thought she was too busy to notice—preparing a meal or watching the children of a woman traveling with the caravan. Otherwise, he talked to the donkey, encouraging the swaybacked beast to step lively and carefully. He speculated about the weather with a man from Jobath, carrying his olive oil into the city. He compared the merits of early and late pruning of fig trees with a merchant who had never turned one shovelful of soil in his life. When they settled onto pallets at the home of kin in Ginae and in the home of a fellow fig grower in Shechem, he turned his back to Miryam and snored raucously. He would have done the same in Berea, but she slept on the roof with a dozen children, while he enjoyed the guest chamber.

Miryam occupied her thoughts—for they were all a tumble with questions about her future, including if Yosef would be part of it—by reciting psalms. She focused on the psalms of deliverance to remind herself of Adonai's might and faithfulness, and then turned to the psalms of praise, where King David extolled the constant love and faithfulness in celebration of Adonai's goodness. As she silently recited the psalms on the road and on her pallet, a picture of her child's mission took shape. The scope of what he would accomplish terrified her and fortified her.

The skies weighed heavily of rain, but only a light drizzle fell from time to time, keeping their clothes from drying out completely. The roads, however, remained passable. Miryam looked to the sky and thanked the Giver of all good things for the pleasure of his favor.

As the caravan skirted the slopes of Mt. Gerizim, a bear lumbered down through the trees and onto the road. A cacophony of complaints rose from travelers and beasts, but the bear simply swayed back and forth, vocalizing his dominance over the land. The drivers stood poised with their staffs but lacked the courage to hassle the bear off the route. The bear finally sat on his haunches, a defiant show of his lordship.

All watched the sun travel across the sky. At a safe distance, the men consulted one another in hushed tones. Their talk of returning to Shechem made Miryam groan inwardly. Finally, a lanky boy lobbed a rock that landed between the bear's front paws. The travelers gasped at such a provocation, but the bear stood laconically and climbed back up the slope into the trees. For the rest of the trip, the boy was called King David, for his bravery and recklessness.

❧

AS THE CARAVAN NEARED Jerusalem, some travelers joined the column, others peeled off to one of the villages that ringed the base of the majestic city. At the road to Ein Karem, Abba tugged the donkey out of line.

Miryam followed, her heart aquiver. She rehearsed, as she had done along the lonely stretches of road, the story of the angel. She didn't want to leave anything out when she told Elisheba, for she knew she had to tell her kinswoman everything.

Elisheba. Known by most as a barren woman, wife to Zekharyah, but she was so much more and worthy of admiration for her piety. Elisheba reminded Miryam of Hannah, Samuel's faithful mother. Surely Elisheba now sang the song of Hannah with a heart bursting with gratitude. Miryam could hardly keep from singing praises herself—and asking questions. She had so many questions. She wished her father would walk faster.

When the gate of Elisheba's house came into view, Miryam adjusted the bedroll she carried and trotted past her father.

"Elisheba!" she called.

❧

ELISHEBA RECLINED IN THE reception room, watching her servant girl, Atalyah, prepare the evening meal. The weight of the growing child against

Elisheba's back crushed like stone against stone. She adjusted a cushion but no relief came.

Delegating all cooking duties to Atalyah had been Zekharyah's idea. It took Elisheba nearly a week to understand his meaning through hand signs. Perhaps she had pretended not to understand to prolong the girl's takeover of the kitchen, but she did appreciate the girl's efforts, if not the results.

"Help me up, Atalyah. This pallet is like lying on a bag of bones."

Elisheba arched into a delicious stretch and shuffled around the room. She itched to reclaim her duties, but Zekharyah had been so attentive in his care, she dared not. The cool, moist air enticed her to the open door.

Three more months. Lord, give me strength.

She heard a call. "Elisheba!"

Elisheba doubled over at the wild tumbling of the child within her, and an effervescent joy percolated through her. An urgency overcame her she didn't understand—until she saw Miryam come through the gate and run to her.

"It's you!" She pulled Miryam into a lingering embrace and breathed in the dust of the road that lingered in the girl's hair. Elisheba knew, she *knew* without any doubt she held in her arms the mother of the Messiah. "Oh, child, he has chosen you!"

She clasped Miryam's hands and kissed them, and then wiped the girl's tears away with her sleeve. "You are a woman given the highest favor and privilege above all others, for your child is destined to bring Adonai great delight."[11]

Eli entered the courtyard, wearing the miles between Nazareth and Ein Karem. His face was grim and his shoulders rounded under some terrible weight. Elisheba could not think what would distract a descendent of Abraham from so great a joy, the fulfillment of a long-ago promise. And more, his daughter carried the Messiah. Eli's gaze froze on Elisheba's large belly, and his mouth fell open.

Just then, Zekharyah stepped from the house, surprise and delight brightening his face when he saw Eli and Miryam.

Elisheba said to him, "I must speak with Miryam. Please make sure Eli gets the refreshment he needs. The journey from Nazareth is long."

---

[11] Luke 1:42b (TPT) *Adonai* substituted for "God."

Zekharyah gestured helplessness.

What was she thinking? Zekharyah excelled at being an attentive husband, but he was still a man. "Atalyah! Come look to the needs of our kinsman!"

Elisheba took Miryam by the hand and led her up to the roof. They huddled together against the winter chill with their backs to the wall. Miryam put her hands to Elisheba's belly. The baby roiled under her touch, and her eyes grew round.

"Now, tell me," Elisheba said, "how did I deserve such a remarkable honor to have the mother of my Lord come and visit me? The moment you came in the gate and greeted me, my baby danced inside me with ecstatic joy!" Elisheba drew Miryam's head to her shoulder, and her arms went around the girl. "Great favor is upon you, for you have believed every word spoken to you from the Lord."[12]

◌ℜ

MIRYAM LEANED HER HEAD on Elisheba's shoulder, content in the mystery of all Adonai had done and would do through her. She knew more than anyone that she was no one special, merely a girl among a nation of girls. There were prettier girls. Smarter girls. Girls from better families. And yet…

Miryam could not sit still. She rose, lifted her hands to heaven, and twirled. She sang, "My soul magnifies Adonai; and my spirit rejoices in God, my Savior, who has taken notice of his servant-girl in her humble position."[13]

She stood before Elisheba, her hands over her heart, overwhelmed by God's attention to her, a very unworthy girl. "For—imagine it!—from now on, all generations will call me blessed! The Mighty One has done great things for me!"[14]

Miryam stood at the parapet, looking up at the great city of Jerusalem in the distance. Even in the descending light, the walls of the city declared

---

[12] Luke 1:45 (TPT).
[13] Luke 1:46b-48a (CJB).
[14] Luke 1:48b (CJB).

Adonai's faithfulness to the humble, for he had brought his people out of slavery to this land.

She sat again beside Elisheba. "HaShem is faithful to the humble, is he not?"

"Yes, my dear, our Lord is faithful to promote the humble, and most especially humble women. Consider Ruth, a committed servant to her mother-in-law. HaShem provided a kinsman redeemer and placed her in a family. And there was Esther who grew up an orphan but rose to great heights in the Persian court. She went boldly before the king to save her people, and HaShem preserved her life. Even Rahab, a harlot, risked her life to hide the spies sent from Joshua into Jericho. HaShem saved her and gave her a place of honor in the lineage of David and your own beloved Yosef."

Could she and Elisheba belong in such a company of women? "Elisheba, we are another chapter in HaShem's story of faithfulness. His mercy flows in wave after wave on those who are in awe before him. He bared his arm and showed his strength, scattered the bluffing braggarts. He knocked tyrants off their high horses, pulled victims out of the mud. The starving poor sat down to a banquet; the callous rich were left out in the cold. He embraced his chosen child, Israel; he remembered and piled on the mercies, piled them high. It's exactly what he promised, beginning with Abraham and right up to now."[15]

---

[15] Luke 1:50-55 (MSG)

Chapter Seven

An Alliance of Women

The three women sat around a low table in the center of Elisheba's reception room. Atalyah washed the days of travel from Ima's feet and massaged olive oil into her cracked feet.

Miryam sat on her hands to hide their trembling. She had anticipated this moment for the three months she'd been with Elisheba. She would, with Elisheba's help, tell her mother that she was, indeed, pregnant. She prayed she could hold onto the contents of her stomach until the deed had been done. Her father and Zekharyah had left soon after the family had arrived from Nazareth to visit Baruch, who would give voice to the story of Adonai they were all living out.

Elisheba and Ima chatted like young brides at the well, Ima often diverting her eyes to Elisheba's large belly and then to Miryam, a question etched on her face. They talked of weather, the health of relatives, the preparation of the *Pesach* feast. Outside, her brothers and sisters fussed over the *Pesach* lamb that had been brought to live with the family. They brushed his snowy fleece and led him around the courtyard in turns. Miryam longed to join them.

When Atalyah left with the silt-filled water basin, Ima settled her gaze on Elisheba and nodded to her swollen belly. "You have been blessed of HaShem, Elisheba, to be full with child even now."

"You mean as an old woman?"

Ima scrambled for words. "You had despaired of ever becoming a mother, and here you are, ready to give birth. I pray it will be a son, so that the name of Zekharyah will live on for many generations."

A gleam lit Elisheba's eyes. Miryam had come to recognize the twinkle meant Elisheba was teasing.

Elisheba asked Ima, "Hadn't Miryam told you I was pregnant?"

Ima looked to Miryam, obviously flummoxed, and back to Elisheba. "I might recall she said something, but I…"

Elisheba took Ima's hand, cooing her name to apologize for her mischievousness. "Channah, dearest, I shouldn't toy with you. Everything we have expected of our futures is changing, and that is challenging, is it not?"

Ima looked to her daughter. "How did you know?"

Miryam was about to remind her mother of the angel, but Elisheba spoke first. "HaShem is using us all in amazing ways. I fear nothing has prepared us, except for his faithfulness to his people from the beginning. Then and now, we are trying to catch up."

Ima looked to Miryam, her eyes pooling with tears. "If you are with child as the angel said…?"

"Miryam," Elisheba said, "your mother and I have many things to talk about. Take the swaddling clothes up to the roof, won't you? Your stitches are so much finer than mine. I would appreciate your help finishing them." She patted her large belly. "This little one won't be long in coming."

Miryam snatched the basket of needlework from the shelf. In the courtyard, the lamb ran under her feet as she left the house, her brothers right behind. She stumbled but didn't fall. "Do not harass the poor thing!" she yelled to the boys. She should have stayed in the courtyard to supervise their play, but she longed for the distance and isolation of the rooftop. She ran up the stairs two at a time.

Spring had not fully bloomed, but the sun warmed the wall where she sat. She tried to thread the needle, but her hands shook so. Instead, she prayed.

Lord, you know my mother's heart. You know she loves you, that she orders her home according to your precepts. Could you not show her, somehow, what you are doing? Miryam put her hands to her stomach. *That you are doing something truly wonderful. And, Lord, I would consider it a great kindness if my stomach would not lurch so. Amen.*

Ima's wail pierced the quiet.

CR

ELISHEBA ROSE WITH SOME difficulty to embrace Channah in her distress. Channah pulled at her clothes, her hair. She balled her hands into fists and dug them into her stomach, bending under the pain of her disappointment.

Elisheba held her words as Channah cried. She could not soften the blow of Miryam's pregnancy. What she had learned in the months of her own pregnancy is that Adonai has his timetable and the power to change hearts of stone into hearts of flesh. She trusted Adonai to meet Channah in her pain, to show to her his goodness. She followed Isaiah's lead, praying Channah would experience perfect peace because she trusted Adonai her Savior, the Rock Eternal.

Channah's sobs quieted. Atalyah brought another basin of water, and Elisheba pushed back Channah's hair to wash her face. She kissed Channah's cheeks and sent Atalyah away.

Channah spoke sodden words. "What are we to do?"

"The story Miryam told you of the angel is true. The child in her womb is of HaShem. Miryam is in no way guilty of shaming her family. She was chosen for the honor of bearing the Messiah."

"But…"

"Do you remember the words of the prophet Isaiah, Channah? 'The Lord himself will give you a sign. The virgin is going to have a baby. She will give birth to a son. And he will be called Immanuel.'[16] HaShem has been waiting for this time, the perfect time, to fulfill his promise, and he has chosen Miryam to bear the child."

Channah kept her gaze on her clenched hands. "This is a hard thing."

"It will be hardest for Miryam."

Her eyes lifted. "She has always been a tender child."

"That's what will make her a good mother."

"The women of Nazareth…"

"I agree, they will not be kind."

"What of Yosef? He could send her before the Sanhedrin." Channah staunched a sob with her fist. "What's to become of us?"

Elisheba drew Channah back into her embrace, rocking her and crying

---

[16] Isaiah 7:14 (NIV).

with her, for truly the road ahead would be difficult for the family.

"Think of it, Channah. Think of how carefully HaShem has encountered Zekharyah, Miryam, me, and now you. He has planned all this from the time of Isaiah, maybe for a long time before that. I believe you are beginning to see HaShem's hand at work." Elisheba patted her large belly. "Isn't that right?"

Channah hesitated, then nodded.

"We have to believe that HaShem is at work in Yosef, too. We don't know how HaShem will speak to him, but because HaShem doesn't leave loose threads, like I do, we know he will give Miryam favor in Yosef's eyes, one way or another."

"Eli will have a hard time believing all of this."

"Even Eli is vulnerable to Adonai's work, no?"

"I pray it will not take ten plagues to convince him."

Elisheba laughed. "Maybe only one or two plagues. Eli is no Pharaoh." She settled back onto her pallet.

Channah knew just how to place the cushions to support Elisheba's aching back. She arranged another cushion under her knees. "Is there anything else I can do to make you more comfortable?"

Elisheba patted the pallet, and Channah sat beside her. She took the woman's hand in hers. "Channah, I believe HaShem chose Miryam because of you. He knew she had a mother of great faith and courage, a woman who would stand by her in this difficult time."

"HaShem could have waited until after the wedding feast."
"But there is Isaiah's prophecy."

"Yes, there is Isaiah. There is *always* Isaiah."

"Miryam is waiting for you. You need to go to her, let her know that you will walk with her through this. Are you ready to do that?"

Channah stood, combed her hair through her fingers, and reworked her braid. "Will you pray for us?"

"Many times a day."

ᙦ

IMA AND MIRYAM SAT on the parapet, fidgeting, taking in breaths to start talking but only letting out sighs. Finally, Ima clasped Miryam's hands.

"How are you feeling?"

"My stomach spins like a dreidel."

"That will soon pass. The baby is just announcing his presence."

"And my breasts…I can barely stand the touch of my tunic."

"That, too, will get better in time."

Miryam wanted to apologize to her mother for all the heartache she had caused, but she wasn't sure doing so would honor what Adonai was doing. Her apology might sound like she didn't agree with Adonai's plan. "Ima, I wish you had seen the angel."

"Then you would be visiting me at my grave, for surely I would have taken one look at the angel and fallen dead to the ground in fright. No, it is much better that it all happened this way. That way you still have a mother."

"Then you believe me?"

"I do, and that surprises me very much. I am not a woman who looks for the mystical. I'm quite happy with the world I can see. The rocks. The trees. The sky. I know HaShem created everything and is in charge of how it all works together, but I am happy to let him do all that without any interference from me. This—the angel, your pregnancy, Elisheba—this is very uncomfortable ground for me. But I cannot deny that something quite extraordinary is happening." Ima gestured toward the house. "That woman has no business being pregnant."

"Neither do I."

"Yes, you're right about that." Ima lowered her head, worked the fabric of her cloak like dough. "I'm not proud of the way I reacted, my daughter. You will understand soon enough that mothers have dreams for their children. In my case, my dreams were simple. I hoped you would be a woman of piety. And you are that. I pictured a man with an upstanding reputation and a strong work ethic to marry you. Yosef is that, certainly. When I saw that dream falling apart…I'm so sorry I doubted you, Miryam."

"Oh, Ima, I would have doubted me!"

"Your father…"

"I know. This will be very hard for him."

"He likes his world just so."

"And Yosef?"

"Together, we must believe HaShem is at work in him, too. At least, that is what Elisheba believes."

"Without him…" Miryam started.

"Yosef may surprise you, so let's put off that worry for another day. We have *Pesach* before us and then a long walk back to Nazareth. We are giving HaShem lots of time to do his work. After all, he created the heavens and the earth in six days. I think he should be able to prepare Yosef's heart to receive this surprise in the same number of days."

"Ima," Miryam put her hands to her belly, "this child will accomplish great things, but I fear he will suffer greatly too. The prophet Isaiah…"

"The prophet Isaiah has an awful lot to say about everything, doesn't he? Well, I'm a simple woman. I can only think on one thing at a time. I suggest you do the same. Your job is to concentrate on having a baby. Once you have accomplished that, focus on the next step. For me, that was getting enough sleep to make it through a day."

Chapter Eight

A Messenger is Born

*T*he pains came as relentless waves pounding the shore. Well before first hour, Elisheba left the pallet she shared with Zekharyah. Feeling her way to the courtyard, she lit a lamp from the embers of the oven.

She stood at her loom and wove by the dim light, shuttling the wool through the warp threads. The tension of her work fluctuated with the pains, drawing the edges in and swelling them out. She would rip the cloak apart later, but for now the rhythm of the work and the clacking of the warp weights soothed her. As she worked, she prayed for strength.

As the sky lightened to gray, a contraction hardened her womb and clenched her lower back with an iron grip. She put her head to the heddle rod and stifled a moan with her fist. Zekharyah found her there. His face registered hurt when she refused his arms, but his eyes quickly turned to pleading. To call the midwife too early was to wear the mark of a novice, to be teased for panicking. First babies arrived only after a long travail, especially if it was a boy. A brave mother looked after the needs of her family as long as she could, so the burden of birth wouldn't fall to anyone else.

She waved Zekharyah off and ambled to the kitchen. Atalyah arrived soon after, adjusting her head scarf, scurrying to take the bread and cheese from her mistress' hands.

"Atalyah, it will do me good to stay busy."

The girl hesitated, assessing her mistress.

"I would appreciate your help stoking the fire," Elisheba said. "Reheat the stew. A man loves his meat, especially on the day he becomes a father."

The girl bustled out the door to do her mistress' bidding. Zekharyah watched her go, looking like a boy who had been left out of the game.

By the time Zekharyah swiped his bowl clean with the last bite of bread, her contractions piled one on another, with no time to recover from the last. She nodded to Zekharyah, and he scrambled awkwardly to his feet. He strode out the door to summon the midwife.

Nechama arrived like an invading general. She exiled Zekharyah to the courtyard with a command to stay out of the house until he was called. He bowed as he backed out the door. Elisheba would have laughed, if a pain had not at that moment gripped her in its vise.

The midwife sat knee to knee with Elisheba. "Well, the day is here, finally. You will see your babe today. Are you ready to work harder than you've ever worked before?"

Another pain stole Elisheba's breath, so she nodded.

"Good. My dear friend, clearly you have HaShem's favor on you."

Elisheba winced at the words. Nechama had been among those who had tormented her for her barrenness in the early years of her marriage, accusing her of a sin that withdrew Adonai's gifts. When Nechama began her studies to become a midwife with old Liora, Elisheba vowed never to use her services. But here she was. And Elisheba's heart swelled with gratitude for the woman's strength and knowledge.

"Usually, with older mothers the delivery is easier," Nechama said. "The womb has surrendered its tiny traveler many times, and the baby is more easily released. You are an older mother, this is very true, but your womb is not tried by many births."

Elisheba groaned with the arrival of the next pain. Nechama put her hands on Elisheba's belly. "Fear will tighten your muscles, Elisheba. Trust me to know what I'm doing. I won't leave you. Breathe deeply. Pull the breath to your toes and let the air out as slowly as you can. Your contractions are regular and getting stronger. That is a good sign."

A soft knock came to the door. Nechama called, "Come in!"

In walked Dalit, a tall and muscled woman Elisheba knew only from the synagogue and at the well. The woman lived with her husband and three young daughters on a farm at the edge of Ein Karem. With no sons to help, Dalit worked side by side with her husband.

Nechama squeezed Elisheba's hand. "Since Miryam has returned to

Nazareth, I asked Dalit to help. When the time comes, we will try the birthing stones, but if you grow tired, you will sit on Dalit's knees, and she will support you."

Stooping over the garden had become difficult in recent years. Standing on two flat stones and squatting for more than a minute would be impossible. Elisheba looked from Nechama to Dalit. "I will take all the help I can get."

Dalit, her eyes bright with excitement, said, "They have set a Torah scroll at the door."

That would have been Zekharyah's doing. He wasn't taking any chances. He gathered all the help he could muster for their son's birth. Elisheba had no doubt in her mind that she carried the boy the angel had announced to Zekharyah. She had already pictured him, an earnest child with a mop of curls and a will of iron.

Lord, you are my place of safety. You give me strength. You are always here to help me in times of trouble...and this, oh Lord, is a time of trouble.

The next contraction robbed her of breath and thought.

"Breathe, Elisheba!"

Adonai, I cannot do this! By your strength, Lord, not mine.

Elisheba labored through midday and into the afternoon. Nechama moved her like a doll through different positions, trying to take the pressure off her back and to bring the baby into a facedown presentation. Each move drained strength from Elisheba.

Nechama held Elisheba's face in her hands. "I've delivered many healthy babies with a face-up presentation, but it's easier for the child to move through the pelvis if it is face down. Let's try one more change." Elisheba leaned against Dalit on her pallet. Finally, Nechama congratulated her. "Your baby has rolled into position and the birth canal is wide open. It's time to push."

Elisheba exhaled. "Thank you, my Lord and God."

She stepped, with the midwife's help, onto the birthing stones and tried to squat, but her legs trembled with fatigue. Nechama pulled a chair to the middle of the room and told Dalit to sit. Then Elisheba sat on her knees.

Dalit whispered in her ear. "My legs are very strong. Lean into me and give me all your weight."

Elisheba welcomed the woman's strength and sagged into her chest.

Nechama kneeled before her. "I'm going to release your waters. That should hasten the baby's arrival."

I have nothing left to give, Lord.

Dalit recited from the prophet Isaiah: "So do not fear, for I am with you; do not be dismayed, for I am your God. I will strengthen you and help you; I will uphold you with my righteous right hand."[17]

Elisheba closed her eyes as Nechama unwrapped a menacing hook from her kit. Water splashed the floor, and Nechama held Elisheba's belly in her hands. "Yes! The contractions strengthen." Dalit leaned forward. Nechama lifted Elisheba's thighs to her chest.

"Push!"

ೞ

ZEKHARYAH WORRIED THE STONES of the courtyard with his pacing, praying for his wife, his son's safe arrival, and that he would be found a worthy father. The musicians arrived—who had called them?—about the time Elisheba's cries intensified. If he owned a voice, he would have told them their psaltery, flute, and *tabret* were definitely needed to celebrate the arrival of a boy, for today his son was going to be born.

The first lusty cries from his son drew him into the house. The midwife startled but turned back to her work. His son writhed with indignation under her hands, first as she sponged the bloody mantel from his body and then as she rubbed him with salt to harden his skin. The midwife scowled at Zekharyah over her shoulder as she worked the bones of the child's skull with her strong hands, reshaping his head from the trauma of birth.

Yohanan looked perfect.

Zekharyah's arms ached to hold the child, to assure himself that he was indeed, finally, a father. He satisfied himself with a quick inventory of the boy's fingers and toes, marveled at the strength of his lungs, and went, instead, to Elisheba.

Dalit covered her with a blanket. Elisheba ran trembling fingers through her damp hair. "You shouldn't be in here, not yet."

His love for Elisheba burned in his throat, squeezed his heart, stung his eyes. He kissed her hands, her face, and tasted the salt of her sweat on

---

[17] Isaiah 41:10 (NIV).

her forehead. His words were sand in his throat. *Know that I love you, Elisheba. Know that I am your lesser by half. More than rubies, my love, you are worth much more than rubies.*

"Why are you here? Go tell everyone, Zekharyah. Tell them all of HaShem's faithfulness."

He put his fingers to his lips and shook his head.

"They will know why you come. Go!"

Zekharyah pushed through the gate and hustled through the narrow streets. Behind him, the musicians played a jaunty tune of celebration for a son born healthy and strong. He met the merchant and the baker and the potter. They all asked about the child. "Is the baby here?" "Have you been blessed with a son?" "Is this the day when HaShem's promise has come to pass?" Zekharyah nodded emphatically, tears streaming into his beard.

Back at the house, Zekharyah received neighbors who came with their hands full of gifts—bread, cheese, figs, even a roasted leg of lamb. One woman, whom Zekharyah had always considered stingy of spirit, handed him a basket of warm raisin cakes. Another carried a bowl of lentil stew. He ushered all visitors to the cradle where his son lay. Men patted his back and shook his hand. Women shyly bowed their heads and rushed to sit with Elisheba to hear her birthing story.

The story of his son's birth filled Zekharyah with awe. His wife outpaced his strength and righteousness, but to hear how she had faced the challenges of birth with such determination and faith humbled him.

CR

BETWEEN THE NIGHTLY FEEDINGS and the constant stream of well-wishers, Zekharyah wondered if he'd ever get a chance to truly know his son. Mercifully, after a few days, the neighbors returned to their homes. Elisheba—by advisement of the midwife—rested on the pallet whenever the baby slept.

Zekharyah lifted the infant from the cradle and carried him to the shade of the almond tree in the courtyard. He opened the boy's blankets and swaddling to study the miracle Adonai had wrought. The boy stared at him with wise, cavernous eyes.

I envy you, my son, fresh from the school of your mother's womb, where you were taught everything of Torah. Although, like the rest of us, you will forget, hold on to these lessons with all of your might, for the law of the Lord is perfect.

Zekharyah stroked his throat and swallowed hard, hoping to loosen what kept his voice silent. *I have so much to teach you, my son—and here I am without a voice, the product of my unbelief.*

The boy grasped Zekharyah's finger.

You are a strong one, and that is a very good thing. You have a big job before you. When your legs are sturdier and your voice grows deep and strong, you will fulfill Adonai's plan, you will prepare the way for the Messiah. You will use your voice more wisely than I.

A prophet. His son was a prophet. Zekharyah's throat burned with unspoken emotion. *To be called as a prophet is not easy, my son. It is a high honor, yes, but the calling exacts a high cost, as well. You will speak for Adonai, and Adonai doesn't always say what men want to hear. They can't strike back at God in their shame, so they take their anger out on his messengers. Adonai seldom works the way we think he should, and that may disappoint you, but he always fulfills his promises. That is what I mean to teach you—Adonai is faithful, my son.*

I will also show you beauty, for Adonai is the author of beauty. Your mother is beautiful, as you have already seen. Zekharyah cradled the boy and gestured toward heaven. *The heavens declare the glory of Adonai; the skies proclaim the work of his hands. Day after day they pour forth speech—even though your father cannot. Night after night they display knowledge. There is no speech or language where their voice is not heard.[18] Glory to God!*

"Zekharyah, what are you telling the boy?"

Elisheba took their son from Zekharyah and nimbly swaddled the boy, straightening his legs and arms as she wound him in the cloths. *Where did she learn to do that?*

"I'm planning the circumcision feast with Atalyah's help. I'm not sure how to celebrate a child born by the announcement of an angel, but it seems right that his arrival should be trumpeted with style and lots of food. Are you in agreement, my love?"

If left to Zekharyah, he would commission a parade with elephants and camels, and a herd of white horses in fine regalia. And yes, trumpets—many trumpets to rival those blown by the Levites at the temple. All of Jerusalem and Judea would be invited to a feast of pomegranates, dried

---

[18] Psalm 19:1-4a (NIV).

apricots, melons, figs, and grapes. There would be cheeses and stacks of bread. Of course, much wine would be poured and a whole lamb roasted on a spit. And, if the neighbor was willing, a heaping platter of her raisin cakes would fill one end of the table.

In truth, no parade would march by, but his heart would be just as glad. He nodded, confirming his agreement to Elisheba's plan with a broad grin.

Chapter Nine

A Name is Given

Zekharyah rose early and sharpened the double-edged knife he would use to circumcise his eight-day-old son. He'd circumcised the sons of many families in the village, acting as deputy to the fathers who could not take a knife to their own flesh and blood. Zekharyah's heart pulsed wildly, yet his hands remained steady. He sheathed the knife.

Elisheba divided her time between feeding the boy and commanding an army of women who helped with preparation of the feast. In the courtyard, the women sang psalms of praise as they arranged platters of cheese and bread on tables. Since the very stones radiated the day's heat, the boy would be circumcised just before sunset, when the cooling breeze swept in from the west.

As the time neared, fellow Abijah brothers squeezed into the courtyard, accompanied by their wives and children. Neighbors he'd known all of his life sidled into scant pockets of space to make room for people he had never seen before. The Lord had, indeed, provided a sparkling sky and drilling sun. Zekharyah led elders into the shade of the almond tree and made sure they had wine to drink. He laughed to himself. *I should be sitting with them.*

He raised his hands to quiet the crowd before they all melted into a waxy puddle from the heat. Elisheba wove through the assembly to stand by his side. She had never looked more beautiful, or tired. He squeezed her hand. His son slept contentedly on a cushion on Baruch's lap. His serenity was about to be shattered.

Zekharyah nodded at his nephew and fellow priest. Baruch filled the courtyard with his clear tenor voice. "Blessed are you, Lord our God, King of the universe, who has sanctified us with his commandments and commanded us concerning circumcision."

The guests responded as one. "Just as he has entered into the covenant, so may he enter into Torah, into marriage, and into good deeds."

The crowd held its breath as Zekharyah unsheathed the knife and bent over the boy. With deft movements, the covenant—the very promise that stretched from Abraham to this fragile child—was in the boy's flesh, never to be canceled or forgotten. The baby's wails broke the silence.

Once the wound was packed with wool, Baruch presented the boy to the guests. Normally, Zekharyah would offer his pinkie dipped in wine to the crying infant, but the angel had said no wine was to touch his lips. Instead, he jostled the boy on his shoulder, but his son continued to howl.

Someone yelled, "Little Zekharyah knows how to make himself heard."

Elisheba raised her hands. "No! He is to be called Yohanan!"

The crowd hummed with surprise.

"Yohanan?" someone muttered.

"There is no one in your family by the name of Yohanan," another said.

Baruch beseeched the crowd to quiet their complaints. He turned to Zekharyah. "You could name him after the grandfather. Barachiah is a fine name. What could be better than being blessed of HaShem?"

"We must remember our traditions," someone called out.

"What else do we have but our traditions under the Romans?"

Elisheba drew herself up, looking imploringly over her shoulder at Zekharyah. He nodded encouragement to her. "We will call him Yohanan, nothing else."

A brother priest stepped forward, motioning with his hands to Zekharyah, shouting and carefully enunciating his words. "What… is…the…baby's…name?"

Elisheba, red in the face, waved her arms before the man. "He is not deaf. He hears everything we say. Shouting at him and waving your hands about does not help. It's insulting."

Zekharyah tapped her shoulder.

"What?"

He gestured as if writing.

"A tablet? You want a tablet?"

He nodded.

The crowd passed a tablet forward from an unseen volunteer. The wax softened by the heat yielded easily to the stylus. When finished, Zekharyah pressed the tablet into Baruch's hands. Baruch read the words and frowned at Zekharyah, who nodded solemnly. Baruch held the tablet over his head and shouted, "His name is Yohanan!"

Zekharyah lifted his hands to heaven. He mouthed, "Give praise to the Lord, the God of Israel!" But to his amazement, his words filled the air.

The crowd pressed in. Elisheba shouted, "I heard you! Oh, Zekharyah, I heard you! Glory to God!"

The people cheered raucously. The elation that rose in Zekharyah felt foreign yet familiar, so very fitting. He felt an unrolling in his soul, like the opening of a great scroll. And with the opening came a surety that Adonai's purposes were being fulfilled in that moment. All that Adonai had promised from Abraham to Moses, every hint of the Messiah in the stories of the *Tanakh* were about to be fulfilled. Even more, the deep longing that had lodged in his people's souls during the horrible centuries of silence would soon be filled with Adonai's presence.

The crowd parted as Zekharyah moved around the courtyard, looking into each face, giving each a blessing. Elisheba walked behind, the child cradled in her arms. Looking into those dear faces, a fresh picture of the Messiah's mission unfolded, one that emerged from all he'd studied from childhood until now. It was time for the benediction that Adonai had been writing on his heart during his season of silence, but not the benediction taught by his father and his father's father. This was a new benediction.

"Give praise to the Lord, the God of Israel!

    He has come to his people and purchased their freedom.

He has acted with great power and has saved us.

He did it for those who are from the family line of
    his servant David.

Long ago holy prophets said he would do it.

He has saved us from our enemies.

    We are rescued from all who hate us.

He has been kind to our people of long go.

    He has remembered his holy covenant.

He made a promise to our father Abraham.

He promised to save us from our enemies.

Then we could serve him without fear.

He wants us to be holy and godly as long as we live."[19]

Zekharyah lifted Yohanan from Elisheba's arms. The child, his son, was so small, so vulnerable. And yet, within him beat the heart of Adonai's most trusted messenger. Adonai could have sent another angel, as he had sent to Zekharyah. But the Lord chose Yohanan.

Zekharyah fingered the embroidery of the swaddling clothes, the tidy blue stitches sewn by Miryam in the shape of Elijah's cup. Under any other circumstances the emblem would be audacious, but for a child who would go before the Lord in the spirit and power of Elijah, the emblem fit Yohanan perfectly.

"And you, my child, will be called a prophet of Ha´Elyon.

You will go ahead of the Lord to prepare the way for him.

You will tell his people how they can be saved.

You will tell them that their sins can be forgiven.

All of that will happen because our God is tender and caring.

His kindness will bring the rising sun to us from heaven.

It will shine on those living in darkness

and in the shadow of death.

It will guide our feet on the path of peace."[20]

CR

BARUCH FOUND ZEKHARYAH ON the roof, savoring the breezes that brought refreshment over the roof tops in the summer and dissipated the smoke of cooking fires. Zekharyah's shoulders rounded as though he carried a heavy load, yet he gazed contentedly at the first stars blinking in the night sky. Zekharyah had asked earlier to speak with Baruch when the festivities wound down, but the celebration had gone longer than expected. Perhaps this wasn't a good time.

"Zekharyah," he called softly, waiting to be invited to join him.

The old man straightened and beckoned Baruch closer with a

---

[19] Luke 1:68-75 (NIrV).
[20] Luke 1:75-79 Ha´Elyon substituted for "the most high God." (NIrV).

welcoming smile. Baruch dragged a chair to face his uncle. He had no fewer than a million questions swirling in his mind. He prayed his uncle felt inclined to answer them.

"You should be proud, Zekharyah. Not since Adonai commanded Abraham to circumcise himself and his household has a more memorable circumcision taken place. This was a day for the history books."

Zekharyah nodded slowly. "Perhaps you should write it down, for the family at least."

"This day won't soon be forgotten. People are already speculating over Yohanan, what he will be when he grows up. I predict all of the Judean hill country will be abuzz by *Shabbat* with people asking the same question."

He waited then, hoping Zekharyah would expand on the question of his son. From what Zekharyah had told him of the angel in the temple and what Zekharyah had prophesied over his son, little Yohanan would someday clear the way for the Messiah. Could it be? Would Baruch live to see the Messiah deliver Israel from her enemies? Had the waiting finally come to an end?

Then why was his soul gripped with fear?

Zekharyah seemed gratified to shelter his thoughts. Baruch scooted his chair closer, leaned forward. "You finally recited your benediction, and what a benediction it was. The words stirred my soul, Zekharyah, but I'm also struggling. We've waited so long for Messiah. Our deliverance is nigh, or so it seems. But deliverance never comes easily or cheaply. The Romans crush rebellion. Anyone they perceive to challenge the emperor's sovereignty is deemed an enemy and mowed down like wheat. Even those standing between the might of Rome and a supposed rebel are destroyed— women and children, Zekharyah. They do not discriminate. You should be careful what you say. If any of this gets back to Herod…"

"I share your concerns. And I appreciate your warning, but HaShem will not be thwarted in his purposes. He is never defeated, not by our worries or a nation's armies. I will use discretion where discretion is due, but something has been set in motion that cannot be contained. As you say, word will spread whether we will it or not."

Zekharyah continued. "My focus, in light of Yohanan's calling, is to prepare him as best I can. He must know the Law better than anyone, and he must obey it. But more than that, the Law must be inscribed on his heart, and that's a very different thing. Having the Law written on our hearts means that we obey, not out of a sense of duty so much as out of a debt of love to HaShem."

Zekharyah placed his large hand on Baruch's knee. "This is a challenging charge for a father, is it not? The only thing I fear is not being given the years to finish the task."

"Zekharyah—"

Zekharyah held the lamp's flame near his face. "See these wrinkles around my eyes? This gray beard? I am old, Baruch. I pray I will have many good days with Yohanan, but nothing is guaranteed. And then who will teach my son?

"Will you, my dear nephew, will you step in when the time comes? Yohanan must be ready for this breathtaking work of preparing the way for the Messiah. Will you help my son become the man HaShem desires?"

Baruch ruminated on the idea that obedience to Adonai is out of love more than duty. How could he teach a boy to act in such a way, if he had never done so himself? "There is no one better equipped than you, Zekharyah, for such a task. Why else would HaShem send the boy to you?"

"In all of your years of studying Torah, has HaShem ever taken the obvious course?"

Baruch shook his head and chuckled softly. "No, never."

"But he has faithfully led his people. We will expect him to do the same with us."

Chapter Ten

Justice Satisfied

awn's gray light seeped through the unfinished roof to bring shape to the shattered table and shards of pottery strewn across the floor. Yosef groaned into his hands, his anger dissipated, his decision made. Where he had once imagined Miryam cooing over their child, he now saw only turmoil and betrayal.

Miryam would, by harvest, be a mother, but he was not the father of the child. What he could not answer for himself was how this had happened. He'd watched Miryam grow from a child into a woman. He'd chosen her for many reasons—she was strong yet gentle, serious but joyful, a woman of charity and piety. He'd never seen her act coyly with any of Nazareth's young men. In the end, with the darkest chapter of the night behind him, he'd decided she had been seduced or violated, by whom he did not know, and the story of the angel was her way of reconciling her sin. He didn't doubt that she believed her own story.

"Son?" His father, Yaakov, stood in the doorway, mussy with sleep, his face creased with worry. He'd heard—all of Nazareth had heard—Yosef's anguished cries through the night. The crack of splitting wood. The crash of pottery against stone.

"I have made my decision," Yosef said.

Yaakov half turned to go. "I will tell your mother to prepare for the journey to Jerusalem."

"No."

Yaakov turned back to the room. "No?"

"I will not put Miryam through such an ordeal." His throat tightened around her name. "We can deal with this here."

"They won't stone her in Jerusalem, Yosef. The Romans wouldn't allow it. Besides, you owe her no consideration. She broke the *ketubah*, not you."

"I will not have Miryam standing at the Nikanor Gate. She prayed there, Father, over a lifetime of holy days in the Court of Women with her family. To have her standing there, dressed in the black of an accused woman, absorbing the taunts of a condemning crowd—such humiliation would destroy Miryam."

"That is the decision of the Sanhedrin, son, not yours. It's obvious she's with child. You needn't worry that they will make her drink the bitter waters."

"No, I'll not waver on this. There will be no hearing before the Sanhedrin, no bitter waters, and no mortification for Miryam in the temple courts. I'm given another option to satisfy her offense before HaShem—I will divorce her, but quietly."

"You do not owe her—"

"Father, *please*. The Law is truly written on your heart, and I know you are a man of justice. But Miryam will definitely bear the repercussions for her sin. The days, months, and years will not be pleasant for her. Her sin will dog her wherever she goes. There is no need to drag her before the Sanhedrin."

With the sweep of his foot, Yaakov cleared a place to sit on the floor. "But you won't recover the *mohar*, my son. It will take years of saving to replace it. You have a house—almost completed—and no wife to live with you here. Yosef, please, all I'm asking is for you to consider your future."

They sat in silence, only the rattle of a nearby cart filled the distance between them. Yosef's mother came to the door, wrapped in a woolen cloak, her eyes red and puffy, her hands clasping her heart. She gasped on a sob that threatened her reserve anew and turned quickly to leave.

Yaakov ran his hands through his hair. "Yosef, I'm your father. I have to ask you one more time—"

Yosef rose and paced the length of the house, scattering broken pottery as he walked. "The child is not mine, Father."

"The two of you are young. You have prepared for a long time to bring Miryam into your home. It would be understandable if the two of you got impatient. This happens. Perhaps—"

Yosef stopped before his father. "As HaShem is my witness, the child is not mine."

"Then what will you do?"

Yosef pried a plank from the table and grabbed a saw from his tool chest. He cut a length of wood with decisive strokes. Then he sharpened a charred stick to a point. "I will write the *get* now, but I will need you to find another witness to sign it."

"You are sure this is how you want to proceed?"

"Yes, but don't ask me to deliver this divorce decree to Miryam myself. I couldn't."

"I will go. I will do this hard thing for you, son. After all, I played my part in bringing this calamity to you." Yaakov stroked his beard, thoughtful. "I'll wait until the time of evening meal. Eli will be home from his work in the orchard. It's best if I hand the *get* to him. He can present it to his daughter. I will stay, of course, and watch as she receives the *get* into her hands, just to be sure." He stood. "Uzziel will make a good witness. Besides, he will still be home. He moves even slower than I do."

"Will he be discrete?"

"We live in a small village, son. How could they help but know?" He put a hand to Yosef's head as he had done when his son was younger. "You are a good man, and you are trying to carry, even now, the weight of Miryam's sin. That is not for you."

❧

YOSEF TURNED FULL CIRCLE in the house he'd built for Miryam. He should put the place to order, not to welcome a bride but to retain what dignity was left to him. He bent to gather shards of pottery.

Yaakov ushered Uzziel into the house. The man scanned the room and sat, eyes downturned. His solemnity heartened Yosef. Others of the village might be less successful at hiding their glee. There is great relief at the exposure of someone else's sin. As Yosef wrote the date on the *get* and signed his name, he swallowed hard on the emotion building in his chest.

The weight of his decision and the finality of it sat on Yosef. Every stone he'd placed in the walls of the home he'd built for Miryam crushed him. He rounded his shoulders against the heft of the burden and dropped his head.

"You're exhausted," Yaakov said. "You won't be good to anyone until you've slept."

Lying down to sleep seemed impossible to Yosef. He'd tried all through the night when the weariness had pulled at him, but his thoughts had barked him into wakefulness each time.

"Your mother has made your pallet ready." Yaakov pulled Yosef to his feet. "There's nothing else you can do today. Go. Lay your head down and sleep. You will need your strength for all that lies ahead, my son."

CR

SUBDUED LIGHT BLED THROUGH the high slit of a window. Yosef bolted upright on the pallet. *What time is it?* He rushed into the courtyard where rain-heavy clouds covered the sun.

His mother stepped away from her loom. "Son, what is it now?"

"How long have I slept?"

"Your father will be home shortly. I'm sure his stomach is grumbling at him."

"I slept all day?" Yosef said.

"You looked peaceful. I let you sleep."

Yosef tied his sandals and grabbed his cloak.

With a quick sidestep his mother blocked the gate. "Where are you going?"

"Father carries the *get* to Miryam. If it reaches her hands, there will be no turning back, the divorce will be final."

"Isn't that what you want?"

Was divorcing Miryam what he wanted? "I...I'm not entirely sure what I want. But I now know that divorcing Miryam is not what HaShem wants." Yosef bounced with his eagerness to reach Eli before his father. "Mother, I have to go."

His mother stood her ground. "Don't do this, Yosef. The woman betrayed you. She sinned before Adonai."

Yosef pushed past his mother and dashed out the gate.

She called after him. "You will not bring her to this house! She is not welcome here!"

He ran the cart-worn path that wound through the village center and out to the valley. By the time he reached the well, he'd wrestled out of his cumbersome cloak and flung it on the stones. He would not allow anything to slow him, and certainly nothing to stop him from getting to Eli's orchard, more than half a mile away, before the *get* made it into Miryam's hands.

His lungs burned as he sprinted past the olive grove owned by Gershom. The man turned his back to Yosef and tended his old cow. There would be more of that. *How will I protect Miryam?*

His sandal strap snapped, and he fell hard on the road. Old Diklah stood from her work in the garden, but when she saw it was Yosef who fell, she batted him away and returned to her work.

There was no time to pick pebbles from his knee and forearm. He left the sandal where it lay and picked his way over the rocky road. Desperate for speed, he cut across a melon patch, striding between mounds to avoid crushing the tender plants. Ofir, the farmer, yelled to his back, "Yosef, get out of my garden!"

His lungs demanded that he slow, to bend over his knees, and breathe deeply. Behind him, the sun brightened the clouds near the western horizon. There would be time to breathe when he got to Eli's house.

As he made the last turn toward his destination, he came upon a caravan of donkeys and camels, their drivers, and some eager salesmen looking to sell their wares. "My donkey will carry you where you need to go! Only fifteen half-shekels, brother!" Yosef ignored the man, running past the animals, and turned off the main track.

Eli's orchard lay near the top of the hill. Yosef's thighs screamed for rest, and his lungs burned like fire, but he didn't stop. Soon he entered the lower terraces of Eli's orchard. The plastered walls of the house shone through the trees. Yosef ordered his complaining legs to run faster.

As Yosef approached the house, Miryam's mother, Channah, stepped into the yard. She fretted the fabric of her cloak, a pained look of betrayal in her eyes.

Yosef bent, finally, to suck in air. "Is. My father. Here?"

"He is on the hill with Eli," she said, flatly.

Miryam stood just inside the door. Yosef thought to go to her, but looked to the hill, instead. There wasn't a moment to waste. He nodded understanding to Channah and met Miryam's gaze. Her eyes were red and swollen. Channah drew Miryam into a protective embrace. He prayed he would have years to explain his actions in their life together.

He started to climb, scanning the trees for his father and Eli. He stopped to listen for their voices, but his heaving breaths covered all sounds. He climbed higher.

Yosef found his father and Eli at the very top of the orchard. The men stood stiffly as Yaakov offered the *get* to Eli. Yosef sucked in a breath and called out, "No!"

The men turned to him, mouths agape, eyes questioning.

Yosef called, "Wait! Don't!" He took the *get* from Yaakov and leaned against the terrace wall, gulping in lungfuls of air. The wood in his hand weighed as heavy as his heart.

"You're bleeding," his father said.

Indeed, rivulets of blood coursed down his shin and arm. There was no breath for words. He waved off his father's concern. He held up his palms to implore patience. When his breathing slowed, he said to Eli, "I still want Miryam as my wife."

Yaakov stepped closer. "Son—?"

"I know, Father," Yosef said, "But something has happened that I can't explain, but I must heed." He turned to Eli with imploring hands. "Will you hear me out?"

"Why should I listen to you? You defiled Miryam and deny it, and now, after shaming me and my family, you want to take her home as your wife? Answer me; why should I listen to a word you say?"

Miryam's future would be difficult enough—the object of scorn and stinging isolation, for few would believe her story. A nod of blessing from her father would fortify her against the coming abuse of all who doubted her. Yosef had never influenced the future of another with his words. He wiped the sweat from his hands and prayed: *Lord, help me.*

"Eli, you have only my word and the word of your daughter that we have done nothing to violate the *ketubah*. I truly understand if that is not enough for you. In your place, I'm not sure it would be enough for me."

Yosef held Eli's gaze and waited, his heart pounding. Although time stood rigidly between them, the orchard sang its song. The ravens voiced their complaints, and the mirth of the mating doves lilted from the trees. Bees hummed in the hollyhocks. The air cooled as the sun slid from the sky.

Eli shook his head. "To tell you quite plainly, nothing that has happened in the last months has made any sense to me. First, Miryam and her angel, and then a most unexpected birth. You have heard of Elisheba?"

"I have heard rumors of a son born to your aged kinswoman."

"They are not rumors," Eli said. "I saw her heavy with child with my own eyes."

"It would seem that HaShem is at work in his own uncomfortable way. He does not change, does he?"

"If you are here to tell me of another angel... Son, I'm an old man. Life has an order—a daughter is betrothed, a son comes to manhood, even death comes at its appointed time. None of this—" Eli opened his arms to the universe. "None of this is happening the way it's supposed to. What will you now add to this madness?"

"Something extraordinary—something I cannot explain away by reason—happened to me today. I'm simply here to tell you what that was."

Eli exhaled resignedly. "If you must."

"Perhaps my father told you that he left me sleeping when he went off to work this morning. I had been up all night, railing mostly about all that has happened. None of this sits easily with me, either. I have never faced a burning bush. I am not a prophet. I'm not even a priest. I am a man who works with his hands. The stones submit to my will. I make wood do my bidding daily."

"Yosef, what are you here to tell me?"

"I had a dream—"

Eli threw up his hands. "You are here to tell me of a dream? My daughter is halfway to being a mother, with no home, no husband, and you are here to tell me a dream?"

When Yosef had lain on his pallet after a night of angst and regret, he would have agreed with Eli—Miryam had no home with him, and he was not her husband. His heart had gone numb toward her sometime in the night. Now he saw everything differently. His heart swelled with love for his betrothed, all thanks to what the angel had told him in his dream.

Eli didn't have the advantage of a heavenly visitor to evoke a change of heart and extract a blessing for Miryam. Only a humble builder with a wooden tongue stood before him. It wasn't in Yosef to construct a convincing argument. He would simply tell of the dream and pray to Adonai that hearing the story would be enough for Eli.

"Miryam says a bright being came to her, here in the orchard. Such a being came to me in my dream. He spoke to me as clearly as we speak to one another now. I have no doubt—I felt this assurance as he spoke—that he was the same messenger who visited Miryam. He called me by name and told me not to be afraid to take Miryam home as my wife, that I wasn't to hesitate. He went on to say that the child is from the Holy Spirit, and that the baby is a son. We're to name him Yeshua—Savior—for he is destined to save his people from their sins."

Eli turned and strode away from Yosef and Yaakov, down the long row of trees. Had Yosef said too much? Not enough? He dropped his chin to his chest, not wanting to watch Eli refuse his request.

Yaakov nudged him and gestured to where Eli walked. The man stopped to lift beseeching arms to the sky, and then walked again toward the orchard's far boundary. He stood there for some time, bowing his head, then looking to heaven, and shaking his head.

Yosef prayed.

Eli walked slowly back to the men. "I am destined, too, but I will be known as a fool in this valley for generations after my death. The people have long memories in these hills. I will be a fool, but my daughter will have a home and my grandson will have a man to call *abba*."

Yosef let out a breath he hadn't realized he was holding.

Eli stepped closer. "When we arrived at the home of Zekharyah, he took me to his nephew's house. I didn't understand why he would do such a thing, but Zekharyah couldn't tell me. He could not talk—not one word. The nephew told me a fantastical story about Zekharyah and an angel." Eli paused and looked directly at Yosef. "But that angel appeared in the temple, where angels belong.

"That angel told Zekharyah that his son would clear the way for the Messiah—the *Messiah*, mind you. His words sounded like a story for children. And your angel says my grandson will suffer for the sins of our people. I like Zekharyah's story better, you understand? Whether any of this happens or not, what do you mean to do now?"

It was a question, but it sounded like a warning.

"First, I have a promise to make to you: I will be good to Miryam and protect her as best I can. Right now, today, I will go home and finish the roof of the house…and tidy up the place. If you are willing, I will come for Miryam when all is in order."

"It would not be appropriate…"

"No, I agree, an extravagant wedding feast would not be well received. Not now, not with everything that has happened and how people perceive the events."

Eli put his hand to Yosef's shoulder. "We will have a small celebration here, away from the center of the village. And then the two of you will go to your home and build the best life you can."

When the day had dawned, Yosef sat in the ruins of his life. Now, as the sun slid toward the western hills, he could once again claim the bride of his heart. The days, weeks, months, and years ahead held no resemblance to the life he'd once imagined for himself and Miryam. It would be hard but perhaps in a strange way better. Weren't the days of securing the Promised Land full of battles? And yet, the Lord went before the warriors, and victory was theirs. The Lord will go before him and his new wife, too.

Chapter Eleven

A Wedding Feast

*M*iryam folded and refolded her woolen cloak, a tunic, and the linens she had embroidered for her life with Yosef. The wool made her skin itch in the cumbrous heat of the loft. She bundled these things, along with her few personal items, to carry to her new home.

She turned around in the small space, to make sure she hadn't forgotten anything. What she meant to leave behind—the pallets of her parents and her four siblings, and the familiarity of their nearness—clenched at her heart.

The wedding tunic she had spent months embroidering lay lifeless across her pallet, resplendent with its red and blue embroidery on the hem, neck, and sleeves. She smoothed the wrinkles from the working tunic she wore. The serviceable garment would be fine for a wedding such as this.

In truth, what sort of wedding she would share with Yosef wasn't clear. She only knew what it wouldn't be. There would be no anticipation, no listening for the *shofar* to sound, no wondering if this was the day Yosef would come for her. Yosef had sent a message with one of his brothers that this should be their wedding day. He did this out of courtesy to her family, as they were hosting the supper, instead of his family.

There would be no processional through the village. She would not be lifted on a seat to be carried from her parents' house to her new home. No torches would light the night, and her friends and family would stay at home.

Her mother-in-law, Atarah, had refused to prepare the wedding feast, so Miryam shared no speculations with the women of her family about the meal. Instead, Savta, Ima, and Dodah worked feverishly to prepare the meal, which, due to the short notice, would be modest. There would be no elders, no guests savoring seven days of feasting, no congratulatory slaps on the back for Yosef. No knowing giggles with her maiden friends.

For the hundredth time that day, Miryam swallowed down her disappointment and blinked back tears. For his great kindness and generosity of spirit, Yosef deserved a bride who looked glad to see him, not one who had been crying most of the day.

Besides, dissatisfaction over temporal things like processions and feasts seemed ungrateful and petty. She had prayed to carry the Messiah, just as every woman and girl had prayed since the time of the prophets. And now the Messiah somersaulted within her.

Oh, Lord, thank you for hearing my prayer. Forgive my shallowness.

Miryam reopened the bundle and added the wedding tunic. With a deep breath to calm her jumbled emotions, she carried the parcel to the yard where the women of the family toiled with grim faces over the wedding supper. This should be the time of day when the women did their weaving in the cooling shade of the fig tree and trellis. Instead, Dodah slapped loaves of bread onto the walls of the gaping oven. Ribbons of shimmering heat rose to redden her face.

Savta mopped her face with a linen towel as she arranged pancakes with dates and grapes on a platter. "This is *not* how a wedding should take place."

Ima caught Miryam's eye and elbowed Savta. "Miryam will have no other wedding day, and a fine husband is coming to claim her. We will be happy with all HaShem has provided. It is a small thing to fulfill the groom's responsibility for a feast, for such a circumstance as this."

Savta shoved the towel into her sash and stood nose to nose with Miryam. "I cannot go anywhere but I hear of this family's disgrace. Everywhere, I tell you. The market. The well. Even the synagogue." She pointed a gnarled finger at Miryam. "All because of you and your angel." She spat the word angel and spittle sprayed Miryam's face.

Miryam closed her eyes against the slap that would surely come, but Savta threw up her hands and stomped into the house. "You stupid, stupid girl!"

Ima wiped Miryam's face with her sleeve. "You should be dressed."

Miryam put her hand to her swollen abdomen. "Wearing such an elaborate tunic doesn't seem suitable."

Ima embraced Miryam with strong, insistent arms. Her mother's breath warmed her ear. "You have nothing to be ashamed of. If anything, you should be celebrated for the honor Adonai has given you."

"Ima—"

"Yes, I know, it is as you have said many times, a very humble calling. And I do agree that motherhood—while it is a gift of HaShem—has a way of correcting any lofty ideas we may believe about ourselves. But, Miryam, there are many, many maidens HaShem could have chosen to carry the Messiah." She pulled back, lifted Miryam's chin. "He chose you. While that truth shouldn't swell your head, it can be a source of strength. You have done nothing to disqualify wearing the dress you so carefully prepared for this day. I insist you go put it on."

A tear escaped down Miryam's cheek. "The sash no longer fits around me."

Ima wiped the tear away with her rough hand. "You will have plenty of chances to wear a sash as fine as yours, perhaps for *Pesach*. In fact, I will wear my wedding sash—if it still fits—to the temple this year, and you can wear yours. No one will recognize us. They will say, 'Who are those finely turned out ladies of Nazareth?'"

Miryam managed a small smile at her mother's imitation of the rich women of Jerusalem. Ima drew her back into her arms. "Oh, my daughter, I will miss you so very much."

A *shofar* blasted, and the women snapped their attention to the sound. The horn blew again, still some distance down the hill.

"They're coming," one of her brothers said.

A man shouted. "Miryam!"

Yosef?

Ima squeezed Miryam to her side. "He's early. He must be anxious to take his wife home."

"Miryam!" Yosef called again.

Ima pulled Miryam into the house and pushed her up the loft's ladder, where Miryam could don her wedding clothes without the prying eyes of her siblings.

Ima called down to Hevel, "Go get Abba! Gather your sisters! Yosef is here!"

Hevel darted toward the door. Miryam yelled after him, "Everyone must wash their hands and faces. You are in charge, Hevel. I'm counting on you."

Miryam held the embroidered tunic to her chest. "Maybe I should have asked Gila and Levana to be my bridesmaids, after all. I didn't expect Yosef to assemble a procession. Will he think I didn't want this day to happen?"

"Daughter, you can look at this day and only take notice of how it differs from what you've held in your heart since you were a girl, or you can discover the day as it unfolds before you, and celebrate the good it holds. Truthfully, Miryam, every bride must measure her expectations against reality. In this way, you are like every other bride since Eve." Ima busied herself with rewrapping Miryam's belongings, singing from the Song of Solomon in celebration of marriage.

Miryam could be sure of some things this day. After the blessing of Rebekah spoken by her parents and then the feast, she would walk down the hill, leaving her family and home, to become part of Yosef's family. She was marrying a man who had gallantly worked to soften the blow of her perceived sin. In doing so, he demonstrated his desire to protect her dignity, and now he was taking on her sin by honoring the *ketubah* that betrothed her to him. Not many maidens knew so much about their new husband's character before they married.

She unfurled the tunic and handed it to her mother, raising her hands over her head to receive it. With the veil in place, Miryam took her mother's hands in hers. "This is the day I marry an honorable man who obeys Adonai, even when it is hard. I am a blessed woman."

Miryam stood beside her mother in the yard as Ima straightened her veil and tugged a sleeve into place. Her heart beat riotously, waiting for Yosef to come into view on the lane. She wasn't sure she could have stood weeks of this kind of anticipation.

Finally, Yosef arrived, grinning sheepishly. Beside him walked his father and one of his brothers. No mother. No aunts. No sisters. Not one friend from the synagogue. She grabbed for her mother's hand.

Yosef came to her, a little winded from the climb up the hill but smiling, a pleading in his eyes she wanted to heed but didn't know how. Her father stepped between them, and Yosef bowed his head respectfully. "All is ready. I have prepared a place for your daughter."

He turned to Yaakov, his father, who addressed Miryam's family, especially her mother. "I have inspected the house. The walls are strong and straight. The family will enjoy many star-filled nights on the roof, and when it rains, they will remain dry inside. No threat will come through the door. A king would envy its stoutness. I deem the house ready for Miryam. It will be a good place to raise many strong sons and some beautiful daughters. The house is, indeed, ready."

Abba pulled a small, linen-wrapped package from his pouch. "I am honored to present this *mattan* to my beloved daughter, Miryam." He took Miryam's hand in his and placed the bundle in her palm.

Miryam opened the linen with trembling fingers. Inside, a chain fitted with ten silver coins glinted in the late-afternoon light. Her mother bent over the bauble. "So beautiful and delicate. It suits you well. Let me help you put it on."

As her mother fitted the headdress in place, Miryam's heart nearly burst with gratitude. She fingered the coins that lay cool on her forehead. In the rush to prepare a feast and to send their daughter to a new family, her parents hadn't forgotten one thing. With her head adorned, Abba took her hand and placed it in Yosef's.

Abba and Ima stood before the new couple with tears in their eyes and recited the blessing of Rebekah, just as she knew they would.

> "Our sister, may you become
>> the mother of many millions!
> May your descendants be strong
>> and conquer the cities of their enemies." [21]

Without the authoritative voice of the master of the banquet, the gathered family shuffled, looking uncertain of what to do next, even though they had attended many weddings over the years.

Yaakov cleared his throat. "I suppose this would be a good time for us to sit down and celebrate the marriage of Yosef and Miryam."

"Yes, let's eat!" Ima said. "Please, make yourselves comfortable at our table."

---

[21] Genesis 24:60 (NIV).

Chapter Twelve

A New Home

Doors slammed as Miryam walked with Yosef toward their home along the narrow streets of Nazareth. A mother gathered her playing children and herded them through a gate, looking scornfully over her shoulder. They had left her parents' home as the sun balanced on the horizon. Now, in the gloaming of the day, the first stars appeared.

Yosef shifted the bundle of Miryam's belongings and took her hand. The strength of his calloused hand assured her that she didn't walk alone, that day or in the days to come. As they entered the empty marketplace, a dog charged through an open gate and barred their way.

Berel's herding dog? She'd shared water with that dog. Now, with hackles raised, he barked as though she meant to steal the family's sheep. Yosef released her hand to charge the animal with a growl and outstretched arms. The dog tucked his tail and ran away.

Even dogs reproached her?

Yosef took her hand again and they walked on. "It's just a dog," he said.

A dog, yes, but the contempt of the whole village weighed on her like a stone.

Not one glimmer of lamplight shone from Yosef's parents' house. No smoke curled from a cooking fire, although it was time for the evening meal. The door stood bolted against the breezes that exhaled through the town at twilight. Even the wedding chambers Yosef's older brothers had built for their brides were closed and shuttered against the most pleasant part of the day, and against Miryam.

Yosef and Miryam walked on without pausing. Their house shared a wall with his parents' courtyard, so the couple walked around the corner to their own fine wooden gate, carved with graceful olive branches.

On her way to the well, Miryam had walked by her new house twice a day over the course of the betrothal. She'd thrilled as the walls rose from the foundation, each course of stone bringing her closer to being Yosef's wife. Yosef's steady progress motivated her better than Savta's taunts to complete her wedding garments.

As she'd carried the water jar, she allowed herself to daydream about what it would mean to be mistress of such a house. She pictured herself grinding meal as small children played. She imagined Atarah, her mother-in-law, taking loaves of bread from the oven, and the easy chatter they made. In her thoughts, the house was full of light and the sound of laughter. The house before her wore the deepening shadows of night like a concealing veil. She hesitated outside the gate Yosef held open.

"I will light lamps," he said.

As he gathered lamps and lit them from embers he coaxed to life, Miryam stepped haltingly into the house for the first time. The door opened into the animal keep. She had hoped to tend a couple sheep and at least three goats. That many goats would produce plenty of milk to feed her family and to make cheese to sell in the marketplace, but the space was too small. Only two goats would fit, maybe only one.

She climbed three steps to the main floor and stood in the middle of the house, turning to take in all that Yosef had created. Without the clamoring of her brothers and sisters, mother and father discussing *Shabbat* plans, the grumbling of Savta, the singing of Dodah, her new home was positively cavernous, although it was much smaller than the home of her parents.

Her betrothal to Yosef had not gone as planned. Who would have expected the visitation of an angel—in, of all places, Nazareth—to upend their lives? And yet, she felt sheltered within the cool quiet of the stone walls Yosef had built for her.

She ran a hand over a wall. It felt like burnished wood. She offered Yosef an admiring smile, and his chest lifted. His careful planning showed in the house's details. A row of niches above a work table provided storage for her cooking utensils and linens, and he'd built shelves on the wall he'd chiseled out of a rock face, the coolest place in the house, for her grain basket, the storage of dried fruit, and the making of cheese.

Yosef gestured to the ceiling. "My father insisted on the biggest timbers for the beams. Wrestling them into place took the better part of a week. All of Nazareth could stand on the roof, and not one piece of plaster would fall from the ceiling."

She nodded her approval. "The beams look very strong."

"There is also a guest chamber on the roof, for visitors or if sometime in the future one of our elders needs shelter." Yosef motioned to the courtyard through the opened door. "Perhaps you noticed that I built stairs to the roof?"

"I've only known a ladder. Carrying the laundry and flax to the roof will be much easier. Thank you."

Yosef slapped the wood of the ladder leading to the sleeping loft. "You won't find a sturdier ladder in all of Nazareth. I know, because I helped my father repair what others have built. You will see, also, that I made the loft roomy. I have slept too many years with brothers elbowing me to settle for anything smaller."

Miryam's face warmed at the mention of the loft, the place where Miryam and Yosef would sleep with their son and all the children who followed. She busied herself with unpacking the linens she'd prepared for her new home.

Yosef coughed into his hand, looking lost in the house he'd built. He brushed away sawdust from the repairs he'd made to the table. "Are you hungry? I could easily start a fire."

Miryam had eaten sparingly of the food her mother and family had prepared for the wedding feast. The awkwardness between the two families had stolen her appetite. Yosef and the men hadn't seemed to notice the tension and ate heartily, if in complete silence. Could he really be hungry after such a meal? "I'm not hungry, but if you are, I can put a meal together."

"I'm fine." He met her gaze with his dark eyes. "I saw that you hadn't eaten much at the banquet."

"Too much excitement, I think. I will go to the market tomorrow and fill the shelves. What Ima sent along, will that be all right until I can bake fresh bread?"

He patted his stomach. "I ate enough for both of us." He nodded to the shelf of pottery. "There were more dishes. Some of them got broken, I'm afraid."

His eagerness to please warmed her. On a shelf, one clay cup and two small bowls sat. "There are only two of us, for now. What is here will suffice."

Yosef picked up Miryam's bundle. "I'll put your things in the guest chamber."

He referred to the room meant for future guests, yet he'd emphasized putting only *her* things in the room. She'd been surprised that he'd included such a room. They had no need for a loft *and* a guest chamber, not with just the two of them, and soon a baby.

He watched her, waiting for her to follow. There was no glint of anticipation in his eye, the very look she'd seen on every groom at every wedding she had ever attended. Mary's heart deflated.

"Yosef?"

He brought a cushion to the low table and invited Miryam to sit with an extended arm. "We have a lot to talk about."

She hadn't expected discussion. She wasn't at all sure she wanted to talk to Yosef about all that had happened. Wouldn't it be easier to simply go about the business of starting their lives together? It wouldn't be long before the tumbling child in her womb would clamber to be let out, and everything would change.

"There is something I need to say, Yosef. I'm so grateful for—"

He clasped his hands on the table. "No, it is I who needs to say something. I should have believed you sooner, Miryam. My pride got in the way. I forgot all I knew about you. I hope you can forgive me."

"Not many men would listen to an angel, in a dream or otherwise. You must know that I believe you were chosen as much as I to parent the child. And as far as I'm concerned, you will always be abba to this boy, and he will be your son."

"I worry that I'm not the best man for the job."

"Your worry tells me you are the perfect man to be his father. You understand that raising this child won't always be easy, and that will keep us both praying, I think."

Their eyes held in the soft lamplight. He was the right man—a very good man—Adonai had chosen for her and for the baby. A small smile creased his eyes. He was so handsome when joy owned his features.

He rose, extended his hand to her. "You look tired. I've made a pallet for you. I'll take you to your room. It's been a long day."

Another thing very different about this day. By now, Yosef and Miryam would have been escorted into the wedding chamber by the friends of the bridegroom. With much cheering and encouragement, and a blessing by their parents, the two would have closed the door on the festivities to be alone. After their first night together, the sheet would have been inspected for signs of her purity and stored away, insurance against any future complaint about her virginity.

Instead, he wanted to usher her to the guest chamber, alone. All the reproach hurled at her over the last weeks had cut deeply, but there had always been the memory of the angel, of Elisheba's welcome, the camaraderie of two expectant mothers, and the confirmation of Adonai's work in her to give her comfort. This rebuff from Yosef cut the deepest. With his rejection clenching her throat, she asked, "You will not join me?"

He looked at his feet. When their gazes finally met, his eyes welled with tears as did hers. "Miryam…"

"Yosef, I am ready to be a wife to you."

"Yes, well, that is good."

"Is there a problem? With me?"

"There is nothing wrong with you. Not one thing. You are beautiful, righteous, and very appealing. But I've given this a lot of thought, and I think we should delay…" He glanced toward the guest chamber. "I think we should wait to start our marriage until the baby is born."

"Knowing what you know, does this child make me so undesirable?"

"Oh no, you are very desirable to me. You are the most lovely woman I have ever seen, and I have longed for this day for much longer than I'm ready to admit."

"Then why, Yosef? If this day has long been on your mind, and you are pleased with me, you must help me understand. Because you know we are not truly married until…"

"Miryam, I remember seeing you for the first time at synagogue. You were sunshine. Every eye was on you for the joy that radiated from your face. This is who you still are—loveliness and piety, a woman beyond reproach. As my time to marry approached, my parents suggested this girl and that over these last years. I waited for you, Miryam. I have never wanted to marry anyone else."

"And yet I am to sleep in the guest chamber?"

"Please remember, Miryam, I'm not an especially wise man."

"You sell yourself short. I see you at synagogue, talking with the visiting rabbis. You ask so many questions, the very questions I wonder about, too. Abba says only smart men ask questions worth answering, and the rabbis don't begrudge their time with you."

Yosef's shoulders sagged. "You will not let this rest until morning?"

She sat on the courtyard stones with only the lamp Yosef carried to encircle them with light. "I will not."

Yosef sat. "All right. I will tell you what has filled my mind these days since I learned of the child. As I'm sure you remember, the prophet Isaiah says that the Messiah will be both conceived and given birth by a virgin. Do you understand what this means?"

She frowned. "Everyone knows that. There is no mystery in those words."

Yosef drummed his knee. "Let me try to say it another way. The *virgin* conceives the Messiah, and then the *virgin* gives birth to the Messiah."

"Are you saying…? Are you saying that the virgin is still a virgin when she gives birth?"

"I think so, yes."

"And you, in your desire to follow HaShem's plan, will sleep in the loft while I sleep in the guest chamber until the baby is born?"

"Yes."

"Is this what the angel told you?"

"This is my own idea, I'm afraid. Our family has been assigned to read the prophet Isaiah, so I'm quite familiar with the writing. Sometimes, as you know, living what we're taught in the Law and the prophets is very difficult, indeed."

"It is true, this arrangement of yours will not be easy."

"It's only a few more months."

"Less, I think."

A smile spread across Yosef's face. "That's very good, a relief, actually." He stood and extended a hand to Miryam and pulled her up. He did not let go of her hand. "I cannot carry the baby for you, Miryam. That burden is yours. Perhaps this is how I'm being asked to demonstrate my love for HaShem, or perhaps my willingness to be his instrument in bringing the Messiah to our people. Whatever his reasons, we are in this together. We will do what HaShem has asked of us, and then we will truly begin our lives, together."

In the darkness of the guest chamber, Miryam lay her head on her arm. Sleep teased her, pulling her into silly dreams, but didn't let her sink into the dark waters of oblivion. She would face her mother-in-law in the morning, for surely the woman's curiosity would not let her stay away. At best, she anticipated indifference from Atarah. She dared not focus on what the worst could be. Miryam would defer to her husband's mother and win her with love, as Ima had instructed her.

Thank you, Lord, that I do not have to share a cooking fire with her.

She let her thoughts travel to the future, when her son stepped into his role as Messiah. Not just Nazareth, but the whole kingdom would erupt in joyous praise. He was to be a savior, and her people desperately needed saving—from Rome, most of all. When he walked among them as a hero of deliverance, they would look differently at her, too. All suggestions of shame would be detached from her name. She recited a psalm as sleep finally tugged at her. "The Lord will save those who serve him. No one who goes to him for safety will be found guilty."[22]

---

[22] Psalm 34:22 (NIrV).

Chapter Thirteen

Rome Demands Its Coin

Yosef and Miryam sat along the back wall of the synagogue. If anyone chose to cast a rebuking look at Miryam during the reading of Torah, they would have to turn away from the reader to do so. Not many wanted to be seen as inattentive to Moses.

And not many listened wholeheartedly on that particular *Shabbat*. Word had just reached Nazareth of another Roman census, which meant higher taxes to follow, for a census was more about assessing wealth than counting citizens.

Rome had already looped a taxation noose around their necks, and they intended to pull the rope tighter. The census had been timed for the greatest gain. Farmers now harvested their fields and filled their storerooms. More revenue could be collected from full storerooms than empty.

Near the door, Miryam's parents sat on the stone bench that lined the room, her siblings sitting at their feet. Her father fixed his gaze on the dirt floor, his shoulders tense, his jaw set. Her mother's eyes flitted around the room until they met Miryam's. How Miryam longed to go to her and find comfort in her arms. Instead, she fretted the fabric of her tunic. Yosef took her hand and squeezed. When would she learn to turn to him first?

As the leader of the synagogue uttered the last amen, Hiram, a farmer, stood. "What of this census? Are we to throw open our coin purses—as meager as they are—every time Rome decrees a census?"

The synagogue leader, Akiva, stood abruptly and raised his hands to the speaker. "Wait, Hiram!" He turned to Miryam's brother, Hevel. "Stand at the door, boy. Keep watch. If a Roman or one of their sympathizers comes near, alert us."

Hevel rose, his chest out, and rushed to the door. He leaned against the lintel, arms crossed over his chest. Anyone passing would think him bored and impatient to be away from the synagogue. Such a clever brother.

"Hiram, my man, you know better than to rant so recklessly."

The man dropped his chin to his chest, flexing his hands. When he looked up, he scanned every face around the synagogue. "I only know that we are barely surviving now. What if the rains delay planting next year? What if the rains don't come at all? What if the locusts swarm? I, for one, will be ruined under the demand for more taxes. I say we forget we ever heard of the census."

Among the farmers, Hiram was the most pessimistic, but to believe Rome could be ignored was foolishness. Rome never mislaid a source of income, not even tiny Nazareth.

Yosef's father, Yaakov, stood and raised a clenched fist. "I hate filling Caesar's coffers as much as you do, Hiram, but there will be no forgetting the census when the Romans ride into town with their spears and clubs."

Another man stood, his face flushed above his beard. "They won't stop at taxes. They will demand an oath of loyalty." He spat on the floor. "I will not—I *cannot*—before HaShem swear an allegiance to a pagan!"

The room exploded with agreement. Again, Akiva lifted his hands to quiet the room. "Listen! Listen!"

"So you can convince us to bow to the Romans yet again?"

"Friends! Listen to me!" But the soft-spoken leader could barely be heard among the angry congregants.

"Our children deserve a better future. All we can promise them now is to be choked to death by the taxes of the Romans."

Akiva stepped onto the bench. "Friends, please, I've received a message from the high priest!"

"Kayafa, the puppet of Rome? What good is he to us? He is more Roman than Hebrew."

Her father joined the leader on the bench, raising imploring hands. "Quiet! My friends, please. Give Akiva a chance to speak. He is but the messenger. He has served our community with faithfulness and integrity for all these years. He is one of us. What we are asked to bear, he must bear also."

Abba turned to Gad, the loudest of those collected. "We all have strong feelings about the unfair treatment of the Romans, but under our leader's direction we have known peace, a precious commodity to be sure."

All gazes shifted to Akiva, who nodded appreciatively at Abba. "I am no happier than you about the census. It means Romans will come to our town, as sleepy and humble as it is, and exert their power over us. They will insert themselves into our most private places—our homes and our storerooms—and they will ask us to be loyal, when we have only one loyalty, to Adonai."

Akiva stepped off the bench and walked to the center of the synagogue, those gathered moving back to give him room. Her father's words had reminded them of the respect due this trusted man. "No, I don't like this new census at all. But the well-being of our inhabitants is utmost in my mind. We must survive this insult to be ready for the day when the Messiah returns. To have him arrive and find us already defeated would be most grievous. It distresses me greatly to agree with Kayafa on this point, but we must cooperate with the Roman census, not to appease Rome but to be strong enough to follow Messiah into battle."

Akiva turned to Yosef's father. "There is more to this census, I'm afraid, and this will affect your family, Yaakov, and anyone else whose ancestral home is in another city. The heads of households must go back to the homes of your ancestors for the census."

The room erupted into chaos again, questions shouted but no answers given, only speculation. "What do the Romans care of our ancestral homes?"

"This has the high priest's dirty handprints all over it, but to what end?"

"Who will feed my children this winter?"

"This from men who have never worked a day in their lives!"

The census could not have come at a worse time. As the head of the household, Yosef was required to return to Bethlehem with his father and his married older brothers, all who had been born there. The trip took four days each way—if all went smoothly, if the weather held. Most believed the census would be a protracted affair as the Romans meticulously inventoried property and possessions, and then interviewed each citizen. Not one Roman official would care that Yosef left behind a pregnant wife nearing her time.

The weeks since their wedding had been a mix of sweet and bitter. In the evenings, Yosef and Miryam spent long hours on the roof, getting to know one another and speculating about what raising the Messiah might be like. But Yosef left far too early each morning for Sepphoris, walking with his father and brothers to continue their work.

The days passed slowly for Miryam in his absence. Yosef's mother Atarah, shunned her involvement in the day-to-day work of the women, so Miryam carried water, ground meal, prepared meals, and gathered bushwood for the fire, all on her own. Everywhere she went, she suffered abuse by the women of the village. She feared being left alone during Yosef's journey to Bethlehem. Would he take her along?

Yosef tugged her hand and whispered into her ear. "Let's go."

‹♦›

ABBA AND IMA STEPPED through the courtyard gate. Ima wrung her hands, looking from Yosef to Miryam and back to Yosef. "She isn't far from giving birth. You would have her do so on the roadside between here and Bethlehem?"

Miryam rose from the cooking fire. "Ima, I am still weeks from giving birth."

"You don't know that. Babies come when babies are ready, and sometimes when they are not ready, always when *you* are not ready. It's foolishness to put yourself in such a dangerous position, with this your first birth. You can't know what will happen. Yosef, talk sense into your wife."

Yosef smiled self-consciously. "It was my idea to take her with me."

"Eli, why are you just standing there? Tell Miryam to stay home."

He shrugged. "She is Yosef's wife now. She will do what he says."

"You know your daughter better than that. It is more like *he* will do what she says."

Yosef beckoned Miryam's parents inside. "Please, sit with us. Have something to drink. We have fresh bread, and Miryam has made some cheese."

When they sat together, no one eating, Yosef continued. "Your concern is, indeed, warranted. But I have—*we* have—our reasons for going to Bethlehem together. For one, Miryam has not been treated well, not by the village or, sadly, by my mother or sisters-in-law. I don't feel right leaving her behind. It's hard enough when I'm gone to work in Sepphoris all day. I would be on the road to and from Bethlehem for over a week, and who knows how long the census will take once I get there."

"Do you plan on taking Tehilla the midwife with you?"

Yosef ignored his mother-in-law's sarcasm. "Tehilla is among those who have treated Miryam most sorely."

Ima's brow creased with concern. "Is this true?"

Miryam raised her tunic to show her ankle. There, a bruise flared angrily. "She threw a rock at me." She took Ima's hand in hers. "We will be traveling with the men of Yosef's family. With such an escort, I will be quite safe."

"And one of these strapping fellows is a midwife?"

"Yosef has many relatives in Bethlehem. Surely, they will know a midwife."

Ima looked from Yosef to Miryam. "Can you be sure they will receive you any better than his family here?"

Yosef put his hand to his heart. "Miryam's right, we left behind a lot of family in Bethlehem. My father has assigned each son to stay with a different family, so we don't overwhelm anyone. Miryam and I will be staying with my cousin Tamir and his family because they have a guest chamber. I promise you, Tamir's family is known for their hospitality. They will love Miryam and welcome her."

Ima rose with some difficulty, and Miryam noticed for the first time that her mother moved with the stiffness of an older woman. When had that happened?

All rose with Ima, and Miryam stepped closer to her mother. "I feel strong, Ima. The walk to Bethlehem is not so much farther than Jerusalem—only a few miles, not many—and I've made that journey many times."

"But never as a pregnant woman, my daughter. Growing a child pulls life from your body. Until now, the changes have happened gradually.

You've adapted to the extra weight, hardly without noticing, but to add a journey and to carry all you will need for your time in Bethlehem…you have no idea."

Miryam had noticed changes—the burning in her chest when she squatted over the cooking fire, how heavily she breathed when carrying the water from the well, how sleep could not be coaxed even with every cushion in the house under her.

Abba pulled Ima near with an arm around her shoulders. "Look at these young people, my wife. They look resolute in their decision. They have thought about all the ramifications. Yosef is now Miryam's protector, and I agree that she would do better to leave the village just now, to give the people here time to move on to the next offense to complain about. Shall we go home?"

Ima pulled Miryam into a powerful embrace. "This is a hard thing you're asking me to accept."

Miryam stepped out of the embrace to look her mother full in the face. "Think on it, Ima. I carry the Messiah. Do you think HaShem will remove his protective hand from me, Yosef, and the child because we leave Nazareth? Didn't David put his trust in the Lord when things went wrong? The Lord is my rock and my deliverer, too. I will take refuge in him. He will be my stronghold as I walk to Bethlehem. And he will be here in Nazareth with you."

◌◌

MIRYAM STOOD APART, LISTENING to Nazareth wake up. Women sang over their kneading. A covey of girls with water jars on their shoulders chatted noisily. Hens complained as their eggs were gathered. Near the gate to Yaakov's and Atarah's courtyard, Yosef helped his father and brothers settle their packs into place.

Today, they started for Bethlehem. The journey ahead held much that was familiar—the roll of the land, the broad Valley of Jezreel—but also promised surprises. On every other trip to Jerusalem and its near points, she had traveled with her family, stopping for the night in households she knew. Each night ahead would mean a new stopping place, each with its own personality.

The second brother, Kalev, dropped his pack at Yosef's feet. "Help me, brother."

Miryam stood tall. Her husband's family respected and listened to him, and well they should. Yosef had packed and repacked his tools until they balanced perfectly. The patience he applied to his craft, he brought to his relationships.

Yosef and the men carried their tools in case the census became protracted. Bethlehem was no bigger than Nazareth and held little hope of employment, but Jerusalem loomed above the town only a short walk away. A skilled craftsman could find work within the teeming streets, doing anything from repairing a cart to shaping cooking utensils, though the pay was not good. The best opportunities lay in building projects, but those lasted months or years.

Miryam groaned inwardly at the thought of a long stay in Bethlehem. She carried the same doubts as her mother about the hospitality she would receive from Yosef's relatives, but he seemed so sure they would welcome her warmly. There was nothing left but to trust him.

The coolness made her nose run. Should she return to their home for a heavier cloak? She dismissed the idea as she would discard a heavy cloak before noon. The walk would warm her, especially as the sun rose higher in the sky. The freshness of the morning air was, however, the harbinger of change, a promise of cooler nights that would bring refreshing sleep, shorter days, and a son.

Before she knew it, the time for *Sukkot* would arrive, her favorite of all the pilgrim feasts. That meant another journey to Jerusalem for the most joyous time of celebration and worship at the temple. Pilgrims slept in tabernacles to remember HaShem's provision in the wilderness and through every season since. But temple worship would only be possible if she wasn't still *niddah* from the birth of her son. She would have to sit out a visit to the temple this year, but the feasting with family would be the same, only better with a son in her arms.

She placed a hand to her expanded stomach. "My son, you will love *Sukkot* as much as I do, I promise."

Yosef strode toward her. "Are you ready?"

Was she? She felt strong, but her mother's warnings echoed in her thoughts. On the other hand, the prospect of getting away from Nazareth cheered her. "This is our first journey together, husband. I'm very excited."

He tested the weight of her pack on her shoulders. "I can carry more. Let me take the food."

She wanted to kiss him, more than she ever thought possible. He made her love him more each day with his attentiveness and his many kindnesses. "You carry more than half already."

"If you feel unwell or uncomfortable, you must tell me instantly. Also, I have warned my brothers, within an inch of their lives, not to act like buffoons. They have given only half-hearted promises to be gentlemen. I can only assure you they will remember that promise until we come to Ofir's melon patch, and then, well, that will be the end of their attention spans. I apologize now."

"Remember, Yosef, I have two brothers, also. They can be disappointing, but they are always surprising. I'm happy to be traveling with yours."

Yaakov called out, "Yosef! Miryam! It's time to go!"

As they joined the men, Yaakov welcomed Miryam. "Stay between me and Yosef as we walk through the village." The eldest brother walked in front, Kalev behind. They hemmed her in protectively. A wave of gratitude washed through her and tears stung her eyes.

Chapter Fourteen

A Lonely Garden

*Y*osef and Miryam walked through the dappled light of the olive grove. The incline was steeper than he remembered, and Miryam struggled against the rise of the slope. Yosef supported her with an arm to her waist, for the climb from the Jordan River Valley had already drained her. Time in a garden was the very thing to rejuvenate Miryam, or so he hoped. He guided her to a level place where his family had often stopped to rest before the final ascent to Bethlehem.

His father and brother no longer traveled with them. Just as Jerusalem had come into view, they had stopped yet again to rest, mostly to give Miryam a chance to catch her breath, although Yaakov seemed relieved for the respite, too.

Yosef's brother Kalev pulled him aside. "Yosef, your wife is very tired. We will walk ahead—not even stop for refreshment—to hurry on to Bethlehem. We will make sure Rut has prepared the guest chamber for you and Miryam."

Rut needed no prodding from his brothers to be hospitable. The guest chamber always stood ready. More to the point, his brothers were not patient men. The pace of a pregnant woman taxed them sorely. He shook his head at their transparency.

"Father seems anxious to see his brother. Take him with you but be mindful of the pace," Yosef said.

Kalev's face fell, but he agreed. His father and brothers slipped into the current of people skimming the eastern boundary of the great city. By sending his brothers and his father ahead, he'd bought Miryam the luxury of quiet and a reasonable pace for the last hours of the journey.

He wet a cloth and Miryam wiped the dust of the road from her face. She sighed as she leaned against the gnarled tree trunk. He regretted not accepting the loan of Eli's old donkey, but riding a donkey wasn't any easier than walking, and the trip would have taken several days more. The beasts balked when not fed and rested on schedule, and sometimes became obstinate for no reason at all. He definitely should have listened to his mother-in-law. The journey had been demanding on Miryam. He would be much more mindful of her well-being in the future.

Her eyes opened, and they lit with the affection that melted his heart. "Are you hungry?"

"Close your eyes again, wife. Sleep if you want. We have plenty of time to get to Bethlehem before *Shabbat*."

"But are you hungry?"

He didn't want to lie to his wife, but he didn't want to trouble her with preparing a meal. "I could eat, but then I can always eat."

Miryam smiled knowingly and busied herself unwrapping the last of their provisions. She'd managed to save a good portion of cheese and two loaves of bread. His mouth watered when she opened a bundle of figs, and his stomach gurgled loudly.

"You *could* eat?" she teased.

He gestured at the feast she'd laid out. "Always, by this time in the journey, we gathered crumbs from the bottom of our packs. How did you manage to keep so much aside? My brothers eat like goats."

"I learned from my mother not to bundle all of the food together. What is laid out will be eaten, and my brothers attack their food like wolves. Besides, it's best to save the sweetest morsels for the last day of the journey when travelers need energy to finish."

So much wisdom in a girl so young. "You prove me right and prudent yet again. I definitely chose the best wife."

Miryam dipped her head as a modest wife should, but did she know how dear she'd become to him already?

She tore off a piece of bread and spread it with cheese. "Are you excited to see your family?"

"I am most anxious to provide you with a comfortable place to sleep tonight. I've spent many feast days in Tamir's and Rut's guest chamber.

You will feel like a queen there. We tease Rut about all of her cushions."

Yosef pictured Miryam sitting at the *Shabbat* table with his family. Just imagining the faces warmed him. "I am looking forward to *Shabbat* with my family. Although you could never accuse my brothers of being quiet, since moving to Nazareth I've missed the energy and joy of being with my Bethlehem family—the uncles and aunts, cousins and grandparents." Would she love them as much as he did? They were a boisterous bunch. "You will know such energy soon enough. For now, enjoy the quiet of this place."

From where they sat on the lower slopes of the Mount of Olives, a breeze carried the whisper of Gihon Spring up from the Kidron Valley. On the far side of the spring, a slope covered with olive groves and vineyards rose to the temple mount. The wall of the temple crowned the rise with its massive walls and toothed parapet.

The solitary gate on the east side of the temple mount, The Gate of Mercy, was closed and barred. Only the High Priest and his entourage traveled up and down the slope along the colonnaded path and entered the temple through the gate. Such pomp for a man who had bid for the office and won it from Roman hands. Before Yosef's eyes, the very emblem of his faith morphed into a symbol of Rome's dominance, and a sorrow squeezed his heart. Reestablishing the Aaronic lineage of the high priest would be the Messiah's work. Would his son walk through the Gate of Mercy?

"Yosef?"

The worry in Miryam's voice alarmed him. "What's wrong?"

"This place. It's so lonely. The ground practically moans."

"Moans?"

Yosef scanned the scene. Olive trees cast mottled shade that shimmied in the breeze. Below them, travelers kicked up dust on the road, and conversations blended into a muffled hum. The squeals of children playing along the spring reached them. Not one Roman defiled the view. The relative quiet anointed him like oil. If not for the coming *Shabbat*, he would stay there all day.

"I don't hear a moan, my wife."

Miryam deftly gathered their meal.

He stilled her hands with a touch. "You haven't eaten, and we still have two hours of walking ahead of us."

She rose without trouble, and he saw in her movements a determination he was beginning to recognize. "I'm not hungry," she said.

He caught her hand. "But remember, I am hungry. Can we not sit for a few minutes more?"

Miryam rejoined him, but she didn't offer what she'd wrapped. Her brow creased with concern; she looked deep in thought. He took the bundles from her lap and reclaimed his lunch. Perhaps she had a heightened sense of alarm due to her nearing delivery, or maybe she worried about meeting his family.

"My family will welcome you, Miryam, I promise."

"What?" she said, as if waking from sleep.

"My family, they will love you."

"Of course, there's no reason for you to stop eating. The shade is so pleasant. Please stay. I will walk down the hill to sit by the spring and wait for you there."

He had never seen Miryam so agitated, not even when he'd arrived at her father's orchard to intercept the divorce decree. "You want to leave right this minute?"

Miryam put her hands to her bulging abdomen. "The baby has never tumbled so."

"Are you in pain?"

"No, not pain. Just… Yosef, it's as if lions are circling. That's how I feel. I can't stay here."

He stood, bobbling the food and their packs. He reached to pull her up. "I'll eat as we walk."

At the bottom of the hill, Miryam turned back to look where they'd been. Travelers stepped around them, turning to see what had made the couple act so inconsiderately. Yosef ignored them.

Frowning at the hill, she said, "What is this place called?"

"Gethsemane."

"Oil press. Well, that seems about right." She turned her onyx eyes on him. "You're familiar with Isaiah, I know you are. There is a passage that speaks of a man who is pierced and crushed for the sins of his people. Who is that man, Yosef? Who could carry the sins of a whole nation?"

"Is there a reason you ask such a question?"

"The man is treated horribly by the very people he delivers. He is despised and rejected. Does that make any sense to you? Wouldn't the people honor such a man?"

"I know the passage you speak about. It's caused more arguments than any other prophecy I know of. Most avoid bringing it up." But not his wife. "The thought of a man being offered for the sins of others...well, that isn't a pleasant thought to consider, nor does it make much sense. After all, we have the temple. Our sins are covered by the blood of our offerings."

She leaned into him, whispered. "Some say, Yosef, that man is the Messiah."

She was worried for the child, not yet born. What words could he offer her? "I see, yes. I have heard this too, but this isn't for us to know, Miryam. Generations will pass before the truth of that passage is known."

"Not if the man is the Messiah." Miryam hugged her pregnant belly. "If the man in the passage is the Messiah, then what will become of our son?"

Yosef took her hand and they joined the column of travelers hurrying home for *Shabbat*. He had no answer for her. None of his reading of Torah had prepared him to walk with the mother of the Messiah. All he knew from Torah was Moses and how Adonai had led him. But then, perhaps, that was enough.

"I can't look into the future, Miryam. I can only look back to see how HaShem has dealt with his people in the past. Think of it, when HaShem sent Moses to set our people free from Pharaoh, his instructions were simple: I am sending you to lead my people out, and I will be with you. HaShem didn't tell Moses about the plagues or crossing the Red Sea. Moses knew nothing of wandering in the desert for forty years with a brood of complainers, or that Adonai's people would worship a golden calf in the shadow of Mt. Sinai. Moses might have stayed in the tents of Midian, if he'd known all that lay ahead.

"Maybe it was HaShem's great kindness that kept Moses from knowing all the trouble he would face. HaShem only told him to start on a journey and to expect his nearness. We don't know much more than Moses, only that you carry the Messiah. We also know he must be born to achieve all that HaShem has planned for him. I'm afraid that falls on you, but I can take you to my family, who will help all they can. The next step is HaShem's, and he promises to be with us."

Yosef believed Adonai was indeed with them, but as they walked he couldn't help turning his thoughts back to Isaiah. The prophet painted a picture of Messiah that contradicted the warrior-king faithful Jews believed would lead a liberating army against Rome. Yes, the Messiah was to reign on David's throne, but the prophet spoke of one even mightier than the shepherd-king, each revelation more amazing than the one before.

The Messiah would be a sanctuary to some and a stone of offense to others—a paradox of a man, both compassionate and confrontational. He is referred to as Ha´Elyon, but how could that be said of anyone, even of a boy conceived by the Holy Spirit? That very Spirit would rest on him, giving him wisdom, counseling him, and endowing him with the might of the Lord. Of course nations would rally to such a man, a man mightier than even Moses.

When Moses came down from Mt. Sinai, he covered his face to shield the people from Adonai's glory, but the Messiah would reveal the glory of the Lord. Would Yosef perish when he saw his son's face for the first time? How could that be, for his son would bring forth justice without breaking what is already bruised or quenching a wick already sputtering. Which of these qualities would bend every knee to his Lordship?

Miryam slipped her hand into his.

"Are you all right?" he asked.

"I was going to ask the same of you. You're frowning so."

He would never be able to hide anything from Miryam, but he would not burden her further with his unanswerable questions. She had enough on her mind. They would live out the answers together, and that idea heartened him. "I might have eaten too many figs."

She stooped to pluck a handful of mint. "Chew some of these leaves. You'll feel better soon."

Chapter Fifteen

No Room

The courtyard of Tamir and Rut erupted with cheers and hearty welcomes when Yosef and Miryam stepped through the gate. Yosef greeted Tamir, who kissed his cheeks, as did Rut.

Miryam took a step back and swallowed hard against the dread she'd harbored about this meeting and how those ill feelings played out before her. Hands lifted Yosef's pack from his back, and he was led to the shade of an awning where cushions had been piled high. Miryam followed, willing herself to be invisible.

A young girl of about eight carried a sloshing water bowl and set it on the ground before Yosef. A younger boy hovered over him with a jar of olive oil for his face and hands. No kisses or basins of water or oil for Miryam. She looked longingly at the guest chamber door, which, oddly enough, stood closed. Surely, their hosts meant to air the room before they settled their guests for the night. The coming days stretched before her, menacing and singular—so much like her days in Nazareth.

Smiling, Yosef stood, his feet still dusty from the road, and knelt before Miryam. He untied her sandals and lifted her feet into the cool water that was instantly muddied. He washed and tenderly dried her feet with a towel handed to him by the girl with the bowl. Miryam fought for composure at the honor he showed her. He was not a servant to wait on her. How many ways could this man surprise her?

She dared not look away from Yosef's eyes to see how his family reacted to his devotion, but not one person spoke. Sandals no longer scuffed the stones. Even the children stopped their play. All was still.

Yosef poured oil into her hands and Miryam massaged the rich liquid into her face. He watched her with adoring eyes, which warmed her cheeks. Miryam rewarded him with a trembling smile, fighting to contain the grateful tears that stung for release.

"There," Yosef said over his shoulder to the crowd, "now you can see how very beautiful my wife is."

The family—a father, mother, a woman who could be a grandmother, an older son with his young wife, perhaps halfway through her pregnancy, and three more sons and two daughters—stood with heads bowed. She worried that Yosef's rebuke had cut the family too deeply, that his preferential treatment of her had only turned their hearts to stone.

Rut lifted her eyes to meet Miryam's gaze. "You honor our home with your presence, Miryam."

Miryam started to rise, but Rut squatted before her and touched her hands. "Oh no you don't. You are our guest of honor, at least for tonight. Please, take your rest here in the shade." Rut stood, turned to her oldest daughter. "Bring our travelers refreshment, and be quick about it. You still have tomorrow's *Shabbat* meal to wrap in straw." Rut bent to kiss Miryam's cheek and offered her an imploring smile.

Miryam saw the apology in her eyes. "Thank you for your warm welcome."

Rut looked to the west, and Miryam followed her gaze. The sun dove rather than set toward the horizon to bring *Shabbat*. "I better get the food to the table."

Not everyone fit around the low table, so the youngest children balanced plates on their knees. The adults sat hip to hip. Miryam watched, studying the family that gave her and Yosef shelter. Tamir smiled easily as he told Yosef about the construction in the city, and by the city, he meant Jerusalem. "There is work here for you, and not for pagans like you work for in Sepphoris. Jewish merchants are eager to show off their wealth in new and bigger homes. I'm building a *mikveh* for a priest. He also desires an embellished gate. If you're as good as your father says, I have a place for you on my crew. If your father's words are empty boasting, you can go back to the bath houses of Sepphoris."

Rut was a watcher. She managed her children with a look, communicating mostly with her oldest girl, Batya, who looked to be near

Miryam's age, perhaps younger. Was she betrothed? Miryam's heart clenched, observing the partnership between mother and oldest daughter, just as Ima and Miryam had worked together.

Ora, Tamir's aunt, was a widow without sons. What a lonesome, vulnerable state for the woman. Fortunately, her family honored her properly by bringing her into their home and under their protection. Miryam had learned through the conversation that Ora inhabited the guest chamber and would continue to do so until she died, meaning there was no room for her and Yosef.

With the dishes cleared and stored, the children were sent to the loft to prepare their pallets. Miryam longed to join them, but to leave the table without her husband would be rude to her hosts. Besides, with the guest chamber occupied, Yosef and Miryam would be sleeping on the main room floor below the loft. There would be no sleep until the whole family retired—and there would be no whispering to Yosef about his family when they did.

Soon after the children, the young couple left for their chamber, the attached residence on the opposite side of the house. Then Ora trundled off to bed, and the animals were let into the keep for the night. Had Miryam known how many people sat at Rut's table, she wasn't sure she would have imposed herself on her hospitality. On the other hand, the thought of sitting alone in her little house in Nazareth—with the disapproval of her mother-in-law seeping through the wall—saddened her. Besides, her place was with Yosef, so she would do all she could to help Rut feed all of these people during their stay.

With only Tamir, Rut, Yosef, and Miryam at the table, Yosef asked if he could speak. "I wasn't sure our story would have reached you yet." He took Miryam's hand and squeezed. "We want to thank you for receiving us into your home and giving us a chance to speak for ourselves. Some have been satisfied to rely on gossip."

Tamir squirmed, looked to Rut, and then back to Yosef. "It's sometimes hard to know who to believe."

"We understand. Our own families have struggled." Yosef finished his wine. "It's been a long day, but we hope you will let me tell our story. Who better knows the truth of something than the ones who were there?"

Tamir looked to the loft. "There is wisdom in what you say, but sleeping children still have ears."

Yosef, too, glanced at the loft. "Then they will hear how HaShem has chosen to use a humble craftsman and a beautiful maiden—for a maiden she is—to bring the Messiah to his people."

Tamir's eyebrows rose and he nodded. "That is a story I would like to hear."

Yosef went back to the beginning of their story, telling how Zekharyah had encountered an angel in the Holy Place of the temple, and that his aged wife had conceived and given birth to the one who would prepare the way for the Messiah. Setting that foundation, he continued with Miryam's visitation by Gavri´el and his own crushing disappointment when he learned of her pregnancy, for he knew he was not the father. And then he told how an angel had come to him in his dream.

Hearing the story from Yosef sparked new wonder in Miryam. Was she truly the maiden in the drama? She marveled that Adonai had chosen her to carry his Messiah, but she did *not* marvel that Adonai had chosen Yosef. He was the perfect man to walk alongside her and to be a father to the boy.

Tamir nodded thoughtfully. "I see in your face and hear the conviction in your voice. You believe your story, and you care deeply for your wife. I will not contradict you, and you are welcome to stay here as long as you have need of shelter in Bethlehem. After all, we have prayed for the Messiah all of our lives. With deep conviction I can say that I want your story to be true."

Tamir worried the wood of the table. "I only ask that you not talk of this in front of the children. In fact, you should keep your story to yourselves. The Romans, while not in a hurry to come to Bethlehem, will arrive for their census soon enough. They are always listening for news of rebellion. That's exactly how they will interpret any talk of Messiah."

Yosef grasped Tamir's strong hand. "Thank you for listening. The months since our betrothal have been especially challenging for Miryam. I hope she will find a respite here. I realize it's a lot to ask."

Rut took Miryam's hand. "It's not so much to ask for the mother of the Messiah. We will do all we can to give you a comfortable place to stay, even though our best accommodations are occupied by our dear aunt, Ora. We pray you will feel at home here, Miryam."

Chapter Sixteen

A Boy in the Wilderness

Paltiel lagged behind the master potter, Merav, staying out of range of the man's fist. Already, Paltiel struggled to see out of his left eye. He did not want to face his family both shamed and blind.

They left the haze that shrouded the potter's house and walked toward the smoke of cooking fires in his village, Tekoa. Behind Merav, Paltiel dodged piles left by donkeys on the narrow street. Women looked up from stew pots, and children paused mid-game. Even the smith stilled his hands at the forge to watch Merav and Paltiel trudge by—Merav muttering oaths against the day Paltiel was born, the boy avoiding eye contact with those he'd known all his life.

At Paltiel's house, Merav stopped at the courtyard gate and thundered his brother's name. "Shemu'el! Shemu'el! Come out here! Now!"

Paltiel stepped back, looking left and right. Where could he go? Where could he hide?

Shemu'el stepped into the courtyard, his eyes traveling from Merav to Paltiel, his face knowing and resigned. Paltiel would give up twenty years of his life to save his brother from this disappointment, but he didn't have twenty years to give. He'd just turned twelve on the sixteenth day of *Elul*.

Shemu'el, older by four years, wore the grime of a day laborer. Had he pounded the flesh of cattle at the tannery or dug a latrine? Shemu'el would consider himself lucky to be chosen at all from among all who waited for paying work. Harvesting was the luckiest sort of work, for the farmer sometimes sent home bruised or infested produce with his workers. Shemu'el didn't look especially lucky at the moment.

"I cannot afford to have your brother anywhere near my pots," Merav roared. "He has clubs for hands and boulders for feet. He destroyed an entire order of urns destined for the Upper City. I will be at the wheel for days, recovering lost inventory. I am now behind in orders for months, all thanks to Paltiel."

Shemu'el pleaded with open palms. "Sir, give him one more chance. He is small for his age, I will grant you that, but he will grow. He is like my father, right? Small of stature but large of heart. No one outworked Abba."

"Your father was a good man, Shemu'el. He welcomed me when I was a stranger in the village. He built my kiln when I couldn't pay him right away. He praised my pots to his customers in the city. I owe him a debt of gratitude, but I don't owe him the bread from my children's mouths. Do not send Paltiel again." Merav threw up his hands, turned sharply, and left, muttering about the boy's ineptness.

Paltiel stared at his feet, gray from clay dust, and waited for Shemu'el to say something, for surely he had plenty to say about another botched apprenticeship. Shemu'el's own apprenticeship had died with their father, and now Paltiel's failure robbed his family of a secure future. The boys had no family to take them in, and their mother languished from a mysterious malady that kept her abed most days.

When Paltiel didn't hear Shemu'el's sandals scuff the courtyard stones, curiosity overcame him, and he looked up. Shemu'el stood with head bowed and shoulders rounded. He sucked in a shuddering breath. His brother, the man who faced down larger men to vie for jobs on the street, now cried before him. Paltiel had reduced him to this.

He stepped closer. "I will go with you to the city tomorrow, Shemu'el. I will work harder than anyone. I will earn what is needed for Ima's medicine."

"You are too small, Paltiel. No one will pick you," he said flatly.

Paltiel had heard this all of his life: *Paltiel is terrible at three-sticks; he jumps like a little mouse. The climb is too steep; Paltiel won't be able to keep up. The figs grow too high for Paltiel; send his cousin, Chuldah. She, at least, has long arms.*

Why did Adonai make a boy who had no purpose under heaven?

During the evening meal of porridge, his mother remained on her pallet in the loft. Every so often, a soft moan floated down, and Shemu'el stopped chewing and looked up. Her distress sounded louder, more demanding than other nights. Clearly, she had overheard all that Merav had said.

Paltiel's friend, Omri, called to him from the street. They played Mancala most nights. The game didn't require the winner to be tall, only smart. But he was in no mood for games. Instead, he added wood to the oven and mixed the next day's bread. He would not forget the salt this time, if they had any.

☙

ON THE DAY BEFORE *Shabbat*, Shemu'el came home early. From the stench on his clothes, he'd spent the day at the tannery. He walked past Paltiel straight for the wash basin and pulled off his tunic.

With his back to Paltiel, he said, "You leave for the high country tomorrow. You will be gone for a few weeks, at least, until there's no grass left for the sheep, or it gets too cold for the old man."

"You mean Reuel? You're sending me into the wilderness with sheep and that cranky old man? For weeks?" Paltiel couldn't imagine a worse fate for himself than trekking through the foothills with the likes of Reuel and a flock of sheep. He enjoyed staying home with his mother. No one complained if he didn't move fast enough or if he carried pots with one hand. On Ima's better days, she took a turn at the quern and told him stories about his father.

Shemu'el scrubbed at his face. "Reuel says the hills around Bethlehem are still lush with grazing. You could be away longer."

After a day with a flock of sheep, Paltiel would smell worse than Shemu'el, but his brother wouldn't care about that. Shemu'el never complained. "Who will look after Mother?"

"Maybe her sister—"

"From Kedesh? Why would she? She's never come before. But maybe, Shemu'el, if we sent word about how sick Ima is, she would come."

"We can't wait to hear from her. Winter will be here before we know it. The coin you earn as a shepherd will keep us in grain, and we can buy some of the herbs Ima needs. There's nothing else we can do."

Paltiel had never slept anywhere but a house or traveled with anyone other than his family. Besides, sheep could not be trusted. They kicked and bit, didn't they? They had teeth and hooves, so they probably did.

This was the true problem: Other animals wandered the wilderness besides sheep—bears, lions, and leopards, all prowling for something to devour. If they couldn't find a fat rabbit, they might eat Paltiel. The thought of going into the wilderness with Reuel filled him with dread. The man hated children. He had thrown a rock at Omri. His brother had not thought this through.

"I don't like shepherds, Shemu'el. They're mean and they smell bad. And they never go to synagogue."

Shemu'el held his head in his hands, his wet hair dripping on the dirt floor. Was he reconsidering his plans to send him to the wilderness? Had Paltiel's arguments shown him his wrong thinking? Perhaps Shemu'el would speak to the smithy again. Iron work required only strength, not great stature.

Now was the time for Paltiel to say something or accept his fate as a shepherd. "I would like working in the smithy, Shemu'el. Nothing to break there, even if I tried. And it's not very far. I could come home every night and take care of Ima."

Shemu'el shook his head. "I'm sorry, Paltiel. Reuel is expecting you at sunrise. Be sure to pack your wool tunic, and you can take my camelhair cloak for when the weather turns."

"Shemu'el? Did you talk to—"

"I tried to talk to the smith. He heard about the pottery, so he wouldn't listen to me." Shemu'el tussled Paltiel's hair. "This is how it has to be."

His brother treated him like a baby. Paltiel swallowed hard on threatening tears.

"It's not shepherds you don't like, Paltiel. You don't like Reuel because he protected his sheep from your annoying friend, Omri. Shepherds do important work. You like to eat, don't you? And stay warm in winter? Have you forgotten that our father Abraham was a shepherd? Have you also forgotten the years Moses chased sheep in the deep canyons of Midian? You do remember, I hope, that HaShem chose David, a shepherd boy, to rule all of Israel." Shemu'el put a hand to Paltiel's shoulder. "You will change your mind about shepherds, I promise."

His brother thought he knew everything about him and, so it seemed, shepherds. Paltiel would go with Reuel, keep a half-hearted watch over the sheep, collect his coin, and come straight home. He doubted that anything would change his mind about shepherding.

൚

FOR THREE DAYS, PALTIEL trailed behind Reuel's flock from spring to spring. Traveling with him were a sorry group of shepherds who had also, most likely, failed more promising apprenticeships. There was Haran who lived up to his name. Like Mt. Moriah, he towered over Reuel by two heads. As he walked, he scowled at the sky, the rocks, even the rare flower, and definitely at Paltiel. Since Paltiel still wore the bruises from Merav's fist, he kept a wary eye on the man.

He kept a cautious distance from old Bet, too. The man limped on the edge of the herd, nudging obstinate sheep back into the fold with his staff. At first, Paltiel thought the man spoke angrily at him and worried he'd done something wrong already, but Bet spoke to people who only occupied his imagination. And by the sound of it, they had treated him shamefully.

If Paltiel had a friend among the shepherds, it was Nogah. Only a year or so older than Paltiel, the boy reveled in the life of a shepherd. Before he stretched at rising, Nogah began Paltiel's shepherding lessons. He reminded Paltiel that sheep wandered off, not out of willful defiance but because they were too interested in the next tuft of grass to look where they were going. Paltiel disagreed. Sheep were stubborn and stupid.

Later, at night, when Paltiel could not keep his eyes open, Nogah named each sheep and their antics of the day. All of the sheep looked exactly the same to Paltiel, and every last one of them demanded his attention, from sunrise to sunset.

If the sheep were tired or anxious, the shepherds settled the animals in the open where a threat could be seen coming, and the sheep rested. If thirsty, Paltiel and Nogah explored wadis for water. If hungry, Paltiel climbed plateaus in search of stubble. No one asked Paltiel if he was tired, thirsty, or hungry. In fact, he rested after the sheep, drank after the sheep, and ate after the sheep. He hated sheep.

Each night of their journey, Paltiel and Nogah collected brushwood to build a sheep pen. They laid course after course of thorny bramble to protect the sheep from wild animals. As they worked, Nogah told endless stories. He told his stories as if these men had faced down each menace only yesterday, but he'd borrowed the stories from his ancestors, all of them shepherds.

"Is Reuel your father?" Paltiel asked as he rubbed olive oil over the scratches on his arms and legs.

"My father was killed by robbers who waited for him at the entrance of a wadi. That, my friend, is another story."

Only when the sheep had been herded into the pen under Reuel's rod, and the count was verified, did the shepherds build a fire and satisfy their hunger. After the evening meal, Bet played his flute. The lullabies quieted the sheep and coaxed Paltiel to his bedroll.

Above him, a cloud of stars hung heavy in the sky. The weight of all those stars filled him with wonder and crushed him with loneliness. Would the God who set all the stars in the sky and called them by name know his name as Nogah knew all of the sheep? He was just a boy, a smaller than average boy, in a big desert under an enormous sky, fatherless and alone. Silent tears spilled into his ears.

On the fourth day, as the sun started its slide to the horizon, Reuel announced they had reached the base camp. The village of Bethlehem squatted on a ridge above them and the Judean hills rolled higher and higher, as green as could be expected after a long, hot summer. Nogah whistled and directed Paltiel to a ruined sheep pen of rock. "We'll be here until the grass runs out, so we'll repair this pen."

"That will take forever."

"We only have until sunset."

The sheep bleated fretfully as Paltiel and Nogah rushed to stack stone upon stone. His arms ached from hefting rock, and his eyelids burned from sun and grit. Paltiel longed to put his head on his bedroll, and although he was hungry, he doubted his arm could lift the bread to his mouth.

Once the sheep were milling in the pen, Reuel lifted his chin to Paltiel. "You'll be a watchman with me tonight, boy. Move your bedroll to the opening of the sheep pen."

One of the men usually served as watchman, sleeping at the open gap in the sheep pen wall. They served as the gate as sure as if a smith had fashioned one of iron. With their staffs close and their rods always in their hand, nothing passed through them to the sheep—not lion nor bear, wolf nor leopard, and certainly no man.

Paltiel held only a woolen blanket. Perhaps Reuel would see how poorly equipped he was for such a job and send him to the fire to sleep. "I didn't bring a rod with me, master."

"I have an extra."

"I have never used a rod."

"You will watch and learn."

"Won't it be too dark to see?" Paltiel asked.

"The fire will burn all night."

"I heard something howl last night, master."

"A wolf. I heard it too." Reuel stood. "Move your bedroll."

Paltiel studied each man around the fire. Bet played his flute, Nogah ate his third bowl of stew, and Haran whittled. Not one of them studied the shadows or bounced a nervous knee. Had they not heard the wolf?

Paltiel gathered his bedding and stood. Bet's song ended, and he caught Paltiel's arm. "The master is showing his confidence in you."

Because he'd never heard Bet speak directly to another human, he should have been honored. Instead, his stomach clenched. If he died in that wilderness, would his mother ever know?

The moment Reuel's head sunk into the wadded cloak he used as a pillow, he sucked in a sticky breath. Paltiel lay between him and the sheep, wide awake. A few sheep huddled in sleep, most nosed the ground for grass, all felt the need to call out, one by one, all through the night. Paltiel fingered the rod in his hands, smooth but for the splinters that had snagged wool, or was it wolf fur?

He dozed, only to be woken repeatedly by a sheep's call, a shift in the wind, or one of Reuel's wet snores. He finally sat up, surrendering to the impossibility of sleep. A waxing gibbous moon cast silvery light over all that lay before him—canyon walls, jutting spires of rock, the sleeping shepherds—and deepened shadows. Nothing moved. Only embers winked in the fire ring. King David had killed both a lion and a bear while watching over his father's sheep. Paltiel tightened his grip on the rod and dropped his head to his knees.

Lord, I do not want to see a lion or a bear, not tonight, not ever.

Chapter Seventeen

A Day's Work

*T*amir yanked Yosef out of the path of a mounted Roman messenger, galloping his horse toward Herod's palace. "Look alert, young Yosef. Romans menace the streets of Jerusalem during the festivals. You'll be ground into powder, if you get in their way."

Yosef brushed the dust of the encounter from his hair and beard. "Miryam's time is near. I'm worried about her."

Tamir stopped him with a hand to the shoulder. "If you can't put your heart into the work today, it would be better for you to return to Bethlehem." He shrugged. "Of course, you will have to explain yourself to our taskmaster the priest."

Miryam hadn't slept well. When the moon tipped toward the western horizon, she left the pallet and went outside. She had often given up on sleep during the last month, so Yosef turned away from the door and pulled the blanket up. Soon, his shoulder ached, one of the children in the loft whimpered, and Rut sang a whispered lullaby. Sleep would not come, so he joined Miryam in the courtyard. They paced together—not talking, clenching hands. Even before a rooster crowed, the door creaked open. Rut carried a bowl of bread dough and an oil lamp.

"Is it time?" she asked Miryam.

"I don't know. Perhaps I slept wrong," she said with a hand to her back. "Such a clenching ache but walking helps."

Rut drew near, a picture of calm knowing. "Walking is good. If this is your time, moving about will help the baby slide into place. If this is not your time, activity will keep your mind occupied. No one is more disagreeable than a woman ready to give birth if the child makes other plans for the day. For Yosef's sake—"

Miryam took the bowl from Rut. "Then I will bake the bread."

Yosef had only agreed to work in Jerusalem that day when Miryam had reassured him that the pains had stopped.

"Her time is close," he told Tamir. "Maybe today, but I don't know."

Tamir pulled Yosef back into the foot traffic. "Then you will help her best by staying and working with me."

The streets of the upper city teemed with merchants and farmers and workmen. *Sukkot*, the most joyous of all the festivals began at sundown, and the household staffs waited for deliveries to prepare the first of a week worth of feasts. Farmers walked hurriedly, burdened with baskets of melons, pomegranates, and squash. Bakers carried trays of honey cakes and date rolls on their heads. Carts rattled on the stones—some filled with jars of wine, others with lambs ready for roasting.

Yosef and Tamir passed marble mansions and glimpsed lush gardens through gates left ajar for deliveries. "Rut will take care of Miryam as if she were one of her daughters," Tamir said, "because I'm pretty sure she likes Miryam much more than her own daughters."

The men laughed at his exaggeration, although what he said held more than a morsel of truth. Miryam and Rut worked side by side throughout the day, sharing the labors of the household, while the daughters required haranguing to complete their chores.

In the evenings, Yosef listened to the two women as they marveled over the perplexing works of HaShem, while the men spoke of typical things like the weather, the rabbi's interpretation of a ticklish passage, and speculated on what the Romans would do next to make their lives ever more miserable. He'd never expected to envy his wife. Perhaps when they returned to Nazareth, just the two of them and their son, it would be him she shared her heart with. For now, he was grateful for Rut. Miryam had blossomed in confidence with the woman's friendship.

Yosef stopped abruptly. "I haven't finished the cradle. Where will the child sleep?"

"You worry too much." Tamir tugged at Yosef's tunic, and they continued on. "The first baby is in no hurry to see his ugly father. You have plenty of time to carve the story of creation and the great exodus on that cradle before Miryam gives birth."

Embellishing the cradle ranked low on Yosef's priorities. He feared he'd already failed at providing what the child needed, a bed to sleep in. What else had he neglected? He'd allowed everything but his son's arrival to occupy his thoughts during their weeks in Bethlehem.

The Roman census takers had ridden into the village with excessive pomp, daring the lowly inhabitants and visitors to defy Rome's authority to collect ever greater taxes. True, the pledge of loyalty they all feared hadn't been required after all, but the Romans demanded an accounting of every hen, every mallet, and every broken sandal a family possessed. With practiced skill the people of Bethlehem feigned resignation before their occupiers, while bewailing the injustice of their greed behind closed doors.

Yosef had welcomed the work Tamir arranged to do for a priest—Amos ben Haviv—who served in the high priestly order under Kayafa. Unfortunately, adding ornamentation to the man's palatial home had been no less disappointing than the work he'd done for the Gentiles of Sepphoris, or perhaps worse, as he never expected a Gentile to act like anything other than a Gentile, with their many gods and hunger for all things carnal.

He'd assumed a priest would be a benevolent master, looking to his spiritual and physical needs, treating him like a son of Abraham, a co-heir. Instead, the priest had demanded longer hours and shorter breaks of his workers, even as the man feasted in his courtyard and was carried to the temple three times a day to pray. The clear, rousing blast of the *shofar* that called the faithful to prayer also reached Yosef where he bent over his carving, but the priest had told him to keep working.

Although there was already a *mikveh* hewn into the limestone under the main house, Tamir chiseled into the bedrock for the *mikveh* they would build for the women of the priest's family. Without any hint of embarrassment, the priest had commissioned them to build a more elaborate *mikveh* than his neighbor. The expertise Yosef had gained working with marble in Sepphoris assured they would fulfill the priest's expectations.

Yosef had assisted Tamir on the *mikveh's* design that mimicked a shell. A graceful spiral of stairs would lower the women into the clear, pure waters to be made ceremonially clean for the temple and to be readied for their husbands. Yosef would carve symbols from the Song of Solomon—lilies, doves, gazelles—onto each riser.

Yosef lamented the extravagance but also regretted that Miryam, the mother of the Messiah, would never use so beautiful a *mikveh* to purify herself. Mostly, he hated entertaining such opposing ideas.

As the master potter, HaShem shaped his people for his glory, making them both beautiful and useful. When Yosef shaped wood and stone into something to please the eye and to be used as a tool, his heart sang with worship to the Creator.

The work for the priest left him flat, especially since the man lived ostentatiously from funds collected at the temple, the very tax collected from worshippers who struggled to pay higher taxes to the Romans. Did widows go hungry and orphans go unsheltered because the priest competed with his neighbor for the largest *mikveh* and the most ornate gate?

Adonai, may it never be!

Nevertheless, Yosef's father had taught him to honor Adonai with the gifts he had given him—whether building a house for a Gentile client or for a Jewish priest misusing the people's taxes. He would do as the priest asked. He would carve a lush vine—the symbol of Israel seen all through the *Tanakh*—on the man's gate. And then he would join Tamir in the building of the *mikveh*, work that would keep food on the table for two years or more. He hadn't yet told Miryam how long the work would keep them in Bethlehem.

Yosef unrolled his tool pouch and ran his fingers over the stout vine he'd carved into the massive cedar gate over a course of days. Five-fingered leaves, as broad as his hand, raised from the wood like worshipping hands. He selected a gouging tool with a broad, curved blade to refine the grape cluster he'd roughly cut with a knife the day before. The spheres were the most challenging to shape and the most difficult to reconcile, for they represented the fruit that came out of the hearts of Adonai's people.

Long ago, a psalmist had written of Israel as the vine, telling how Adonai had transplanted the vine from Egypt and cleared the ground of stones, and then planted only the choicest plants. This was how Adonai's people liked to see themselves and how they were intended to be, but Adonai reaped only bad grapes from his vines. The sound and reliable stock the vinedresser had planted had turned wild, bearing fruit only suitable for the birds. And so, Adonai had taken away the hedge that protected the vineyard. The boars from the forest—the Assyrians, the Medes, the Persians, the Greeks, the Romans—had ravaged the vineyard.

How will your Son recapture the hearts of such men to lead them against Rome?

The sound of steps on the garden walk pulled Yosef out of his lament and set his hands to carving. His work released the sweetness of the cedar. Ben Haviv led a visiting priest, bedecked with a headdress that required him to dip his head to enter the shade pavilion. From the ornamentation of his cloak, Yosef judged the visiting priest to be of higher rank than ben Haviv. A serving girl scurried to offer a platter of fruits and cheeses. Another poured wine into silver chalices.

Yosef stopped his work and stood with head bowed, waiting for ben Haviv to dismiss him.

"Slacker," ben Haviv bellowed. "Get back to work!"

Heat rose from Yosef's chest to his face. He nodded to acknowledge the command but waited for the men to lower themselves onto the couches to turn his attention back to the gate.

The visiting priest gestured toward Yosef and spoke in Greek, the language of learning and the tongue Yosef had learned among the people of Sepphoris. "You are comfortable speaking in the hearing of a laborer?"

Yosef had worked among the wealthy and privileged long enough to know that craftspeople were to be admired for their work but were not to be conspicuously present. He longed to join the ants between the cracks of the stones.

"Him?" ben Haviv said, almost spitting the word. "He's a Nazarene. You know what coarse speakers they are. Speak freely, Good Master, no one of consequence will listen in today."

Yosef let out a breath and picked up a sharply angled gouge to separate two grapes from the wood. The work required concentration he wasn't sure he possessed after the soul-crushing encounter with his employer, so he made shallow cuts and slowed his pace, praying the men didn't tarry in the garden. He didn't mean to eavesdrop, but Miryam enjoyed hearing about the people he encountered in the city. Besides, they sat so close he could smell the remnants of incense on their robes.

Ben Haviv talked around a fig in his cheek. "I'm surprised to see you, ben Sapir. *Sukkot* starts at sundown. Surely you have guests and preparations."

Ben Sapir leaned in and lowered his voice. "The census drags on and on, and Herod demands daily updates to pass onto Rome. The people don't openly rebel against the census, but there are discouraging reports. When the census takers get close, villagers move their belongings in the middle of the night to avoid an accounting of their wealth. This has slowed the progress of the census to a crawl, while Roman soldiers search every wadi and cave for the fortunes of our people. An unfavorable report puts Herod's governance in a poor light, and pressure from Rome means pressure on Kayafa, as well. I can tell you with great certainty that no one, neither Herod or Kayafa, is happy."

"Yes, yes, I hear what you're saying, ben Sapir. But what more can we do? We encouraged the people from the beginning to comply with Rome's demands. Are we to go out into the villages and take the count ourselves?"

"In a manner of speaking."

Ben Haviv slammed his cup down. "That's preposterous! The man has no sense of propriety. The priests of Adonai do not go on errands for Rome."

"You can tell him that when your head is on the chopping block."

Ben Haviv finished his wine in a gulp. "The man asks for the impossible. Of course the census has slowed. The city teams with pilgrims for *Sukkot*. Who is left in their villages to be counted? It's utter chaos out there."

"Then we must use *Sukkot* to our advantage. The pilgrims are coming to the city from all over the region. We will simply send our people into the streets to speak with them, to encourage their cooperation, and to warn them that not cooperating carries a steep price."

"To act as an agent of Rome… I don't know."

Ben Sapir flipped a dismissive hand. "The question has been settled. We will do as Herod asks. To do otherwise is to unleash his wrath, and he always strikes at the top. You are smart to keep that in mind." He stood, and ben Haviv scrambled to join him. "Herod is most anxious to fade from the attention of Rome on this matter. To show just how desperate he is, his secretary hinted at a gift to enrich the temple's treasury if the census is finalized before the month of *Heshvan*. That is your charge, ben Haviv. Make it so."

Yosef's gouge slipped and a fat wooden grape rolled from the cluster. He looked to where ben Haviv stood to see if the priest had noticed the marring of the gate. The priest took no notice, for his face drained of color as he watched ben Sapir leave.

Yosef took a chisel to the wound in the wood. With decisive strokes the wood surrendered the insult. No one would ever notice a missing grape, but Yosef couldn't believe what he'd just heard. The priests of the Aaronic line actually cooperated with Rome to injure the people they were meant to serve. Their partnership with their occupiers soured their stomachs, but their collaboration proved too profitable to refuse. His blood grew hot in his veins. He would never tell Miryam what he had heard.

When the time came to gather his tools for the trip home, he hefted his pack to his shoulder and paused. Herod's grand theater rose beyond the garden wall, the seat of Gentile thought that opposed HaShem and his people. To the west, Herod's palatial fortress dominated the horizon. These were the sorts of places where Yosef had pictured men scrambling for their weapons to engage the Messiah and his armies.

But opposition lay closer, more familiar. He took in all the priests worked to protect—the marbled mansion, the opulent couches, the lavish gardens. *Lord, these men and others like them won't tolerate what your Son is coming to do. They will resist him if he threatens their comforts and their positions, and how can he not? This world must be capsized to turn it right again.*

The temple rose above all of Jerusalem—majestic, imposing, the one place the world still made sense. Through Moses, Adonai had ordered the coming in and going out of the faithful, the times for prayer, and the atoning sacrifices. Wouldn't the temple be the rallying place for the Messiah's cause? Instead, with leaders like ben Haviv and ben Sapir, would his son's greatest resistance come from the seat of HaShem's holiness?

No, he would not tell Miryam what he had heard that day, and he wasn't sure how he would live knowing what lay ahead for his son, either. Although the thought of returning to the priest's house sickened him, he would return. He would carve the most luscious vine ever imagined, for Messiah was coming to restore the vineyard to its glory, and he wanted the gate to reflect that promise.

Chapter Eighteen

The Silence is Broken

*M*iryam paced a tight circle in the small house of Tamir and Rut, pressing her head to the support post when a pain gripped her. She breathed deeply as the midwife, Tzillah, had instructed her and released each breath into her arms and legs. When she did, her muscles softened but only until the next pain came.

The pains had been regularly spaced since the hour Yosef left for Jerusalem, but now they grew in intensity. Was it too late to change her mind about this assignment? She'd watched her mother deliver her sisters. The toil of delivery loomed before Miryam, and she worried a prolonged labor would disturb the working of the household of her hosts.

The children had been dispersed, the youngest to neighbors, the older to collecting palm fronds for the *sukkah*. The fretful goat tethered in the courtyard complained about her banishment. Yosef and Tamir would be home from their work before the sun set for *Shabbat*, the first night of *Sukkot*, but would a meal be waiting for them?

Rut and Miryam had been working for days to prepare special treats for *Sukkot*. The men had erected the three-sided *sukkah* on the roof, where the family would eat their evening meals for the coming week, and where the children would beg to sleep, just as the children of Israel had slept during their time in the wilderness. *Sukkot* would not wait, and hunger did not take a break for the birth of a baby.

Rut ground nuts she would use to stuff dates. Her calm presence, her encouraging words, and the distraction she provided with stories of a houseful of sisters soothed Miryam, but she couldn't help worrying about how others fared.

Her family traveled each year to Jerusalem for *Sukkot*. In doing so, they proved a merry spectacle for their fellow travelers, singing psalms and reciting long passages of Torah. Picturing her family together in their *sukkah*, so close to her in Jerusalem, made them seem even farther away. She'd hoped her family—in truth, her mother—would have pushed past Jerusalem to celebrate this year in Bethlehem with her and Yosef, and the babe that now commanded a seat at the table.

Oh, Ima, I wish you were here.

Tzillah arranged the birthing stones on the floor and positioned a chair behind for Miryam to rest when the hard work of pushing began. The setup was familiar. Old Yemima had done the same for her mother.

"Miryam?" Tzillah said. "Rut and I have delivered many babies together. Her own babies, yes, but also the babies of her sisters and other women of the village. We make a good team, and we will take good care of you and your baby."

Tears choked in Miryam's throat. "My mother—"

Rut left her grinding to embrace her. "Let's walk together, dear one. You are doing an amazing job. So calm for a first-time mother. The moment the child arrives, we will send word to your parents. In the meantime, Tzillah and I won't leave you for a moment."

"But *Shabbat*."

"Yes, Miryam, *Shabbat* is sacred and not to be dismissed. But the Law provides for babies born on *Shabbat*, too. The tiny ones, their mothers, and those who help with birthing are not forgotten. You are called to the most noble of labors, the birthing of a child."

Miryam recalled her mother rising from her birthing bed to prepare a meal for her family. "But this is also *Sukkot*. There's so much to do. I should be helping you."

"Your son has chosen a joyous time to be born. We celebrate HaShem's faithfulness in the wilderness, the forging of a nation from mere slaves. Just think, every year your son will have two things to celebrate— his birthday and Adonai's redemption—with all of Adonai's people. And this child, more than any other ever born, will be cause for celebration."

The tightness started in her back and reached to her belly button. How much longer could she do this? The question was meaningless. She would continue until the baby was born—in a few minutes, an hour, a day, or two. The cramping would not stop until the muscles had exhausted themselves or the baby was born. She crossed her arms over the back of the chair and laid her head on her arms.

Tzillah touched her back. The pressure irritated Miryam, yet she needed the midwife near. "Are you breathing?" she asked.

The question seemed nonsensical. Of course she was breathing. The pains were intensifying. She nodded in hopes of silencing any more of the midwife's questions.

"Are the pains strengthening?" Tzillah asked.

"Oh yes." The words came as a moan.

"That's very good, Miryam. Your calmness is letting your body do its job." Tzillah swept Miryam's loose curls from her face. "Daughter, I have heard your story, the one you tell of the angel. Not since Shifrah and Puah stood up to Pharaoh's decree has a midwife been called to so worthy a task. Today, in this house, the Messiah will be born. Are you ready?"

CR

SUPPORTED BY RUT AND Tzillah, Miryam squatted on the birthing stones. The sun cast long beams on the far wall through the west-facing windows. Her legs shook with fatigue. She'd never been this tired. "Yosef. Has anyone heard from Yosef?"

"I sent Penuel to the crossroads. He will tell Yosef to hurry, that his son is coming today."

The midwife put her hand to Miryam's swollen belly. "No more talking, daughter. Save your air for the work before you. You must listen and do as I say. If you do, your son will be here soon."

Tzillah sat on a low stool before Miryam. Rut stood behind, arms clasped under Miryam's arms. "It begins, Miryam…listen…listen…okay, breathe in…deeper…good…hold it…push!"

Miryam expected the push to feel good, productive, as she'd heard her mother say. Nothing happened. The child didn't move.

"Keep pushing."

"It hurts!"

"You are stronger than the pain, Miryam. Push through it."

Miryam pictured wineskins swollen with new wine, taut and thinned by the pressure within. To break the skin was to release the pressure. She bore down, willing the skin to burst.

"Stop pushing." Tzillah and Rut lowered her onto the chair.

Already? But nothing had changed. The child remained high in her womb.

This became the rhythm: breathe in, hold the breath, and push until Tzillah told her to stop. Shadows filled the room. The air cooled. Rut lit a lamp. The voices of anxious relatives floated to Miryam. Was Yosef among them?

"You must save your strength. Breathe in and release your muscles."

Miryam doubted her muscles would do her bidding, to relax or to push. She'd been pushing for what seemed like hours. Her mother had travailed for a far shorter time with her sisters. But much longer for the sister who had been born without breath. Miryam swallowed down panic.

Rut cooled her face with a wet cloth. "Let me wipe the worry from your face. Everything is going beautifully. You are doing very, very well. The baby will be here soon."

Miryam's back clamped into a fiery knot that stretched its tendrils around her abdomen and pulled. A moan escaped her lips.

Tzillah signaled to Rut and they hoisted Miryam onto the birthing stones. "Breathe. Breathe. Don't tense." Rut squatted with her, supporting her with strong arms. Miryam noticed a tremor as she leaned against her legs. Rut was getting tired, too.

"Deep breath in. Push."

The midwife knelt before Miryam, feeling for the baby's progress. "I feel the head, Miryam. Push through the pain."

"I can't."

"You can, dearest. Just a little bit more."

When they lowered Miryam to the chair again, she questioned if she'd seen an angel at all. Would HaShem ask her to do the impossible? Would she labor the rest of her life? Since HaShem gave her the child, shouldn't he ease the birth?

Rut wiped Miryam's face again. Tzillah offered her a spoonful of honey. Miryam turned her face away.

"You need strength to finish your labor. Borrow the energy of the bees,

Miryam."

She opened her mouth. The sweetness roiled her stomach, but she mouthed the gooey sweetness until it dissolved down her throat.

Tzillah cupped Miryam's face in her hands. "You are so close. Only a push or two, and your son will be in your arms. This is when girls discover what it means to truly be a woman. You have strength you never needed as a girl, strength that lays dormant until it's needed. It is a gift from HaShem. Call upon that strength now, and it will come."

Back on the birthing stones, Miryam prayed. *I do not have a woman's strength, Lord. My flesh and my heart are failing, but you are the strength of my heart and my portion forever.*[23] *Help me.*

Tzillah's words proved true. Yeshua emerged from her womb with the next searing push. The babe pierced the darkness with his penetrating cry until the midwife placed him, still slippery with birth fluids, on her chest. He looked as if he'd been dipped in whitewash, his thick, black hair pasted to his head. His vulnerability squeezed Miryam's heart. She asked for a linen towel to wrap him against the room's chill.

"Your work isn't yet done," Tzillah said.

Miryam knew what the midwife meant. There was the afterbirth to deliver. She waited for the next pain to add what strength remained to this final expulsion. In the meantime, she put her cheek to Yeshua's damp head, felt the heat of him bleed into her. The love she'd planted for her son in the orchard all those months ago now swelled to an enormity she couldn't fathom. It strengthened and enfeebled her at the same time. How could this tiny, helpless babe be the suffering Messiah Isaiah told about? She longed for such a Savior, the One who would bear the sins of many and make intercession for the transgressors, but this babe could not bear such weight. Could he?

Adonai, I will carry your Son, but you must carry me.

YOSEF CRADLED HIS SON against his chest as Miryam slept on the pallet. The child smelled of the olive oil rubbed into his skin. Tamir's family slept together on the roof, satisfying the children's pleas to do so and giving Yosef and Miryam the night to be forged into a family.

He carried the baby to an oil lamp to study his features, to marvel at

---

[23] Psalm 73:26 (NIV).

the tininess of his hands, his ears, his feet. Most surprising, the child looked like every other newborn he'd seen. Nothing regal in this child. Nothing in the way he looked would draw attention and certainly not affection, except from his mother and father. Love for the child chiseled a deep ache in Yosef's heart.

From the pallet, Miryam said, "Do you plan on holding him all night?"

"His father has already neglected him enough. This poor child of a carpenter has no bed to sleep in. The least I can do is hold him through his first night."

Miryam gestured to an indentation on the floor by the pallet. "The goat has agreed to share her manger."

On cue, the goat bleated, as if to say she had been bamboozled out of her manger, for someone had filled the recess with straw and covered it with a linen sheet.

"No finer bed had ever been offered to king or child," Miryam said.

She sat up and rummaged through the bag she'd carried from Nazareth. "Bring him here. It's time I swaddled him in the cloths I embroidered."

Miryam cradled the child on her thighs and deftly wrapped his legs together and his arms against his sides. She tucked the embroidered end of the cloth through a layer of the swaddling and laid it open across his chest.

Yosef fingered Miryam's fine stitches. "A lion?"

"The angel told me Adonai will give Yeshua the throne of his father David." She lay the baby in the makeshift cradle. "David's line goes back to Judah, the fourth son of Jacob, who promised the scepter would never depart from Judah. The Lion of Judah, that's our son, Yosef."

The world tilted and swayed when Yosef tried to reconcile what Miryam believed about the child and what he knew of the leaders who exercised authority over HaShem's people. Would Herod bend a knee to a king born of a craftsman and his wife? Would the Romans politely acquiesce to the Lion of Judah, the true ruler of Judea? Would the high priest step into line with a Nazarene and do his bidding? He couldn't imagine such a shift of power, not from the likes of Kayafa and his sycophants, or the Romans, or their puppet king. What could he do to help his son?

A passage from Isaiah came to Yosef's mind:

He will swallow up death forever.
Adonai Elohim will wipe away
the tears from every face,
and he will remove from all the earth
the disgrace his people suffer.
For Adonai has spoken.
On that day they will say,
"See! This is our God!
We waited for him to save us.
This is Adonai; we put our hope in him.
We are full of joy, so glad he saved us!"[24]

Yosef chuckled to himself, shaking his head in wonder. The baby sleeping in the manger was the Messiah, the *Messiah*. When the child grew to a man, he would not require his help to do anything. Adonai promised to save the world through this babe, and Adonai is never foiled in his plans.

---

[24] Isaiah 25:8-9 (CJB).

Chapter Nineteen

Good News!

Paltiel woke to the shouts of men and the frantic bleats of sheep. Light shone around him, brighter than daylight but not warming, only revealing. The light glowed from within every shrub, every stubble of grass, and the boulders that littered the desert. It ignited every crystal. The sand sparkled like water. There were no shadows. He couldn't take his eyes off of what only hours earlier had been brown and drab.

A strong hand clamped his arm and pulled him toward the sheep pen. Stones tumbled from the wall as the shepherds scrambled inside. One cracked against Paltiel's ankle. The rod he had hugged to his chest all night fell from his hand. He reached for it, but Haran told him to leave it with a voice clogged by fear. Another hand pushed Paltiel's head down.

Paltiel cowered with the other shepherds, face to the ground, behind the stone wall he and Nogah had stacked to protect the sheep. The pen seemed pitifully insubstantial. The men whispered urgent prayers.

"Adonai, have mercy!"

"God, deliver us from our enemies!"

"Come quickly to help me, O Lord my savior."[25]

The sheep, now quiet, stood like statues. Their eyes shone white as they stared unblinking past the shuddering shepherds to the sky. Whoever stood on the other side of the wall was tall. Very tall.

A giant? Twenty giants?

Against such a foe, Paltiel could never make a stand or even escape.

---

[25] Psalm 38:22 (NLT).

But he might be able to help the others escape. He had nothing to lose by trying. He didn't know how, but he would divert the giants' attention to give the other shepherds a chance to escape into the nearby wadi. If his efforts proved unsuccessful, Paltiel would at least die in a way that brought honor to his family and not the shame his many failed apprenticeships had brought to their door. And if he succeeded, perhaps he would become a hero in one of Nogah's stories.

He crawled out the opening of the sheep pen to where he and Reuel had lain moments earlier. He kept his head down, his eyes on the sand, lest he offend the giants with his brazenness. Besides, he would surely lose what little courage he possessed, if he saw who or what stood before him. He gripped the rod, said a prayer, and stood to face his enemy.

The being before him, for he could not have been a man, although he had the form of a man, rose to the height of a date palm. The whitest, purest light shone from him. His hair, his face, his clothing, and even his feet glowed the brightest light Paltiel had ever seen. The being bowed his head in greeting. The rod again slid from Paltiel's hand. All plans of distracting the being evaporated, for his legs and arms had turned leaden.

Behind him, the shepherds whispered, but too softly for Paltiel to understand. Shouldn't one of those men come to talk to the being? His first attempt to call Reuel came out as a squeak. He cleared his throat. "Reuel, there is someone here to speak to you, our leader."

Paltiel heard only more worried whispering from the men. To keep so powerful a being waiting didn't seem wise. Paltiel returned the greeting with a nod and tried to smile. His lips trembled, and he probably sneered instead. Perhaps if he closed his eyes, the being would leave as he'd come. If not, at least Paltiel would not see the giant creature raise his hand to strike him dead. He squeezed his eyes shut and whispered, "Reuel? Please. Come out."

There was a shuffling of feet. A grunt. A collective gasp and a sniffling cry.

"I'm here, boy."

Paltiel opened his eyes to see that Reuel stood beside him, his skin ashen and his hands trembling.

The being raised his hands, as big as a cart's wheels, as if to say everything would be all right. In fact, he smiled like it was his birthday, and his mother had baked raisin cakes to celebrate. Paltiel would choke on his mother's dry raisin cakes or anything else he put in his mouth in that moment.

"Don't be afraid."[26] The being's voice vibrated in Paltiel's chest.

Paltiel took a step closer, for Reuel stood mute, and someone had to speak for the band of shepherds. "As you can see, we are *very* afraid. I'm sure you understand why. Look at yourself. You're huge. We only have sticks to fight you. If you're going to kill us, please do so swiftly and mercifully, for we are only humble shepherds." Even an honorable death had lost its appeal, so he added, "It would be a great kindness to spare such lowly servants as us."

The being smiled wryly and shook his head. "You've got this all wrong. You must listen carefully, because you are being called—from youngest to oldest—to be witnesses of Adonai's faithfulness." He motioned to the shepherds who still hid behind the sheep pen wall. "Come forward, shepherds, to receive a message directly from Adonai."

Bet and Nogah shuffled forward and stood behind Paltiel and Reuel. Haran stood rigidly with the sheep.

"I'm here to announce a great and joyful event that is meant for everybody, worldwide: A Savior has just been born in David's town, a Savior who is Messiah and Master. This is what you're to look for: a baby wrapped in a blanket and lying in a manger."[27]

Behind Paltiel, Bet voiced the questions that niggled at him as well. "In Bethlehem? In a manger? The Messiah? A king would surely be born in a palace and in no other city but Jerusalem."

Instead of answering, the angel—for who else would bring a message from Adonai?—shouted, "Glory to God in the heavenly heights,"[28] and a cacophony of voices joined him. "Peace to all men and women on earth who please him."[29]

As the angel's praises got louder, the forms of other angels emerged from the brilliance, filling the sky with a crowd too numerous to count and too raucous to contain. Some shouted. Others sang. A parade of

---

[26] Luke 2:10a (MSG).
[27] Luke 2:10b-12 (MSG).
[28] Luke 2:14a (MSG).
[29] Luke 2:14b (MSG).

trumpeters marched across the sky, followed by drummers that quaked the ground. Joy rained upon the shepherds and swirled around, until the ragged group could not still their voices one moment longer.

Nogah leapt and spun. "A Savior is born! A Savior is born!"

Reuel clapped his hands and raised them to the sky. Bet knelt in the sand, his hands clasped over his heart. "You haven't forgotten us, Lord!" Haran sat on a boulder and wept, but not the weeping of a sad man, but the kind of weeping that cleanses a soul from regret. Paltiel joined Nogah, dancing as King David had danced before the ark of the covenant, or so he hoped, for he had never danced before.

The shepherd's praising went on until the voices of heaven quieted and faded to the typical sounds of a desert night—the crickets' chirrups, an owl's mournful call, grasses rubbing in the breeze. The shepherds stood, faces raised, waiting in the faint starlight.

"They're not coming back," Haran finally said.

Reuel added kindling to the embers and blew until small flames pressed against the darkness.

Nogah bounced on the balls of his feet. "Let's go!"

"It will be safer by daylight," Reuel returned, adding wood to the fire.

"The angel said to go now."

"The angel said we would find the baby wrapped in a blanket in a manger. Baby's sleep a lot, young Nogah, almost never at night. We will find him just as well by daylight."

Haran grunted.

The men turned to the large man and waited for what he might say, but he didn't utter a word. It was Bet's voice that interrupted the silence. "We have been given a great honor. Perhaps we are so unused to such a happening that we have forgotten the message: The Messiah and Master has been born. Our people have waited for him for a long time, too many years to count. I must go see what HaShem has done. Who will go with me?"

"If we wait until daylight, we can take the sheep with us," Reuel said.

"They will slow us down, nibbling at every blade of grass between here and Bethlehem. We can be there in an hour if we leave them behind."

"If a cheetah doesn't attack and scatter them, a pack of hyenas will," Reuel countered.

"I will stay," Haran said.

"Don't you want to see the Messiah?"

"I am not worthy."

"Look around," Bet said. "None of us is worthy. We're nothing but shepherds. But the angel came to us, not kings or princes or wealthy merchants, not holy men or priests. HaShem sent the angel to us. We should go. We should all go."

Reuel rubbed his eyes with the heels of his hands. "Bet is right. We cannot delay a response to so great an announcement. These are my sheep. I will stay with them. The rest of you will go. I will follow at daylight with the sheep and meet you at the city's well."

Paltiel had never been to Bethlehem, but they'd seen it from a high ridge on their trip up the mountain. The village wasn't large or small, but there were many houses that looked alike. "How will we find the baby? The angel said only that he was born in David's town. Will we knock on every door in the village? People won't like that—waking their animals and their children."

Bet shrugged. "Perhaps that is what HaShem intends. Who should sleep on such a night as this? The Messiah is finally here." He paced before the watching shepherds, stopping to pound his palm with a fist. "I will do the door pounding, and I will not stop until we find the Messiah. If I make someone angry, so be it. I will knock on the next door. If someone throws a rock at me, that is a small price to pay. If you intend to lay eyes on the Messiah tonight, follow me."

Bet touched a torch to the campfire. Soon, blue and yellow flames licked the night, casting a soft glow over scattered bed rolls and cloaks. "I will go before." He handed another torch to Haran, who hesitated. "If HaShem had not intended the message for you, Haran, he would have struck you dead. Take the torch and walk behind. We will be in Bethlehem in less than an hour."

"Let's go!" Nogah shouted.

Bet walked resolutely into the night, followed by Nogah and Haran. Paltiel stood beside Reuel, watching the men go.

Reuel put a hand to Paltiel's shoulder. "You handled yourself well tonight, young man. You stood to face the angel while the rest of us trembled with the sheep."

"I was really scared, Reuel."

"We were all frightened, but you managed to find just enough courage to do something. I'm proud of you."

Paltiel let Reuel's words settle into his heart.

"Now, you better catch up to Haran's torch, or you'll be walking to Bethlehem in the dark. Hyenas hunt at night, you know."

Paltiel hesitated. Hadn't Reuel taught him that two shepherds were better than one?

"I appreciate that you are willing to stay with me, boy, but I would never forgive myself for keeping you from so glorious an event. A Messiah is born but once. It's time for you to go and welcome him."

☙

MIRYAM ADJUSTED YESHUA'S SWADDLING by lamp light and wrapped him in the blanket she'd woven. Her arms savored his nearness, but weariness tugged her to sleep off the travail of birth. She brought his face to hers, felt his milky breaths on her face, and touched her lips to his downy cheek.

You've worn me out, my son, and you're not even a day old.

She laid him in the manger and blew out the lamp. The goat in the animal keep complained half-heartedly. "Good night, goat," she whispered. Yosef already snored softly beside her. She reached from the pallet into the darkness and rested her hand on the sleeping baby. The weight of fatigue pulled her into a dreamless sleep.

She woke to the whispering voices of men, Yosef and others she did not recognize. Her heart thumped wildly. She felt for Yeshua. His chest rose and fell under her hand. "Yosef? Who's there?"

"Go back to sleep, Miryam. I'm sending some crazy shepherds away."

"Are you the mother of the Messiah?" an unfamiliar voice called to her. "An angel told us to come. To see him."

Miryam pressed herself to sitting. "Yosef, you better let them in."

But Yosef pushed the door closed. The bolt thudded into place. "Miryam, we don't know who these men are. They speak in riddles about a sky full of angels. We have a sacred honor to protect the boy."

"But Yosef, they saw a crowd of angels. In the sky. Celebrating Yeshua's arrival."

"And don't forget the bright light. They were quite taken with a light that seemed to glow out of the rocks. How could that be possible?"

"Yosef, who are we to contradict the message an angel delivers to anyone? For whatever reason, HaShem wanted these men to know his Son had arrived today. You really should let them in."

"The hour is late. They can come back in the morning. We will all be better for having slept, at least a little."

She made to stand. "Yosef, I want to hear their story. Please, open the door."

He pulled Miryam into his arms and cradled her head to his chest. Miryam marveled at his strength sheltered in tenderness. Not much could tempt her to step out of his protection. But the shepherds. Their story. What had the angel said?

Yosef said, "You won't rest until I let them in, am I right?"

He knew her well for having only lived together for a short a time. Miryam smiled. "You are correct, my husband."

Yosef kissed her forehead and opened the door. Miryam lit another lamp and stood between the door and the manger, just in case.

An old man stepped through the door, bent with his years and favoring one leg. He lowered his head and held his hands to his chest. "Mistress, is he here? Is the Messiah under this roof?" His voice was filled with awe and tinged with disappointment. "I have knocked on many doors."

Miryam took the man by his elbow and led the way. She lifted the lamp over the manger. "He is here, sir." The baby slept in the dim ring of light, snug in the manger bed, unaware of celebrating angels and sojourning shepherds.

The man gasped, covering his mouth with a hand. "He sleeps in a manger."

Yosef stepped into the light. Behind him, the other shepherds stood, eyes round, mouths agape. Yosef said, "I have started a cradle. With the traveling from Nazareth and the long days in Jerusalem, well…"

The old man lowered to his knees before the child, and the other shepherds joined him. "It's a good thing you didn't finish that cradle. The angel said we would know him because he lay in a manger. We have interrupted the sleep of many households in search of this child, but none of their little ones slept so."

If the angel knew where the babe slept, what else did he know? Miryam asked, "Did the angel say anything else?"

Bet frowned and rubbed his forehead. "I'm not so good at remembering as I used to be."

Paltiel stood. "If it pleases you, mistress, I remember everything the angel said."

Miryam extended her hand to the boy to urge him closer. "Tell me everything."

Paltiel told the whole story, from the first blaze of light to the celebration that filled the sky. Miryam could only smile and nod, so familiar were the proclamations about her son.

"Mistress," said Paltiel, "you don't seem surprised by my story."

"Have you told me everything?"

"You should know that we hid in the sheep pen when the angel appeared."

Miryam nodded. "I climbed a tree."

"Then you've seen an angel, too?"

"Yes, and angels are a marvel. But what you must remember from this night is that HaShem didn't forget his people, Israel. Every promise he has ever made will come to pass, and this child is his very best promise. He is tiny and helpless now, but he will grow to be a Savior."

"For the whole world," Paltiel added.

The whole world? When Miryam stood in Bethlehem, it was hard to fathom even Nazareth or Jerusalem, places where she had been, where she had lived. Yet those were tiny compared to Rome, which truly was the whole world—Greece, Egypt, Gaul, Lusitania, and many other places that were unimaginable to her, only names that she'd heard in the markets. Her son would be the Savior of all those people? The Gentiles as well as the Jews?

She picked Yeshua up, held him to her chest, and stepped out of the ring of light. Could she share him with so many, most of them Gentiles? *No, not this night. Not yet.* The day would come when the demands of his heavenly Father would require her to relinquish him to his calling, but not when he was so small, so helpless. She turned back to the shepherd boy, intending to send him and his friends away.

The boy's chin dropped to his chest. "I have nothing to give him."

Already her son evoked a response from those who met him., and already she felt the tearing of separation.

What you ask of me, Lord, is very hard.

A tear slipped down her cheek. "You have given him a wonderful gift, boy. You believed what the angel told you, and you came to make him feel welcome. I will never forget what you have done."

Miryam looked into the faces of all the shepherds—the old man, the giant, the young man with the dancing eyes. "I will never forget that all of you came to welcome Yeshua. I will tell him all about you and this night when he is older."

Each shepherd stepped forward to watch the child sleep, and Miryam marveled at how they responded to the tiny babe. The large man bent over Yeshua, his shoulders heaving with his cries until he uttered a thank you and rose with a broad grin across his face. She wasn't sure what had transpired, for the child never stirred. The younger man with a shock of wild curls bent low, studying the boy's face. "I will remember you always."

The shepherds shuffled out the door. Over their heads, the sky had brightened to gray. The older man turned back. "I won't see the boy grown to be a man, but I will tell his story for all of the days I have left."

Miryam carried Yeshua to the pallet and curled her body around him. Her son would wake for a feeding soon. And it wouldn't be long before Rut's family stirred on the roof, creaking the rafters and the children crying to break fast. Yosef nestled behind Miryam, draping his arm over her waist. Within moments, Yosef's breaths deepened and his arm grew heavy.

Miryam did not try to sleep. She repeated the shepherds' story over and over in her mind, careful not to add or subtract one detail. It was a story she would retell all through the life Adonai granted her.

One question made her smile: What would she say to those who gathered to hear? Would she say that the most amazing part of the night was that Adonai had filled the sky with his angels to celebrate Yeshua's arrival, or would she marvel before everyone that Yosef could sleep after such a wondrous night?

Chapter Twenty

Purification

*E*lisheba handed her six-month-old son, Yohanan, to Rut, who bounced the complaining child into a tentative contentment. "He would suckle every hour of the day," Elisheba said. "He is a greedy little creature." The women who stood inside the entrance to the *mikveh*—Ima, who cradled Yeshua against her chest, Rut and her daughter-in-law, and Miryam—laughed knowingly.

Ima's familiar chortle gladdened Miryam's heart. Bethlehem seemed more like home with her mother there. Soon, however, Abba would feel the pull of the orchard and her family would return to Nazareth, without her. But not that day, so she pushed all thoughts of farewells aside and simply enjoyed the company of the women around her. After all, Yosef would soon take her and Yeshua back to Nazareth, as well.

Elisheba turned to Miryam. "Yeshua arrived at the perfect time. Here we are, all gathered after seven days of celebrating HaShem's provision for his people in the wilderness. We have waved our branches and boughs, rejoicing before Adonai for his goodness. Doing this reminds us of our utter dependence on him.

"And now…" Elisheba scooped the sleeping Yeshua from Ima's chest and drew him to herself. With her cheek to his head, she closed her eyes. The women watched, waited. A knot cinched Miryam's throat to see Elisheba's love for her son.

Elisheba opened her eyes and looked into each woman's face and then rested her gaze on Miryam. "And now he has sent his most prized and perfect provision in this new babe. Our salvation is near. Adonai be praised."

Elisheba kissed Yeshua's head and handed him back to Ima. "It's a very good thing we are together to celebrate his arrival and to share this moment with you, dear Miryam, when you go from *niddah* to *tahor*. How can our hearts possibly contain so much blessing? To return the blessing to Adonai, we will try."

Elisheba took Miryam's hand. "You have been a mother for just seven days, but those days have challenged and delighted you as no other passing of days. Am I right?"

The sight of Yeshua sleeping serenely against Ima's chest swelled Miryam's heart with a love that was both exquisite and excruciating. She'd never been more tired or happy. Her eyes burned with tears, and she nodded.

Elisheba continued. "Birth is separation, a separation brought by much painful laboring. This child, whose tumbling and hiccupping became as much a part of you as your own heartbeat, has left the comfort of your womb forever. His leave-taking is a wondrous miracle and a kind of loss.

"There is yet more to the separation, Miryam, for the blood that brought life to Yeshua has sloughed away from your body, now useless and dead. This encounter with death makes you *niddah*. Immersion in these waters will make you *tahor*. You will be made clean to enter the temple…and to reunite with your husband."

At the thought of uniting with Yosef, as only a woman and her husband can, her stomach bloomed with warmth and her heart thumped in anticipation. Miryam's face grew hot. She bowed her head, draping her flushed face with her hair.

Rut stepped close. "Let me help you with your tunic."

Miryam pulled the tunic over her head and handed it to Rut, who then stepped back into the company of the women.

Elisheba smiled broadly. "It is time, Miryam. Descend into the waters—like all faithful daughters of Adonai before you."

Miryam took the first step, and her skin constricted with the briskness of the water and erupted with goose flesh. The shock of cold stalled her. Behind and above her, the women stood at the arched entrance to the *mikveh*, singing Ima's favorite psalm of praise. Their voices reverberated off the barrel ceiling.

"Great is Adonai and greatly to be praised;
his greatness is beyond all searching out.

Each generation will praise your works to the next
and proclaim your mighty acts."[30]

Ima's chilled hand touched Miryam's shoulder, and she whispered into Miryam's ear. "Do not hesitate, my daughter. The water will not get warmer by your waiting. It's best to step quickly into its depths and receive the newness of HaShem's cleansing."

Miryam nodded tightly and descended into the spring-fed water. To her knees. To her thighs. She gasped when the water touched her stomach. Since she'd clung to her mother's tunic, Miryam had longed to join the women of her village and the long line of her foremothers at the *mikveh*. She had never considered that the coldness of the water would bite so.

"Go on," Ima coaxed.

She took another step, and the water covered her breasts, soothing the sting of Yeshua's suckling. She drew a breath, crossed her arms over her stomach, as Ima had instructed, and continued. The last step was steeper than she'd expected. Before she could panic, her feet settled on the stone bottom. The water lifted her hair and stunned every inch of her, but the water no longer clawed, only refreshed.

I receive this new birth, Adonai. Make me acceptable in your sight.

Miryam rushed into the towel that Rut held open. The hands of the women burnished the cold from her skin, and she dressed quickly. The women erupted into another psalm as they walked through the streets of Bethlehem.

"I will bless Adonai at all times;
his praise will always be in my mouth.

When I boast, it will be about Adonai;
the humble will hear of it and be glad."[31]

Yeshua's breaths warmed Miryam's neck as they walked back to Rut's house. He arched and stretched, so she patted his back, hoping to delay his awakening. His cries for a meal would overwhelm the women's songs.

Although something had altered for Miryam in the *mikveh*, everything about Bethlehem remained the same. The narrow streets, the greetings of

---

[30] Psalm 145:3-4 (CJB)
[31] Psalms 34:2-3 (CJB)

neighbors, the scent of lentil stew wafting from cooking pots. In a season of changes—marriage, motherhood, a new family—she finally felt a part of something big and lasting. And yet, she also felt different—a part but apart. She suspected these feelings had to do with being Yeshua's mother, but she wasn't sure why. Only the passing of days and the unraveling of Adonai's plan would tell her that.

I will wait on you, Lord.

Ima put an arm around her shoulders. "Daughter, we must turn our thoughts to the circumcision celebration tomorrow. Your father packed five jugs of honey and a heaping basket of figs, the best we've seen from the orchard in years—so plump and sweet. Your guests will be delighted.

"Elisheba has agreed to make her raisin cakes, and Rut will bake some almond breads. Surely, it will take little convincing for your father to buy some good wine. So you see, daughter, we will celebrate Yeshua in grand style. Will you roast meat for your guests?"

Just as Ima had warned, time was short for women to reflect on the wonders of Adonai. She kissed the whorl of hair at Yeshua's crown. "Yosef went to the butcher right before we left for the *mikveh*. He will bring home some chickens."

"There's nothing better than roasted chicken," Ima said and rejoined the singing. "Taste, and see that Adonai is good. How blessed are those who take refuge in him!"[32]

Miryam was grateful for her mother's enthusiasm over roasted chickens. She had hoped for a leg of lamb, but Yosef had counted out coins from his purse and come up short.

CR

YOSEF STOPPED MIRYAM BEFORE she entered the gate. His eyes glinted with a secret that needed telling. "Come with me," he said. "I want to show you something."

While men enjoyed a festive celebration, they believed the food came to the table without a hint of planning or labor. She'd seen this played out between Ima and Abba all through her childhood. And now Yosef wanted to show her something when she had mere hours to prepare for all who

---

[32] Psalm 34:9 (CJB)

came to the circumcision and naming of Yeshua? "Yosef, there's much to do before tomorrow. Can it wait?"

"No."

"No?"

"No."

What could be so important? The women had put their hands to their baking even as Miryam and Yosef stood outside the gate, talking. Surely, tomorrow or the next day would be soon enough to see something. "Yosef, the baby will soon wake up hungry."

"It's not far. We'll be back in a few minutes."

Was he blind to what went on before his eyes? "Yosef...?"

"I promise you will like what you see," he said, squeezing her hand.

No, he did not see the women working or notice his son squirming. She would have to follow him. "It's not far?"

"No, not far, but we should go now."

With that, Yosef led her across the street from Tamir and Rut's house and up a narrow alley. The stones gave way to a rutted path as they climbed higher, past small houses where children played in courtyards and mothers squatted before cooking fires.

She was about to insist Yosef take her back to her work, but he stopped suddenly. He gestured to a courtyard gate that hung haphazardly from its hinges, a look of triumph on his face. "This is it. Only 233 steps from Rut's gate to here."

The house before Miryam gaped open but silent. From the stand of weeds growing through the stones, no one had tended the house in a very long time. The bread oven lay in shards across the courtyard.

"Let me show you inside," Yosef said, pulling her through the gate. "It needs a new ladder to the loft. That's why the landlord discounted the rent. I will build a new one, of course. All it really needs is a good sweeping. I'm sure we can be happy here."

Miryam stopped at the threshold. "Happy *here*? What about our home in Nazareth? Why would we...?" She leaned into the open door. One corner of the loft sagged precariously. The table only looked good for firewood. Animal dung filled the keep. "Yosef, why here when we have a beautiful home—a home that you built—in Nazareth?"

Yosef pulled on his beard as he often did when she pressed him with questions. In her arms, Yeshua mewed and stretched. She didn't have time for ambiguities. "Yosef?"

"The work is good in Jerusalem. In fact, there are two years of work at the priest's estate. If we go back to Nazareth, I will have to scrounge for work in Sepphoris or see what tools the farmers might need—and farmers don't pay much. For all I know, there won't be anything for me to do."

He hadn't thought this through. "You hate working for the priest."

"It's steady, good-paying work. I do complain, but the work is a gift from HaShem. I don't want to offend his generosity to us. Besides, Tamir agreed to do the work for the priest, knowing I would bring a certain set of skills to the job. It wouldn't be right to abandon him in the middle of the work."

Yet they had to settle for chicken over lamb? "How can we afford to rent a house?"

"I have run the figures over and over. We will have to skimp, especially at first, but we should—with the blessing of HaShem—manage to save some of my wages and go back to Nazareth with a little in our pockets when the work runs out."

The house smelled of mouse urine and moldy straw. "You will help me clean this up?"

"Tamir has offered to help with the loft and ladder. I'm sure Rut and her daughters can lend a hand with the sweeping, as well."

Of course Tamir had offered his help. His family had graciously bent, and in some cases suspended, their lives to accommodate Yosef and Miryam, for nearly a month. They shouldn't impose on them any longer, especially if the work was in nearby Jerusalem.

Yosef's eyes lit with hope. "You agree?"

Miryam met his gaze. "I went to the *mikveh* today."

He smiled. "Yes, I know."

"I am no longer *niddah*."

"Yes, I know this, too."

"It is a good thing for us, especially now, that we will have our own house—as long as the work is good here."

"That crossed my mind as well."

C03

WHILE EVERYONE ELSE SLEPT, Yeshua woke Miryam complaining of hunger. She quickly lifted him from his manger bed and wrapped them both in her woolen cloak. The babe frantically sought his meal, so she put him to her breast and carried him outside and up the steps to the roof. The quarter moon pierced the eastern horizon like a curved blade. To the west, the indigo sky sparkled with the stars that Abraham could not count.

She sat in one of the sling chairs the men used during their evening Torah talks, grateful for the chance to reflect on the day. The women had laid a bountiful table for the circumcision celebration. Neighbors and friends of Tamir and Rut had carried every manner of savory and sweet delight to the courtyard. Their generosity astonished Miryam, who could not name half of the people in attendance. Their presence spoke to their respect for Tamir and Rut but also to their curiosity. Everyone wanted to see what a Messiah might look like.

Some in attendance only flitted a glance, not wanting to seem too eager for a look at the newborn Messiah. Perhaps putting their support behind so young a prospect seemed too risky. They might be found the fool if proven wrong, which wasn't hard to understand, for other men had come claiming to be the Messiah and disappointed them.

A small group of attendees had frowned their disappointment when they stepped forward to meet Yeshua. It was all Miryam could do not to shoo them away. What did they expect of a newborn? He had not been born with a sword, only a heavy burden of responsibility, the deliverance of a whole nation, a whole world. The job of raising a son strong enough to manage so weighty a charge fell to her and Yosef, with the help of HaShem.

Still others, like Elisheba and Zekharyah, and the family they had traveled with, moved around Yeshua with reverence, spoke in hushed tones, whispered prayers of thanksgiving to Adonai. How she appreciated their faithfulness.

Miryam understood the questions and uncertainty that Yeshua caused. Who was this babe in her arms? On one hand, Yeshua was like any other newborn. He required frequent feedings and even more frequent changes, which kept Miryam at the washtub all through the day. Some days his naps came regularly, giving her dependable time to assist Rut with meal preparations and other household duties. The next day, Yeshua napped like a cat and demanded continual feeding, frustrating any plans she'd made for the day.

On the other hand, this child was marked by El Shaddai, Ha´Elyon. He came from a promise of an angel and an encounter with the Holy Spirit. A company of angels had announced his birth to, of all people, shepherds in a nearby field—and they'd sought out the child to worship him. And Adonai had sent his messenger angel to Zekharyah and even to Yosef. She was especially grateful the angel had reassured Yosef of her fidelity.

Lord, don't let me forget who this child is and where he came from, even if I'm not sure where he's going.

The celebration had given Miryam a glimpse of the challenges Yeshua would face in his life. There would be curious people, willing to take a brief look and to listen until his words stung or offended. There would be people who eagerly came close because others they admired had witnessed his worthiness. Some of those would find their own reason to be loyal to Yeshua or to withdraw their devotion. Still others would see in him what they had longed for but couldn't name. Those followers would march through Hades for Yeshua.

The babe's head lolled, and he released her breast. She put him to her shoulder to work the air out of him.

"My son, you will win the hearts of the faithful with your goodness and strength of character. I pray I am the mother you need, when you are small and when you answer your true calling."

Chapter Twenty-one

A Day Like No Other

*S*him´on entered the temple through the Women's Gate. He scanned the crowd, his heart beating wildly. "Lord. Adonai. Open my eyes to see the deliverance of your people Israel."

He'd woken that morning confident his prayers had been answered, and that the promise he had wheedled out of HaShem so many years ago had finally been realized. The impression had come to him like a drink of cold spring water on a hot day: The Messiah would show himself at the temple this very day.

From his vantage on the Nicanor Steps, Shim´on watched. Below him, rabbis debated the finer points of Torah with their disciples. Women bent their heads in prayer. Priests busied themselves with preparations for the morning *Tamid* sacrifice. Men, lost body and soul in their devotion to Adonai, rocked as they prayed. On the far side of the Court of Women, the eastern gate yawned open to the Court of the Gentiles, where merchants hawked their wares—lambs, turtledoves, pigeons—and the moneychangers competed for business.

Not one person in the growing throng looked like a Messiah. None of them carried themselves with the confidence of a vanquishing warrior. There wasn't a savior among them. No, they looked like beggars, pleading for a morsel of goodness. The promise of the Messiah had grown stale in their mouths. To spit the hard morsel out meant all hope had died. His people were not the kind to relinquish hope, not when they could recite story after story of HaShem's faithfulness—from Abraham to Moses.

Shim´on slumped to the step and held his head in his hands. In the misty place between sleep and wakefulness, beckoning had pulled at him. Had he heard correctly? The sense of Adonai's presence had been so immediate and clear that he half expected the Son of Man to be standing over his pallet when he opened his eyes. He'd surely felt his breath on his face.

"Lord, I heard you, I know I did."

Using the gaps in the stones to pull himself up, he stood again. His hips burned like fire from the grating of his joints. In his determination to reach the temple when the gates were first opened, he'd not taken a moment to rest on the long, uphill walk from the Lower City. He pushed the pain aside to scour the faces flooding through the gate.

Too old. Too young. Too tired. Too female. Too stooped.

"Show me, Lord!"

Worshippers waited, sheltered by the colonnade. Every last one of them proved disappointingly unremarkable. Still more worshippers pressed through the gate, taking their places among those who milled in anticipation of the morning *Tamid* offering. Early arrivers shifted to make room. Shim´on couldn't be sure some faces had not avoided his scrutiny. Could he be in the very place the Messiah had walked and missed him?

"Lord, I am only a man! Help!"

Shim´on fingered the tassels of his *tallit*, untangling the fringe, reciting the commandments of Torah as he'd done since a boy. The familiar act calmed his heart. His eyes settled on a young couple bringing their new baby boy to the temple to be ransomed, for they waited their turn to pay five shekels to the supervising priest.

He'd seen the mother and child earlier, talking respectfully to another priest and dropping coins into the third trumpet for the wife's purification, just as the Law commanded. The couple were dressed in the rough cloth of the poor, but they moved with dignity and piety. Both covered their heads to pray as they waited for the *magrefah* to sound and the *Tamid* sacrifice to begin.

The vignette of the little family warmed him, reminding him of the times he had visited the temple with his dear wife, Edhah, after the birth of each of his seven children.

All but the couple and their child grew fuzzy. The voices of the people sounded as if they came through water. Shim´on knew in that moment that the baby in the mother's arms was the Messiah. *The* Messiah. He laughed from a deep place. "A baby!"

Worshippers turned, frowning at his outburst.

He shrugged at them. "He came as a baby, and he is *still* a baby!" The people dismissed him with a wave of their hands, so he turned to find the couple again. "Of course he came as a baby." He slapped his forehead. "Where is my mind? A *child* is born to us, just as you said! A *son* is given, just as you promised!"

He stopped and raised his shaking hands to heaven. "You like surprising me, don't you?" Tears of relief filled his eyes, for the days of silence were past. "Adonai be praised!"

Shim´on eased down the stairs, mindful of his aching hips but moving as quickly as he dared. He would not miss a chance to meet the Messiah, infant or not. He excused himself as he wove through the people, catching sight of the blue and red embroidery of the mother's veil as the people parted.

Shim´on stopped abruptly before the couple. His gasping breaths disturbed their prayers, and by the puzzlement on their faces, alarmed them. Distressing the young family had not been his intention.

He smiled his most reassuring smile. "I am Shim´on. I have waited my whole life for the Refresher of Israel to come. And here he is. A baby. Just as HaShem promised."

The husband looked to the wife, a question knitting his brow. Perhaps Adonai hadn't yet told them about the babe?

"I assumed you knew," Shim´on added quickly. He gestured to the child. "I speak about the babe." A realization dawned in the old man. "Of course! It is for *me* to tell *you*. Where should I begin?"

A soft touch alighted on his arm. He looked into the warm eyes of the wife. Had he ever been as young as she? She smiled with a kind of knowing that said she was glad to share her story.

The wife spoke. "Would you like to hold him?"

Shim´on's arms shook with fatigue. His legs ached to sit. He'd been in such a rush to get to the temple that morning, he hadn't grabbed his walking stick. Did he dare take the child—the Messiah—into his arms, the child who was destined to hold the government on his shoulders? Would he drop the babe in his hubris? Could his clumsiness extinguish the remnants of his people's hope?

Miryam didn't wait for Shim´on's reply. She offered the babe, and he received the child to his chest. The Messiah surely felt the pounding of his heart. The babe looked up at him with wise, inquisitive eyes. The knots of discouragement that had snugged tighter and tighter throughout Shim´on's life—with each offense of the Romans, with each disappointment in his own people—now loosed, unraveling and slipping away. With the release, his chest heaved a sob he could not staunch. Tears flowed down his cheeks and into his beard.

The presence of Adonai crowded out everyone and everything. He rocked the child with each exhalation of gratitude, reveling in the glory of Adonai, awash with a joy that threatened to explode his heart.

"Now, Adonai, according to your word,
> your servant is at peace as you let him go;
for I have seen with my own eyes your salvation,
> which you prepared in the presence of all peoples—
a light that will bring revelation to the nations
> and glory to your people Israel."[33]

The babe's parents stood wide-eyed before him. Did they know, *could* they know what it meant to be mother and father to the Messiah? Shim´on kissed the child's head, and the father received the child into his hands.

Although Shim´on considered following the little family home to spend his last days watching the child grow, he dared not burden them with his presence. Besides, his grandson's family would fret over his disappearance. Instead, Shim´on offered a *brakha* over the threesome: "Blessed is he who allows us to see the unfolding of his salvation."

No sooner had the words left his mouth, when another message came to him, a message from Adonai for the family, but especially for the mother. He took her hands in his. "Daughter, a painful sword will one day pierce your inner being, for your child will be rejected by many in Israel."[34]

The youthful blush of her cheeks faded at his words, but there was more to say. He kissed the backs of her hands and took in a shuddering breath, for he had never dreamed he would be called upon to deliver such

---

[33] Luke 2:29-32 (CJB, "salvation" substituted for *yeshu'ah*, "nations" substituted for *goyim.*)
[34] Luke 2:34 (TPT)

a message to his Messiah's mother. "And the destiny of your child is this: he will be laid down as a miracle sign for the downfall and resurrection of many in Israel. Many will oppose this sign, but it will expose to all the innermost thoughts of their hearts before God."[35]

The girl started to speak, but her words caught in her throat. He waited, hoped, that more words would come for her, words of consolation for the young mother. But not one word more came. Adonai, in his wisdom, granted the girl enough insight to guard her heart from disappointment, and yet he graciously withheld what she could not bear.

CR

ANNA SUBMITTED TO HAVING the youngest of her order of widows, Rivqah, tie her sandals. The older woman's aged body robbed her of the dignity of doing that simple task for herself. Not only did her back seize when she bent, but she coughed and couldn't stop. Laying down proved especially irritating to her belabored lungs. Her chest rattled like bones in an ossuary.

Rivqah rested her hands on Anna's knees. "You haven't recovered your strength from the celebration of *Sukkot*, my dear lady. Perhaps one day added to *Shabbat* will restore your vigor."

Anna snorted dismissively and presented her hands for Rivqah to pull her to standing. The prayers of the people in the temple courts reached the humble rooms where she lived with her band of praying widows below the colonnade. She was late already.

Rivqah pulled her to standing, handed Anna the walking staff she depended upon, and voiced a *brakha* over the woman. "Blessed is he who gives us strength when we are tired."

"And when we are stubborn," she added with a wink.

"Oh yes, especially when we are stubborn."

Anna reminded herself to be more tender with Rivqah. Not more than three months had passed since the girl had entered the ranks of widowhood and spurned her brother-in-law's offer to marry, as if one brother could substitute for another. How the girl reminded her of herself.

Now Rivqah insisted on being Anna's caretaker, whether she wanted

---

[35] Luke 2:35 (TPT)

one or not, and she did not. It was the Lord who sustained her. He alone
carried her and rescued her. When her spirit wearied, he gave her the wings
of an eagle to soar, although her soaring seemed much closer to the ground
these days.

She could not deny that her pallet had enticed her back to its comfort
after her rising that very morning. She was, indeed, tired. Her feet shuffled
forward, her lungs pulled in breath after breath, her eyes took in the fuzzy
images of worshippers milling in the Court of Women, and no one was
more surprised than she that she rose to serve her Lord yet another day.
He was her strength.

She found a sunny spot at the base of the towering lanterns that
illumined the courtyard during *Sukkot* and leaned against the stone. She
positioned herself to watch the people making their way from the eastern
gate to the Nicanor steps to worship Adonai.

"Lord, I am yours to direct as you will. Show me who needs an
encouraging word from you, and I will deliver it. Show me who is hurting,
who stumbles under shame, who is lonely, or heartsick, or in a captivity of
disappointment, and I will pray for them, because you are faithful."

A breeze lifted Anna's veil. She pushed away from the tower to stand
taller. "What is it, Lord? Show me who is in need, and I will serve to
promote your glory."

There. With Shim´on. A young husband with his wife and babe. The
girl looked as if Shim´on had pushed a knife into her heart.

Anna had tried time and again to explain to the other women of the
order just how the voice of Adonai sounded in her ears—A clarity, like the
shock of *mikveh* waters. The authority of the spring winds, pressing to be
heard. Even the giddiness of joy like a mountain stream rushing to the
valley. The women had listened to her, nodding kindly yet dismissively,
and walked away.

Watching the face of the young mother, Anna heard Adonai's voice,
telling her she looked upon the mother of the Messiah. The girl's
woundedness made sense to Anna, for no other mother would suffer
more. She gripped her walking staff and inched her way toward the family
in the company of Shim´on.

By the time she reached them, her lungs struggled for breath. She clung
to Shim´on's arm for support, although the man was no steadier on his

legs than she. "Shim´on, introduce me to my Lord and his family."

Shim´on laughed. "Praise Ha'Elyon, we have lived to see this day, Anna. But I am embarrassed to say that I haven't inquired of their names. My head was too jumbled by other questions."

Anna shook her head, but she understood Shim´on's neglected manners. They stood in the presence of the one they'd prayed to know their whole lives, and HaShem had granted that they would meet the child who would become their deliverer.

She asked and discovered Yosef and Miryam were parents to the baby Yeshua, a name assigned to the child by Gavri´el himself. The whole marvelous story spilled from Miryam in a steady stream of wonderment. Anna made a note to query Zekharyah when the Abijah priests next served in the temple, if she lived enough days to do so. Only Adonai knew the number of her days.

Miryam peeled back the blankets that encased Yeshua. His legs, already thickening from the richness of his mother's milk, lashed out at the freedom. Anna touched his palm, and his fingers closed around her gnarled thumb. How fresh and new was the babe's skin next to hers, but how ancient and holy was he, as well.

What will these fingers touch, my Lord? Will you carry a shield and sword, or will you lift up the oppressed and comfort those who mourn?

The deep resonance of the *magrefah* filled the courtyard. The time for the *Tamid* sacrifice had come. A shiver snaked its way along Anna's spine as the babe's gaze met hers. The leadenness that had dogged her spirit and her legs vanished. Anna tucked the child's blankets around his bare legs and under his chin, and then bent her face to his.

"You'll have to excuse me, my Lord. There are many who have faithfully awaited your arrival and the redemption of Jerusalem. I must go tell them you have finally come. Blessed is he who remembers his promises to his people." She kissed the babe's forehead, smiled a farewell to his parents, and headed for the chambers of the widow's order.

That evening, when the widows gathered for the evening meal, Anna looked from face to face. Some she had lived and prayed beside for many decades. Others, new to the order, still wore their widow's rags. All of them had a vision of a redeemed Jerusalem, one that drew rather than repelled its residents to seek HaShem with fervor and faithfulness. These women deserved to hear first that their vision was coming true.

"Ladies, my fellow servants of Adonai and his purposes, today proved to be a day like no other."

Chapter Twenty-two

Wise Men from the East

*B*ilal stood among his fellow Nabataean Magi, waiting for King Aretas IV to acknowledge their presence. One subject after another bowed low and requested Aretas' intervention in a dispute or brought news of neighboring kingdoms. The senior member of the Magi, Ridwan, clenched his jaw as he waited.

It seemed to Bilal that the king bided his time, although he had no way of knowing if the king delayed their interview or not. Bilal had never stood in the king's presence before this day. He prayed there would be few such command appearances in his future. His hands shook and his knees had turned to pooled wax.

When they'd broken their fast that morning, Ridwan had reminded Bilal of the stakes. King Aretas held his throne by a thread due to his volatile relationship with Rome. Not only did he look for threats from outside his realm, but amongst his loyal subjects. To be noticed could prove dangerous, unless a Magus were acknowledged for serving with distinction and humility. Bilal prayed he would not be noticed at all.

He kept his eyes on the scrolls opened on the table before him—the star charts as familiar as his own fingerprints and the prophecies of Isaiah. Soon enough, every eye in the room would be on him, for he had been the one to discover the propitious movement of planets, the moon, and a comet. He didn't trust his voice to come out above a whisper. Not only did he stand before the king, he stood before his stepfather and superior, Ridwan. He prayed his performance in court would lessen the tension at home, for his mother's sake.

"Enough!" the king bellowed, and with that one word, the petitioners scattered like mice. "I have waited months to hear from you, Ridwan. Tell me, has the time finally come to strengthen our alliance with the old snake, Herod?"

Ridwan bowed his head in tribute. "Yes, my lord, we have diligently studied the night skies—"

"Spare me your posturing, Ridwan. Tell me what you've found—nothing more, nothing less."

"If it please my lord, the intricacies of the skies and what the prophets have foreseen—"

King Aretas flipped a contemptuous hand. "Is there a Magus among you who can speak plainly?"

Ridwan hesitated only slightly before he bowed and gestured toward the table where Bilal stood. The other Magi backed away to leave Bilal and his scrolls alone in the center of the room.

This was not part of the plan. Ridwan spoke for the Magi. As the senior among them, he basked in both the glory and the shame of missed readings of the stars. Bilal's role was to point to scrolls and say only a few words. He would trade his dioptra for a drink of water.

"This is Bilal, my lord," Ridwan said, acknowledging with a deep bow he had displeased the king. "The youngest of our order."

General Nahyan, the king's highest-ranking military advisor, whispered into the king's ear. The king, in turn, studied Bilal for a long moment. Bilal tried to swallow away the tightness of his throat, but it was too dry.

"You are a Jew," the king said, both a question and accusation.

"Yes, my lord, by my mother." Bilal's voice rose an octave higher than normal.

"Does she pine like all Jews for Jerusalem?"

Bilal took a breath to speak, but the king continued.

"She and all Jews have lived peaceably among us for nearly 600 years. When Nebuchadnezzar destroyed Jerusalem, we opened our gates and homes to all those left behind. Does she still weep for the temple courts?"

"She is content in Petra, my lord, but it is as you say. The temple is very important to my mother. As a girl, she went there three times a day to pray."

"And you, a man who struggles to grow a decent beard, do you pine for Jerusalem, too?"

Bilal straightened, raised his chin. "I am Nabataean, my lord."

King Aretas worked his chin in thought. "Tell me what you have found, boy. Briefly."

Bilal scanned the star chart. For months he'd spent every clear night studying and recording the movements of the planets and a comet that raced across the sky. His gaze shifted to the scroll of the Jewish prophet Isaiah, opened to a description of the Messiah and outlining his mission. Every day, from sunrise to sunset, he bent over the prophet's writings. Bilal stole what sleep he could in the shadowed hours of dusk and dawn.

He'd discovered the night sky shouted its proclamation that something, actually some*one*, would bring peace and justice to all the nations. A king of unrivaled power and righteousness had been born to the Judeans.

As thrilling as a conjunction of Jupiter and the moon were to Bilal, it was what he read from the prophet Isaiah that thrilled and gave substance to the hope he'd inherited from his mother. Since all that Isaiah had prophesied about the recalcitrant Jews played out exactly as he'd said, Bilal trusted the prophet's voice even more than the stars.

King Aretas, too, revered Isaiah, but like all Nabataean kings he looked to the stars to perfectly time his political maneuvers. He craved an alliance with Rome's puppet king, Herod, who held the keys to the trade routes that had enriched the Nabataeans. Herod also controlled the port of Gaza, the gateway to faraway riches. More than securing trade routes, Herod's favor meant improved status with Caesar Augustus, whose approval would secure King Aretas' throne.

"My lord, as you know, Judea is associated with the constellation Aries. Furthermore, the planet Jupiter and the moon are associated with royalty. Jupiter, at this time, is rising in the constellation Aries, but with a lunar occultation, which, of course, in and of itself, is very exciting. Even more so when taken into consideration that Jupiter is at his helical rising."

King Aretas' face flushed crimson, and he spoke through his teeth. "Speak plainly, boy."

Bilal clasped his hands behind his back to hide their tremor. "The royal planet Jupiter is rising with the sun and is embraced by the moon." The king still scowled, so Bilal added, "This points to an amazingly powerful royal presence in Judea." The king's expression did not change. "The Jews have a new king, my lord."

The king's brows came together and then relaxed. He stood. "General Nahyan, we must be first to pay tribute to the new king. Gather the choicest of what Nabataea has to offer—gold from the mines of *Mahd adh Dhahab*, 150 talents of frankincense for the Jews to burn in their temple, and 50 talents of myrrh to perfume their women and medicate their old men. No one else in all the world can match the quality and abundance of these gifts. That old snake will take notice, and he will be hungry for more."

Aretas paced before all assembled. "We must make a show of our strength and wealth. Assign your best fighters to escort and protect so rich a tribute—fifty men at the head of the caravan and fifty to guard the rear. Each camel's treasure is to be guarded by two warriors.

"Ridwan, you and your fellowship of Magi will accompany and present the tribute to the new king. And for the sake of our sovereign future, let this young man do your talking."

Bilal felt the cut of Ridwan's sideway glance.

The king continued. "You will be clothed with the finest silk from the orient, for you will represent me before Herod in his court. Choose for yourselves the best desert steeds of my stable, for you must enter the gates of Jerusalem as envoys of a worthy ally. When Herod sees you on the backs of my prized stallions, he will grow green with envy."

The king pivoted sharply and left the throne room, followed by his advisors. Nahyan roared, "You have your orders!" Bilal stood among his brother Magi, stunned by the king's edicts, especially the role he would play in the king's plan.

Bilal worked to wind the scrolls with fingers that resisted his will. Ridwan, clearly disgusted by Bilal's ineptitude, lent a hand. The two Magi brought up the rear of the contingent of learned men, walking hurriedly through long torch-lit corridors and into the bright sun—Ridwan before, Bilal struggling to match his pace. Bilal recognized the man's hurt pride in the rigidity of his shoulders.

They descended from the heights of the palace on stairs chiseled from the red stone cliff to the canyon floor. Once they were out of hearing of the palace guards, Bilal scurried to catch Ridwan and grabbed his arm.

The man shook off Bilal's grip but stopped to face him. "What is it?"

By upstaging his stepfather in front of the king, he had shamed him. Bilal would spend the rest of his life working to undo the damage of those few moments, but he couldn't start now. The message the sky had conveyed and his responsibility to deliver it to the right audience, took precedence over all. He ignored Ridwan's indignation, for now. "I didn't finish my presentation."

"According to the king, you have said more than enough."

"Master, this new king announced in the planets and stars, he will not be a typical king. The prophet Isaiah has much to say about him. He is from the line of David, a direct descendent of Abraham, our father. He will be a blessing for all the nations."

Ridwan looked askance at Bilal. "You don't expect to go back in there and explain all this to the king, do you?"

That was precisely what he wanted to do. "King Aretas is expecting a mighty ally in this new king of the Jews, someone to fortify his forces in battle and to solidify his standing with Rome." Bilal leaned in, lowered his voice. "This king of the Jews will, indeed, bring justice to the nations, but he won't do it with a show of force. He won't even raise his voice. He will make things right, but not by might. Have you ever heard of a king like that?"

"Does it matter how he makes things right, if we wake up one morning and the Roman dogs are no longer breathing down our necks?"

"I had only hoped to discuss—"

"You will learn, my apprentice, as your years of service accumulate, that all kings are conundrums and contradictions and…dangerous. Tread carefully, Bilal." Ridwan lifted his chin toward the Magi's observation towers on the top of the cliff. "We have much to prepare before we leave for Jerusalem."

Bilal's mother waited for a report of his first meeting with the king, and only she would appreciate the disequilibrium he suffered, for the new king of the Jews was like no other. Not only would he speak softly and walk with care among the weak, he would suffer horrifically and sacrificially. "If it please you, master, I will follow in a few minutes."

As Ridwan walked away, he spoke over his shoulder. "Give my regards to your mother. And then follow as you say, and do so quickly."

CR

CHANAN WALKED THE STREETS of Jerusalem dressed as a middling merchant, not so richly attired that vendors fawned for his coins and not so shabbily dressed that he would be shooed away by wary shopkeepers. As the captain of Herod's spies, he gathered reports from sellers of fruits, cloth, and utensils positioned all over the city. He listened and watched for anything of interest to the king, which meant any sign of rebellion or treason. It was Chanan's job to separate the idle laments of beleaguered men from the voice of a truly seditious threat. His job grew more difficult by the day.

Chanan sidled up to one of his spies posted within view of the Tekoa Gate on the southwest side of the city. The man sold trinkets to the Jewish pilgrims who flooded the gates for each of the feasts. With Chanukkah just behind them, the streets were relatively quiet, hopefully giving the man more time to listen than to haggle.

"Have you anything to report?" Chanan asked.

"Nothing."

Gathering information occasionally required an incentive, as his spies could develop a conscience. "I have been authorized to sweeten our arrangement. Any information you give me will be richly rewarded…if I find it useful."

The merchant refolded a fine woolen veil. The color of the wool reminded him of the summer hills around Shiloh, but that was a dangerous thought to have. "It's as though the streets have gone silent," the man said under his breath. "I have nothing—"

At that moment, a column of Nabataean foot soldiers marched through the gate, coming two by two to fit through the narrow passage, but they came steadily, their gazes fixed ahead, their backs straight, with blades half the height of a man strapped to their backs. So impressive was their appearance, Chanan almost forgot to count their numbers as they headed into the city. By the time he counted forty, his heart pounded in his chest. He supposed word about the visitors had already reached the palace from those who scouted the hills and stood at the gates, but should he follow to see where they headed?

He had no time to answer his own question. After the soldiers came an imposing brotherhood of Magi, mounted on the high-stepping horses the desert dwellers prized for their speed and endurance. On the streets of Jerusalem, the steeds spoke of wealth and power like nothing else.

The breeze caught the silken garb of the Magi, coloring the drab winter streets with brilliant shades of blue and red and yellow. He estimated twenty-five Magi. Chanan had never seen the Nabataeans make such a show of their arrival.

He was about to step into the parade and accompany the foreigners to their destination, but the sight of pack camels plodding through the gate stopped him. One animal after another, a seemingly endless line. He counted thirty camels, each accompanied by a driver and two armed guards. Then fifty more foot soldiers marched through the gate, followed by the supply camels and servants who supported the caravan with their cooking skills, and those strong enough to erect the elaborate tents the sons of Ishmael preferred. When the last Nabataean walked through the gate, Chanan estimated their numbers to be 300 strong.

He ran to speak to one of the guards escorting the treasure-laden camels. His years as a spy had taught him the most valuable information came from those who worked within hearing distance of their masters. "Who are your masters and what do they want in the city?" he asked the man in Aramaic, the language of commerce.

The man shrugged. "No one stoops to tell me their plans. You better ask them," he said, lifting his chin to the front of the column.

Chanan girded his cloak and ran to catch up with the envoy of Magi. Winded, he walked beside a lesser Magus—his beard embarrassingly thin—and asked him what business he had in the city, switching to the language of knowledge, Greek.

"We've come to pay tribute to the new king of the Jews."

Chanan sucked in a panicked breath. A new king? Only Herod sat on the throne, and he was past siring new princes, or so Chanan thought. There had been no new heirs born into the household through Herod's remaining sons, either.

The Magus disturbed his thoughts. "Do you know where the new king is that we might deliver the tribute sent by King Aretas IV, the king of the Nabataeans?"

Herod had murdered his own sons for alleged disloyalty. He would not welcome news of a new king of the Jews. The spectacle of the Nabataean's arrival gathered a growing crowd of gawkers. As people ventured closer, the Magi asked everyone they met about the location of the new king. Knowing such talk of kings and uprisings had unleashed Herod's wrath on the innocent before, most clamped their mouths and scurried away.

Dread slid a knife along Chanan's spine. Could one of the murdered sons' wives have given birth to a son and gone into hiding? He prayed it were not so.

Chanan adapted an effect of surprise and pleasure, turning to the young Magus. "I'm sorry to say I don't know, young man. But that's exciting news—a new king! I better tell my wife or lose my life over my silence."

The young Magi laughed knowingly as Chanan turned to race back to the palace. Chanan wasn't happy to be the first to tell Herod the news that would surely ignite the king's wrath, but he feared more being the man who *didn't* tell Herod first.

Chapter Twenty-three

In Herod's Court

The youngest of the Magi, the boy with the pitiful beard, held a half-dozen scrolls to his chest. Dressed in silk the color of lemons, the boy drew Chanan's attention as he fidgeted in his nervousness. An older Magus calmed his movements with a sharp elbow. When the boy looked to see who might have witnessed the rebuke, his eyes met Chanan's and worse—they held.

The boy looked to be considering breaking rank with the other Magus and striding over to Chanan. To what end? Could the boy be that naïve about the workings of Herod's court? This was no party. To discourage his foolishness, Chanan scowled, shook his head tightly, and melded into those who crowded the throne room—Jewish religious leaders, visiting Roman officials, and merchants, all awaiting Herod's arrival.

Chanan, dressed this day in the ostentatious robes of a wealthy merchant, positioned himself on the edge of the gathered merchants. They came to offer exotic luxuries in exchange for preferential contracts. Their endless speculation on prices and markets usually bored Chanan, but this day they whispered only about the presence of the Magi and the religious leaders.

From Chanan's new vantage, he watched the boy, who stood with his head bowed, his lips moving, praying. At last, the boy knew how to stand before Herod.

Kayafa and his muster of peacocks had also been called into this audience with Herod. They stood huddled around Kayafa, leaning in to hang on his every word. Chanan stifled a laugh, for their lofty headdresses clashed like swords. They weren't frequent visitors to the court. The religious leaders preferred sequestered chambers for their meetings with Herod. Roman collaborators were not celebrated among the Jews.

The door to Herod's anteroom opened and whispered words caught in throats. Heads snapped up. Shoulders squared. Roman soldiers struck their chests in homage. The boy edged behind his superior.

Good choice, my friend.

Herod strode in. Chanan had seen the old man shuffle painfully through the palace halls on the arms of muscled aides. This show of strength would cost the old man, for he would drink bitter willow tea in his bath that night.

The king surveyed the crowd, nodding greetings to those he knew. His eyes alighted on the Magi, singling out the leader who had elbowed the boy. The king respectfully bowed his head, and then gingerly lowered himself onto his throne.

Ever the statesman, Herod performed the role of a kindly grandfather, eager to hear from his beloved charges. What every man in the court knew—with the exception of the boy in yellow, perhaps—was that Herod trusted no one, liked no one, feared everyone. He acted out his paranoia with precision and ruthlessness. Herod's court was the most dangerous place in Jerusalem.

Herod spoke. "Honorable Magi of Nabataea, you honor this court with your presence. As you know, my own beloved mother was a princess of your court."

Resplendent in his blue silk cloak, Ridwan stepped forward and bowed at the waist. "We are the ones honored by so gracious a welcome, my lord. We come at the bequest of our high lord, King Aretas IV, to pay a fitting tribute to your newly born king of the Jews on his behalf."

Blackness clouded Herod's eyes but only for an instant, and he was again the munificent patriarch. "Yes, yes, we have heard of your inquiries all over the city. How is it you have come to know about this new king? Of the Jews, you say?"

"We are people of the stars, my lord, as I'm sure you know." Ridwan pulled the boy in yellow to stand beside him. Surely, no one expected the lad to open his scrolls for the king. "We've come prepared to give you a detailed report of what we have learned, but my lord's time is precious.

Suffice it to say we are quite sure that a king of extraordinary power and influence has been born."

If the Magus had declared war, his words would have held less threat to Herod. In their huddle, the religious leaders exchanged sideway glances and murmured their worry. The soldiers put their hands to the hilts of their swords. The merchants inched closer to the door.

The king smiled warmly, a glint of light in his eye. Chanan half expected him to offer the Magus a sweet from his pocket. "You were right in coming here, as we must beg to be numbered among this new king's loyal subjects." Herod tented his fingers to his chin. His left eye fluttered. "And where, pray tell, was this king to be born? Did the stars tell you *that*?"

The Magus stalled his answer, measuring his words. He'd no doubt caught the malevolence behind Herod's question. "No, my lord, nothing so specific as a place of birth, only that Judea has been blessed by a new king."

Herod pivoted to the religious leaders, and their murmurings stopped. "Surely, Kayafa, you are privy to such information. No doubt the prophets of old have quite a lot to say about such a king."

Kayafa fretted his beard, adjusted his cloak.

"Speak, man, or…" Herod let the threat hang in the air. He looked to the Magus, rubbed his clean-shaven chin. The dignity of the Magus must have reminded Herod to stay in character, for a small smile creased his lips, and he looked back to Kayafa, whose face streamed sweat. "Do you know anything of a birthplace for a powerful king?"

Kayafa gestured one of the younger men in his company forward. It seemed to be a day when the elders were willing to sacrifice their disciples. Unlike the young Magus, the lesser Pharisee's beard reached his chest.

"I am Nakdimon, my lord. I have spent my life studying prophecy, but I must warn you, as one of the men entrusted with interpreting the Law, those ordained by the God of Abraham, Isaac, and Jacob."

Herod sighed. "Yes, yes, young man, we know you are important in your own mind. Get to your point."

Nakdimon squirmed. "The heavens declare the glory of God, and the sky indeed proclaims his handiwork. It is Adonai their maker, and no one else, who gives names to each star in the sky. The Law guides us, not the stars."

Nakdimon looked at the Magi and back to King Herod. "But people who look to the stars for their flimsy predictions and supposed interpretations are like stubble. According to the prophet Isaiah, they will be burned up. To listen to them is to bring the wrath of Ha´Elyon."

Herod shook his head and tsked. "My good friend, Nakdimon, I fear our friends from Nabataea will think you ignorant, since you have avoided answering my question. I will give you a chance to right that misunderstanding: Where is the king to be born?"

Nakdimon looked to Kayafa for direction, but the High Priest averted his gaze, leaving his protégé to navigate the dark waters alone. The young man cleared his throat. "He will be born in Bethlehem, in the land of Judah, according to the prophet Micah. The prophecy states: 'And you, little Bethlehem, are not insignificant among the clans of Judah, for out of you will emerge the Shepherd-King of my people Israel!'"[36]

Herod's expression did not change with the pronouncement, but Chanan had clearly seen the machinations of a plan whir behind his eyes. The babe—wherever he laid his head—would not live much longer.

"Bethlehem? You're sure?" he asked.

"Yes, as improbable as it may seem, Bethlehem is the birthplace. But you must know, my lord, we do not and cannot put any stock in the astrological prognostications of these men."

Herod pulled himself to standing by the arms of his throne. Clearly he was done with being a grandfather, kindly or otherwise. "This audience is finished." He pointed to the lead Magus and the boy in yellow. "You will stay. The rest of you, go."

Chanan loitered at the end of the column of merchants. He glanced to the boy in yellow. Their eyes met again. Oh, that Chanan were a magician or soothsayer, that he could speak to the boy across the silence without words. He would tell him to speak plainly to the king, to tell him everything he knew, not holding anything back, for Herod had ways of finding out truth no matter how deeply it got buried. And Chanan was one of his most effective diggers.

☙❧

[36] Matthew 2:5 (TPT)

A CHILL COURSED THROUGH Bilal's veins, although he and Ridwan had left Herod's court hours earlier. The king spoke lies with his lips and the dark truth with his eyes. If they traveled to Bethlehem, the child would be dead by the next morning. If they didn't accomplish King Aretas' bidding, they could never return home to Nabataea.

Bilal left his tent and joined the council of Magi who lounged after the evening meal. The tent billowed, and the poles creaked under the strain of a coming storm. They were now clothed in the garments of the road, colors that blended with the desert. Bilal sat beside Ridwan and accepted a cup of tea from a servant girl.

Bilal waited for his master to speak first, but Ridwan seemed content to keep his own counsel the whole night long. Perhaps he, too, stewed in the aftermath of standing in Herod's court. Bilal leaned in and spoke only for Ridwan's hearing. "What will we do?"

Ridwan frowned. "What will we do?" he said loud enough to silence the Magi who crowded the tent. "What else is there to do but to obey our king?"

His master's assertiveness was meant to cow Bilal. But if he didn't speak for the new king, who would? "I told Herod when Jupiter first rose with the sun, and exactly when the planet and the moon joined in Aries. He knows when the child was born, and thanks to the Jewish leaders, he knows where he was born. I tell you, Herod means to find the child and kill him."

"I cannot argue Herod's ruthlessness with you. He is that and more, but you saw things that were not there, my young apprentice—a product of your inexperience. I entered the court alert to Herod's duplicitous ways. I saw none of it. He received the news with good humor, and dare I say it, a sense of expectation. I sense a new age of cooperation between two great kings. King Aretas will be pleased at our success. We have done as he asked and will pay tribute to the new king.

"We will let this storm pass, and then we will take one more reading of the sky before leaving to confirm what that pompous Nakdimon said about Bethlehem. Now, let the serving girl pour you some of the fine Roman wine Herod gifted us." With that Ridwan shifted to join the most senior among the Magi, giving Bilal his back. The tent filled with the conversations and laughter of his fellow magi.

Bilal pushed away the next cup the girl offered and left the tent. The scent of rain filled his nostrils. Rain always gladdened the heart of desert dwellers but not this night. Rain meant clouds that veiled the night sky, and Bilal desperately needed to see what the stars had to say about the new king. Would the child survive to the end of the week?

The stars hid from him, but he remembered his mother's face when he'd told her about the Shepherd-King of Israel. She all but ignited with joy, enhancing even more the regular planes of her face. Would the death of the new king snuff her light and mar her beautiful countenance with grief?

With no moon or starlight to guide him, he trudged to the small fire that burned outside the tent he shared with the lowest echelon of Magi. A man bent over the fire to add a log. From his cloak, he was not one of the Magi.

Bilal stopped outside the ring of light. "Who's there?" he demanded, but his voice broke.

His father's advice—to treat a stranger as a friend was better than expecting a foe—came to him. He cleared his throat. "Do you need shelter from the storm, stranger?"

The stranger kept his tongue. Bilal waited, allowing his eyes to adjust to the dim light. The indistinct shape of a man dressed for travel emerged from the darkness. When the man lowered his hood to the fire's light, Bilal finally recognized him as the man who had questioned him as they'd entered the city, and, more troubling, the man he'd locked eyes with in Herod's court.

"What do you want? Speak or leave," Bilal said, more out of fear than authority.

"I was in the court today."

"I remember you. You are one of Herod's men?"

The stranger shrugged and seemed genuinely unsure of the answer.

"Do you mean to follow us to Bethlehem?"

"I am under no orders from Herod to do so. I watched from a secret vantage as you told the king about the message you read in the sky. Your face lit with wonder and hope as you spoke. It has been a long time since I've felt anything but dread. I would like to accompany you, to this king you have announced."

"I'm no diplomat, so I will ask you plainly. Do you mean to kill the child?" Too late Bilal realized he had no weapon to stop the man, and no skill to use one if he did.

"Hope is what I seek, young man, the kind of hope you spoke of. I've wondered for many years how I would finish my days in Herod's service. I cannot end my service, I know now, without something or someone to follow into the future, someone to trust and respect. Your new king sounds like such a man."

Bilal wasn't equipped to outwit the man before him. He had many years on Bilal, all spent in the service of a merciless king. Bilal didn't want to lead him to the Shepherd-King, only to watch him thrust a sword through the child. "What pledge can you give to assure your good intentions toward the new king?"

The man thought, added another log. Finally, he captured Bilal's gaze across the fire. "No one knows I have a family. I've seen too many men lose their loved ones by a supposed slight against Herod. I will give you my true name, and I will tell you where I have hidden my wife and daughter. If I betray your trust, you own what I hold dearest, and you will master me."

"You are willing to pay a high price for this hope you crave."

"Tell me when you are leaving. I will follow behind. You may never see me, but I will follow."

"When the skies clear." Bilal looked to the sky to see if one star pierced the gloom, but the autumn storm had erased all that glittered. When he turned back to the man, he was gone. He prayed his carelessness had not condemned the new king to death.

The next morning, Bilal found a slip of linen paper in his boot. On it was written the name of a Jewish man and the description of a home and vineyard in Shiloh, along with a woman's name and what must be the name of his daughter. Bilal folded the paper and slid it into a pocket of his cloak.

CR

TWO DAYS LATER, PUDDLES left by the storm reflected a glistening sky. The Magi climbed a hill on the outskirts of Jerusalem, muddying their boots and clothing, to observe what message the stars held. Bilal followed

Ridwan to the crest and then pushed farther to an outcrop of rock that opened to the horizon. He set up his dioptra, pointing the sighting tube to the south and west toward Bethlehem. He adjusted the protractor along the arm of the tube and settled in to wait for night. He made no fire against the chill, for he needed his eyes to be night-ready to read the sky.

When the last hint of daylight fell into the western horizon, and the sky deepened from indigo to onyx, Bilal rubbed his hands together to warm his fingers for precise positioning of the dioptra. He whispered a prayer and bent to align the sighting tube with Jupiter.

Bilal's heart stopped and restarted with a thump. He rubbed his eyes and knelt again to view the sky. What he saw drained his body of blood, for Jupiter had halted and reversed its motion. Halted and reversed. No one alive had ever seen such a thing.

With fumbling fingers, he raised the dioptra's sighting tube straight up until it aligned with the comet. The head of the comet pointed directly to the position of Jupiter. The last piece of the puzzle was in place. He recited the coordinates over and over until he found Ridwan where he'd left him.

"Have you written the coordinates down?" Ridwan demanded.

"I had no ember to light the lamp."

Ridwan lifted a cinder from the small fire he'd lit and touched it to the lamp's wick. He thrust paper and a sharpened stick of charred wood at Bilal. "Write it down."

The rest of the Magi returned to their camp hungry and cold, with only three hours to dawn. Rather than bed down, they seized the opportunity to celebrate the confirmation of their destination and the near end to their mission. They poured Roman wine and ate a feast of roasted lamb and vegetables.

All except Bilal, who deeply regretted putting his trust in the mysterious man from Herod's court. He felt, even then, the eyes of the man on him. Although telling his stepfather about his arrangement with the man threatened to destroy any improvement in their relationship—if there was indeed any to boast about—Bilal had to tell Ridwan what he'd done.

Ridwan, however, had also bypassed the celebration to sleep. He'd left instructions with his aide to not awaken him for any reason, especially if that reason had anything to do with Bilal. The boy backed away from the aide, bowing low, and apologizing for any disruption he may have caused. On the morrow, the journey to Bethlehem would not be long, but it would be fraught with angst.

Chapter Twenty-four

Journeys

*B*ilal fidgeted in his saddle. The caravan lumbered up the narrow canyon, wending around boulders recently released by the rain. The overburdened donkeys of merchants making their way to Bethlehem slowed the pace further.

He looked behind every rock, scanned the heights of the canyon, studied every face of fellow sojourners as they passed. If Herod's man traveled among them, picking him out of the milieu proved impossible for Bilal.

A melon bounced down the path, spooking his horse, and the column stopped. Farther up the trail, a cart had overturned. This was Bilal's chance to find Ridwan and confess his alliance with the enigmatic man. Without his stepfather's help, he could not hope to protect the new king. Bilal urged his mount into a trot.

Bilal found Ridwan sitting on a boulder with his head in his hands. The sight of his stepfather in distress quickened his heart. He hurried to him and chanced a hand to Ridwan's shoulder. "Master, what ails you?"

Ridwan raised his head, and Bilal saw a troubled man in the crease of his brow and the tension of his mouth. "Master? Is there something I can do?"

Ridwan considered Bilal's offer for a long moment. Bilal looked ahead to the place where the cart had been righted. Its owners collected the runaway melons and reloaded their cargo. The caravan would soon be on its way again.

Ridwan put his hand atop Bilal's, a rare intimacy between the two.

"You have been my apprentice for these three years, Bilal, my son for longer. You know me as a man of reason and science. I measure. I record. I make no hasty conclusions. And this I have taught to you as well, have I not?"

"Yes, my master, no one is more precise with their measurements or more rigorous in their investigations." Bilal thought back to the hours they'd just spent in the Judean hills, observing Jupiter and the moon, calculating the path of the comet. "Have I miscalculated, master?"

Ridwan looked at him quizzically. "Why would you...? No, my son, your calculations are accurate."

"Then...?"

Ridwan pulled Bilal to sit beside him and lowered his voice. "I had a dream like none I've ever had before. A man stood before me as real as you are to me now. My mind was clear, not in a tumble of questions as dreams usually arouse. I knew without being told that the man was a messenger from God, Abraham's God, the God of our father Ishmael. God sent this messenger to me, of all people. I remember every word he spoke."

Bilal had overheard his Jewish mother discuss the tenants of her faith with his stepfather many times. She brought the subject up again and again, although Ridwan ridiculed her piety for just one God. He also forbade her to teach about Yahweh to Bilal or his younger brothers and sisters, an edict his mother had ignored. Now, his stepfather believed this same God had sent a messenger to talk to him.

"What did the messenger say, master?"

"We are not to return to Herod. He intends to kill the child, just as you said, my son. I should have listened to you. The messenger told me so. After paying tribute to the child—make no mistake, this child is more than worthy of our tribute—we must chart another path home. We will use *tariq siriyun*. No one would dare think we are stupid enough to travel through such a dry and forbidding land."

Bilal's heart fell to his stomach. "Master, we are 300 strong. The camels. The horses. Surely, we will all perish."

Ridwan patted his knee. "I forget you are not a traveler, my son. You have no need to know the varied and hidden routes our ancestors carved out of the desert. But thanks to our wise forefathers and skilled stoneworkers, there are cisterns full of rainwater that have satisfied the thirst of traveling Nabataeans for centuries, and they will quench our thirsts as well. The cisterns are well hidden, I assure you. You have no reason to fear."

Not once had Ridwan spoken to Bilal with such familiarity. They spoke only of the intrigues of planets and stars, not anything so intimate as dreams. And never had Ridwan ever called him son. Less than never had Ridwan admitted he was wrong—and Bilal was right. He could not keep secret from his father any longer what he knew about Herod's man. "Master, I must also tell you something."

"About the man from Herod's court? The messenger also spoke of him. The man has his own duty, although he doesn't know yet what it is. I see now that if God wants a man to know something, he has his ways of making it so."

א

MIRYAM ADDED ONION TO the lentil stew. The flavoring would please Yosef, so she was glad she'd joined Rut on a foraging trip into the hills. She sat back on her heels to watch as Yeshua played with the wooden blocks Yosef had made for him. The toddler erected towers and knocked them down, laughing heartily from his tummy, and then turned to make sure his mother had seen his cleverness. When he tired of that game, he built pens for the toy sheep Yosef had carved for him.

In just a few days the boy would be two years old. Being the mother of the Messiah had turned mundane in a most comforting way. The boy was hers to love and enjoy in the rhythm of the days. Yosef went to work in Jerusalem each morning, leaving mother and son to work and play together. As she ground flour or spun yarn, she told Yeshua the stories of Gavri'el visiting her in the orchard, of the shepherds who came to greet him, and of their extraordinary meeting with Shim'on and Anna in the temple courts.

She meant the stories to teach Yeshua that his story and Adonai's purposes were intricately entwined, but they also reminded her how close heaven had moved to earth with Yeshua's birth. She expected Adonai to step into her life at any moment.

Yosef took his responsibilities as abba of the Messiah seriously. He told Yeshua stories from *Tanakh* each night and recited Psalms as the child fell asleep. Their lives as a family were good and sweetly ordinary. She touched her swollen abdomen. Was there room for another child in her heart and in this family?

"Hello, mistress!"

At the gate, a young man dressed in the garb of the desert people waved for Miryam's attention. What could the man want with her? Did it matter? She hurried to pick up Yeshua and backed toward the house's open door.

"My husband is not at home." The instant she uttered that sentence, she regretted her words, for now the stranger knew she was alone. "I mean to say, he is on his way home. I'm expecting him at any minute."

CR

THE WOMAN BACKED AWAY from Bilal, holding her toddler son protectively. Her reaction mirrored that of nearly every man or woman he'd spoken to since arriving in Bethlehem. He'd reassured each one, but now the business of finding the new king started to rankle. What had he ever done to elicit such suspicion? His irritation wouldn't help, so he spoke as reassuringly as he could.

"Mistress, I mean you no harm. My fellow Magi and I are looking for the one the stars and the prophets told us about—a new king to the Jews. We are here to pay tribute on behalf of King Aretas IV. Your cousin—Rut, I believe—suggested that I talk to you. Are you Miryam? Is this the child? Have I found the right house?"

The woman's gaze came up, and she took a step closer. Perhaps she could help him. "You have found the right house. And this child in my arms is the one you seek."

When Bilal had first arrived at the house, he believed himself to be at the wrong place, so he'd counted the number of houses from the main road several times before deciding he had found his destination. Before him stood the humblest of dwellings, smaller than his sleep chamber back in Petra. Only recent stone repair kept the shack from collapsing into a pile of rubble. This was not what he'd expected of a new king's residence.

The woman—Miryam—wore clothes that were clean but worn, and she looked to be halfway toward motherhood again. She seemed about Bilal's age. And the child? Quite truthfully, nothing remarkable stood out. He wasn't exactly homely, but no one would call him handsome, either. But he watched Bilal with deeply intelligent eyes, unlike anything he'd observed in his half-brothers and sisters.

"I should ask you some questions to affirm your identity, I suppose," he said.

The young mother frowned. "What sorts of questions?"

What sorts of questions, indeed. He had no idea. "I should confer with my master."

"Your master? Then you're not traveling alone?"

"You are correct. I travel with my master and twenty-three other Magi, plus a hundred or so military guards, the camel drivers, the cooks, and probably thirty attendants."

She stepped back again. "Can your questions wait until my husband returns?"

"We are in some hurry to get back to Nabataea. Unless your husband returns quickly, it would be preferable for me to gather my party together and return as soon as possible. Is that agreeable?"

Miryam frowned at her small courtyard.

"Please say that you are agreeable," Bilal said. "We are all so very anxious to fulfill our duty to our king and to honor your son with a proper tribute."

Miryam chewed her bottom lip. "I suppose it would be all right for you to bring your friends." She gestured to the courtyard. "But they cannot all come at once."

CR

CHANAN WATCHED AS THE Magi talked excitedly among themselves. Only the twenty-five Magi stood before him. The rest of their entourage camped to the east of the city. Knowing the Magi would eventually gather here and discuss the outcome of their search, he'd sat at the well since dawn, drawing suspicious looks from women collecting water. Evidently, they'd found the child. How accommodating of them to do his work for him.

When he raised his eyes, the head Magus strode toward him. Chanan closed his eyes, feigning sleep. Perhaps the man meant to stride right past.

"You are…" He read from the paper Chanan had written for the boy. Chanan's blood turned cold. "Adlai ben Naftali?"

He sat upright. "You are mistaken, stranger."

"I suppose such contrariness flows in the blood of spies, but let me ask you this: Are you comfortable with the mystical, ben Naftali?"

"Not particularly."

"Neither am I, so I will tell you plainly: You are meant to meet the new king of the Jews. Don't ask how I know, just know that I was told to invite you to join us."

"And what if I'm not this ben Naftali you've been told to invite…by someone or other?"

The Magus chuckled. "You are this man, ben Naftali. There's no sense continuing this charade. We mean no harm to you. We are scientists and stargazers. In fact, you pose a much greater threat to us than we do to you, since you work for Herod, and we have no intention of returning to him."

Men who defied Herod didn't live long. "Friend, I would be careful what you say."

The Magus held up the paper with Chanan's birth name and the names of his family written in his own hand. "I do, indeed, intend to be careful. I've made several copies and given them to my subordinates. If you bring harm to the child in any way, I will put these names into the hands of dangerous men."

He paused then, met Chanan's gaze with fatherly concern. "I doubt such precautions are warranted. I have heard about you directly from God, and for whatever reason he has to care about you, you are meant to accompany us to the child-king's house. I will not force or cajole you to take part in such an honor, ben Naftali. Come, if doing so suits you."

I have heard about you directly from God? Part of Chanan itched to dissolve into the streets of Bethlehem and race toward Jerusalem, back to his predictable yet precarious life as Herod's captain of spies. It was what he knew.

But part of him, a part he'd not dared access since leaving his father's house, wanted to know if HaShem could stand the sight of him, at least enough to invite him to meet this child, the new king of the Jews. Was there room in Adonai's kingdom for the likes of Chanan, for the likes of Adlai ben Naftali?

He stood and followed the procession of Magi up a narrow alley, as though the new king of the Jews lived in a hovel. Preposterous.

CR

MIRYAM, BY THIS TIME, was a student of how people reacted to Yeshua. She'd seen men weep with relief and joy. Some grew somber and introspective. Others were as indifferent to him as they were to all children.

Women watched Yeshua as if Miryam could not see, compared him to their own children. Were they as bright? Were they taller or shorter? Who had said their first word before the other? Was Yeshua a pleasant or a disagreeable child?

The Magi arrived at her gate with great splendor and dignity, but when their eyes alit on the boy, the men pressed through the gate, falling to their faces before her as she held Yeshua in her lap. They prayed in their own tongue, so she could not understand what they said, but, clearly, they understood whom they worshipped.

The senior Magus—she learned he was named Ridwan—orchestrated the rotation of Magi into the courtyard, so eager were they to enter yet reluctant to leave. Each bowed respectfully to her. All brought gifts, some that required two men to heft. Yosef would have to build them a bigger house to fit it all.

When the fervor of the Magi's devotion mellowed, Ridwan asked Miryam to tell the story of Yeshua's birth, since the Magi had heard rumors in the village of angels and dreams and wanted to hear about everything from her.

Miryam looked past the gathering of Magi, hoping to see Yosef walk up the path from his day of work. The position of the sun told her he was still many hours from returning. In all that played out before her, a sadness tainted her joy for not being able to share this moment with him. They would surely sit on the roof for hours that night, for there was so much to tell. For now, she was content to tell her story to eager listeners.

With a mountain of unfathomable treasure before her, Ridwan approached her at story's end with a deep bow. "There is one more who wishes to pay tribute to the babe. He is not one of our number."

"He is a friend?"

"Not yet, mistress, but the road ahead of us is long. If we are to be friends, we will be nearly brothers by the time we reach Petra again."

Miryam wasn't sure about welcoming yet another stranger without Yosef at home. "Will you stay close?"

"He wants to speak to you alone."

Miryam pulled her now-sleeping son closer. "I don't know."

"Since you are a woman who has encountered one of God's messengers, perhaps it will be meaningful to you that an angel came to me in a dream, just as he did to your husband. The angel told me about this man. He implored me to invite him to meet your son. Afterward, whether you grant the audience or not, he will come to live among the Jews of Petra, of which my wife is a member. His name is Adlai ben Naftali."

A Jew. A son of Abraham. He is no stranger. "Bring the man."

Naftali stood outside the gate, his head down, his hands over his heart.

Miryam walked to the gate. The man backed away. "Sir, will you not join me in the courtyard? I have a stool for you."

The man didn't move, but Yeshua stirred in her arms. "Sir? What is it you wish to say? You do understand that I am but a mother, a wife, a daughter. My siblings find me overbearing and boring. My cousins—some of them, at least—think I'm crazy. My grandmother can't look at me without crying."

Her words didn't move the man, but Yeshua stretched out of his sleep, opened his eyes, and smiled at his mother. She greeted his wakefulness with a kiss, and then stepped over the gate's threshold, hoping to reassure the man he was among friends. Besides, shadows grew longer, she had not yet baked bread for their evening meal, and Yeshua would soon be hungry.

The man shrunk from her and fell to his knees on the hard ground. "I am what my people hate more than anyone else, even more than the Romans. I am a collaborator, mistress. I deserve the deepest Sheol and know it." His gaze met hers. Tears spilled down his cheeks. "Is there hope for me, mistress? Will your son accept me into his kingdom?"

A collaborator in my son's kingdom? May it never be!

And yet.

And yet there was Isaiah's suffering Shepherd-King, the sacrificial lamb that haunted her thoughts and dreams. Miryam drew Yeshua to her shoulder, but the boy turned back to the man, his chubby face puckered with worry at the man's tears.

Naftali hung his head again and wept quietly. Wouldn't this weeping man, this collaborator, know better than anyone that he needed a sacrificial lamb to be pierced for his transgressions, to be crushed for his iniquities? Who more than a man freed from his weight of guilt and shame would be a more loyal servant?

"Sir, it is not for me to judge your worthiness for my son's kingdom, but, I think, it is for men such as yourself that he has come. Until he is ready to take his throne, we are to prepare the way. Honestly, I don't know what that means, but a starting place—just as you've already arranged—is for you to return to your faith."

The man's weeping redoubled, and his forehead touched the ground.

Miryam looked up and down the alley. Her neighbors, already suspicious of her, would never understand why a man had prostrated himself on the ground before her. She wasn't sure why he had done such a thing, either. "Sir, won't you rise and talk to me? *Please*."

When Naftali stood before her, Yeshua raised his arms to the man, stretching across the distance between them and threatening to fall to the ground. Naftali caught the boy just in time, drawing the babe into his arms and weeping softly.

◌ℜ

MIRYAM WOKE TO THE sound of tools clashing against one another. She looked over the loft's edge to find Yosef packing his tools, all of them, into his pack by lamplight. The cock had not yet crowed. "Yosef, it's too early for you to leave for Jerusalem."

"I was just about to wake you. We're all leaving the instant we're ready to do so."

"To Jerusalem?" Perhaps it was finally time to go home to see Ima and Abba. "To Nazareth?"

"No. Egypt."

She checked that Yeshua slept soundly and climbed quickly down the ladder. "Egypt? We know no one in Egypt. What is this all about?"

Yosef paused to look at her. "What else? Gavri´el came to me in a dream."

"Again?"

"Believe it or not, I pointed that out to him." He took Miryam by the shoulders. "He came with a warning, my love. Herod already knows the Magi have outwitted him and have left for Nabataea without telling him what they found. He is dispatching men to seek out Yeshua for himself. The warning was most urgent. We have no time to lose. We must leave within the hour."

Miryam gestured to the gifts left by the Magi—chests of gold, frankincense, and myrrh. "We can't carry all this, Yosef."

"We will take what we will need and leave the rest. What good would it do us if we are dead, for that is what Herod intends for us? Perhaps an unexpected deposit into his treasury will soften his bite. We can only hope." He kissed her forehead. "I'm sorry to ask you to travel again when you are heavy with child."

Yosef looked as though the weight of the world sat upon his shoulders. "I feel strong, Yosef."

"That's good, love, for we must travel quickly. We'll keep our eyes open for a donkey to buy, but that might be a day or a week away. Pack what we'll need for the journey, not what you think we'll need for a long stay. The gifts of the Magi will allow us to buy what we need once we get to Elephantine. I don't know how long we'll be gone, perhaps until Herod dies."

Elephantine? She'd never heard of such a place. At least she'd known of Bethlehem before she'd traveled there with Yosef.

With her heart pounding in her chest, Miryam looked to her kitchen, then to the linens and things they would need to sleep in the open. Definitely the wool blanket Ima had woven as a wedding gift. Definitely as many clouts as she could carry. But not the cradle Yosef had made for Yeshua.

Yosef caught her looking at the cradle. "I'll make him another, I promise."

"What about Rut? Tamir? My parents?"

"We will find a way to send word."

The house that had seemed little more than a shack to her two years earlier, now held the memories of her young family, of new love, and new friends, of Yeshua's first steps, and of many *Shabbat* meals with Tamir's and Rut's family. This was home.

"Miryam," Yosef prodded.

She opened a linen sheet and filled it with what they would need. Into her satchel, she dropped the bread left over from supper and the last of the figs her father had sent from home. She gingerly added a pot of his honey and shored it with clouts.

With a sleeping Yeshua at Yosef's shoulder, they left the courtyard without a backwards glance. They turned south at the end of the alley. Inside the gate of Tamir and Rut, they left a bundle of gold coins wrapped in linen. They did the same for a distant cousin of Yosef's who had played the role of *savta* to Yeshua, and a newly married couple who owned only one bowl, and the widow who whispered prayers over Yeshua at the well each morning.

In the urgency of their leaving, Miryam felt a tearing but could not stop to indulge her sorrow. They walked without stopping. It helped that they walked downhill, heading toward the coast where a road had been built by the Romans to Cairo. The scope of the journey overwhelmed Miryam, but the reason they fled quickened her step and set her resolve. She had no trouble keeping up with Yosef.

They stopped at midday and found a tree for shelter away from the road. Miryam spread a sheet. After a meal of bread, cheese, and figs, they lay down for a nap. As weary as she was, sleep would not come. Instead, she watched as Yosef and Yeshua slept. The thought of Roman soldiers seeking her son kept her alert. But, truthfully, she had no idea what she would do if even one legionary marched into their camp.

Would Adonai bring her, Yosef, and the babe this far only to allow his plan to falter? He pried his children from mighty Egypt and brought them to the Promised Land. He used the unstoppable Assyrians as his "rod of anger" against an idolatrous Israel, and then rebuffed their army from Jerusalem's doorstep, slaying 185,000 soldiers in one night. Even Babylon came running at God's whistle to judge rebellious Israel.

Did Adonai now tremble because of Herod, a mere puppet of Rome?

Miryam's weariness overwhelmed her as she lay next to her son and husband. She recited the words of the psalmist as a prayer, "I will lie down and sleep in peace; for, Adonai, you alone make me live securely."[37] Sleep pulled at her, and she surrendered.

When she awoke, Miryam found Yosef and Yeshua sharing a piece of bread. "Are you ready to continue?" he asked.

With her pack heavy on her back, she looked down the long road that cut a shelf into the mountain and disappeared around a bend. In the far distance a shimmer of blue pooled. Yosef said it was the ocean. Could anything be that big? Could any road be so long? How many such roads would her family travel until one led back to Nazareth and the future God had for her son?

She couldn't know, but she knew without question that when they reached the end of that road, there would be a story to tell. And that story would change men's lives.

"Yes, I'm ready. Let's go."

---

[37] Psalm 4:8 (CJB)

Chapter Twenty-five

A Christmas Prayer

Thank you, Good Father,
for filling the silence with your Son Jesus.
He speaks clearly of who you are and how you love.
Sometimes, our lives are too noisy to listen,
so please quiet our hearts and open our ears
to hear all that you have for us.
And sometimes, Lord,
it's hard to believe you sent such a wonderful gift,
that you even want to know us at all.
Remind us daily that Jesus took the form of man,
not to be served but to serve,
and to give his life as a ransom.
The blood he willingly shed on the cross
pays the debt of every hurtful thing
we have ever done and
welcomes us into your family.
We open our hands and our hearts this day
to receive that gift.
Jesus, you were sent to us with a long list of jobs,
and we're so grateful you didn't shirk from any.
You still comfort the brokenhearted,
announce freedom for captives and set prisoners free.
You exchange the ashes of our lives for beautiful crowns.
We humbly thank you.
This Christmas and all through the coming year,
we commit our ordinary selves to join you
in your mission of love and deliverance.
We love you.
Amen.

Chapter Notes

Chapter One: "A Silent World"

Abijah: One of twenty-four divisions of priests that served in the temple. The Abijah division always served for the eighth rotation, which helps biblical scholars estimate the time of year Zekharyah served. Some use this information to determine the most likely time Jesus was born since the months can be counted ahead to Yohanan's birth and then to Yeshua's birth.

Levites: These were priests also but considered of lower rank. They, too, inherited their calling through their fathers, all from the tribe of Levi. They manned the temple gates, announced the time of sacrifice with the call of the *shofar*, cleaned the temple, slaughtered some sacrificial animals, and performed in the temple choir and orchestra.

Quern: Ancient Israelites ate a diet dominated by flat loaves of bread. To meet the need, the women spent three hours each day grinding grain into flour. They used a quern formed from two flat, round stones stacked on top of each other. The top stone rotated around a center rod, and a peg on the outer edge served as a crank to rotate one stone against the other, grinding the grain into flour.

Temple Priests: About 18,000 descendants of Aaron served as priests in the temple. That many priests could not serve all at once, so they were divided into twenty-four divisions. Each division served two nonconsecutive weeks each year, always at the same time. Their service was various and rigorous as there were two sacrificial offerings each day, one in the morning and one in the afternoon. Jobs were not assigned in order to avoid the appearance of favoritism but also to squelch ambition among the priests. Instead, lots were drawn each day for the various duties. A priest was only eligible to burn the incense once during a lifetime of service.

Chapter Two: "In the Temple"

Kayafa/Caiaphas: The high priest at the time of Jesus' birth, although he didn't come to the office in the usual way. Aaron, the brother of Moses, was the first to hold the office of high priest. According to Exodus, all subsequent men to hold the office were meant to be of the Aaronic line and to be the spiritual leader of Judaism. Kayafa was not of the Aaronic line. Instead, he was appointed by the Roman prefect, Valerius Gratus, who preceded Pontius Pilate. He served as high priest from AD 18 to AD 36. Such a long term of service speaks to his diplomatic skills. He kept a relative peace between Rome and Judea during his years of service. Kayafa is best known for the role he played in orchestrating the trial and death of Yeshua.

Shofar: Made of a ram's horn, the shofar was a musical instrument that called ancient Jews to prayer, worship, and battle. For instance, a Levite priest blew the shofar from the parapet of the second temple three times a day to call the faithful to prayer. Shofars are still sounded to call Jewish worshippers together.

Chapter Three: "A Betrothal"

Betrothal: Similar to engagement in that a man and a woman have agreed to marry, but also very different in important ways. Betrothal happened as a result of an understanding between two families. In fact, the bride and groom might never have met. Betrothal was a time for the bride and groom to prepare for marriage. The bride collected her personal belongings, forged new relationships with her family, and prepared her wedding clothes. The groom built a house for his bride attached to his father's house, where she would live with her husband and join her new family. As binding as marriage, the only way out of a betrothal was divorce.

Ima: The familiar Hebrew word for "mom." Pronounced *ee*-ma.

Ketubah: Once the terms of a marriage were agreed upon, the groom formally proposed to his prospective bride by presenting her with a *ketubah*, a formal document that specified the marriage terms and expectations. In essence, the *ketubah* is a contract. The groom's intent to consecrate himself to her was also included in the document, and once they toasted her acceptance of the *ketubah*, he did not drink wine until their wedding celebration, perhaps a year or more later. The bride kept the *ketubah* in safe keeping throughout her life.

Mohar: After the young man described his financial assets, skills, and other qualities that made him a desirable husband, the *mohar*/bride price was negotiated. The prospective husband wasn't purchasing his bride; he was compensating the family for the loss of their daughter, for what she contributed to the running of her parents' household with her skills and labor.

Sepphoris: A city with a rich and dynamic history, which means plenty of conflict. Sepphoris at the time of this story was being rebuilt by Herod Antipas after a Jewish-led rebellion eventually failed, leaving the city in ruin. Called "The Jewel of Galilee," the city boasted two Roman theaters and is still known for its elaborate mosaics. Selected for the provincial capital government, Sepphoris thrived under Rome and rewarded their occupiers with loyalty. Craftsmen builders from nearby villages, including Nazareth, found consistent employment restoring the city.

Craftsman/Tekton: *Tekton* is the word translated from the Greek in the New Testament as "carpenter," but the word has a broader meaning of "craftsman" and could include "stone mason" or "builder." In light of the scarcity of wood and the abundance of limestone in the Holy Land, it makes sense that craftsmen would diversify their skills to find steady employment. Also, Yeshua frequently uses metaphors from the building trade in his teaching. That's why I've written Yosef as a man of many talents.

Torah: When believing Jews refer to *Torah*, they mean the Five Books of Moses—Genesis, Exodus, Leviticus, Numbers, and Deuteronomy.

Chapter Five: "An Angel in the Orchard"

Shabbat: The Hebrew word for *Sabbath*, meaning "to cease" or "desist." The day commemorates God's creation of heaven and earth in six days, and his rest from his labor on the seventh. *Shabbat* goes from sundown each Friday to the completion of nightfall on Saturday. The day is marked by a complete cessation of labor, but it is also meant to be a day of pleasure. The regulations about *Shabbat* are the main feature of Mosaic Law. In the first century and now, *Shabbat* is a time of sacred assembly and worship.

Synagogue: There is no place in the Mosaic Law that speaks to the establishment of synagogues or how they were to be run. Evidence of their appearance points to the time after the destruction of Solomon's temple and the Babylonian exile. Before that time, only the temple was meant as a place of worship. It's thought that the people needed a place to gather and study *Torah* until the temple was rebuilt. A town with ten or more men (a quorum by Jewish standards) had a synagogue, bigger villages had more. The buildings were used as a community center, as a hostel for travelers, and for regular worship and study of *Torah*. Men and women worshipped together in the synagogues of the first century, and the women were counted among the ten individuals needed for a religious quorum. The spiritual and business concerns of a synagogue were administered by a layman, not a rabbi, referred to as leader or president.

Tamid Lamb: The word *tamid* means "standing," as in a perpetual or continual sacrifice. Two male lambs were sacrificed each day in the temple, one at dawn and one at twilight, as directed in Exodus 29:38-46. The sacrifices were left on the fire around the clock, sending up a perpetual column of smoke. These were communal sacrifices for the atonement of the Jewish people.

Wedding Chamber: The groom builds a room for his new bride during the year of their betrothal, referred to as a "little mansion" in John 14 by Yeshua when referring to his preparations for us in his Father's house. Usually attached to the father's house with a common wall, this is where the groom and his bride will spend the first seven days of their marriage alone, and continue to live thereafter. The groom cannot claim his bride until the father of the groom examines the wedding chamber and declares it suitable.

Chapter Six: "Two Mothers"

Caravan/Travel: Travel in first-century Palestine was quite common. Devout families fulfilled a pilgrimage to Jerusalem each year for Passover, and many also traveled for the two other pilgrim festivals, Pentecost and Tabernacles. Itineraries found from the time suggest travelers typically walked twenty miles per day. The distance from Nazareth to Ein Karem is about ninety miles, making the trip a four-to-five-day journey. As you can imagine, travel had its challenges and threats in the first century. Wild beasts—Asiatic lions, Syrian brown bears, Judean desert leopards—

remained a threat until the end of the nineteenth century. Far more likely, however, were attacks by bandits as we read about in the story of the Good Samaritan. Dramatic changes in elevation added to the difficulty of travel. For these reasons, people rarely traveled any distance alone, and women would never travel without a male family member. Caravans gathered in villages along trade routes, and gave travelers the best chance of arriving at their destination without harm. As to where travelers found shelter along the way, hospitality was an absolute necessity for Jews and not considered merely good manners, but a moral imperative. Biblical law specifically sanctified hospitality toward the stranger, for Jews were once strangers in Egypt. Most travelers stayed with family or friends along the way to avoid any chance of defilement that staying under the roof of a Gentile would bring.

Mount Gerizim: Much Jewish history happened in the shadows of Mount Gerizim and Mount Ebal that stand in the geographical center of the land God gave to Abraham and his descendants. Abram met God there almost 2,000 years before Miryam traveled that way to visit Elisheba with the Messiah growing in her womb. Abram built an altar at that time to commemorate God giving the land to his offspring (Genesis 12:6-7). Moses commanded Joshua to build an altar on Mount Ebal (Deuteronomy 27-28) when the people finally crossed into the Promised Land and defeated King Ai, which stands to the northeast of Mount Gerizim. Half of the people stood in front of Mount Ebal and half in front of Mount Gerizim. In this lush setting, the people heard Joshua read the Law of Moses (Joshua 8:34). Sychar, where Yeshua met the woman at Jacob's well, sits nestled in a valley between Mount Ebal and Mount Gerizim, where the Samaritans built their own temple.

Chapter Eight: "A Messenger is Born"

Musicians at a Birth: Jews celebrated the birth of a son with serious celebration. When a woman went into labor, a band was summoned to announce the fortuitous birth of an heir. They were sent home if a girl was born.

Torah School of the Womb: According to the Talmud, the time a child spent in his mother's womb was the best time of his life, for all through gestation the fetus was taught the entire Torah. As the time of birth drew near, an angel visited and struck the child on the mouth, causing him or her to forget all that they had learned. This legend may explain, at least in part, the devotion and care given to unborn Jewish children.

Weaving: The women of first-century Palestine were charged with weaving cloth for the family's clothes. They sheared sheep and goats for wool, and then the wool was carded, spun into yarn, and dyed. Flax was grown for linen, but wool was more common and affordable.

Primitive looms leaned against the wall of courtyards in the temperate months and inside the house during the rainy season. The warp threads were tied to weights made of clay or rock that hung close to the ground, keeping the thread taut. The heddle bar separated alternating warp threads to speed weaving.

Chapter Nine: "A Name is Given"

Circumcision: God commanded Abraham to circumcise himself and his household as a symbol of the covenant made between God and him in Genesis 17. And this command was meant for all of the generations that followed. Circumcision was to take place on the eighth day of a son's life, and also at this time, the son was named after a living relative. No one expected Zekharyah and Elisheba to name their son Yohanan, because they had no relatives by that name.

Elijah's Cup: Because Elijah did not die but was taken directly into heaven, and because Malachi 4:5-6 prophesies his role in the coming of Messiah, Jewish tradition often spoke of his return. In fact, a seat is always left open for Elijah at every *Pesach* Seder in hopes he will usher in the Messiah that very night. And so, his cup is a symbol of hope for Hebrews.

Tanakh: This is the compilation of Jewish texts—*Torah*, the Prophets, and the writings—known as the Hebrew Bible.

Chapter Ten: "Justice Satisfied"

Bitter Waters: According to Numbers 5, a wife suspected of infidelity was brought to the priests in the temple, which meant a journey to Jerusalem. There, she was stripped of all jewelry and clothed in black garments. Dust from the floor of the temple was added to a jar of water and given to the woman to drink. These were the bitter waters. If she was guilty of adultery, the waters brought a curse and miscarriage. Only the innocent walked away unscathed. Women who were obviously pregnant were not forced to drink the bitter waters.

Get: The only way to terminate a marriage under Jewish law was for the husband to write a *get*, a bill of divorce. Since a betrothal was considered as binding as marriage, a divorce was required to end the union. The husband could write the *get* on anything, but it had to be witnessed, written, and signed within one day to be valid. Once the *get* was put in the wife's hand, the divorce was final. The only way to interrupt the process was to stop the messenger before the *get* touched the wife's hand.

Honor/Shame Culture: All ancient and most non-western societies today are honor/shame cultures. To understand what would happen to a girl who became pregnant under suspicious circumstances, it helps to understand how an honor/shame culture works. I find contrasting the honor/shame culture to the western right/wrong culture the best way to come to an understanding.

The west is an individualistic culture. To reach mature selfhood, a person is expected to internalize a sense of right and wrong, meaning they choose right behavior on the basis of their conscience. The battle for moral rightness is internal, and punishment—a guilty conscience—is also internal.

The honor/shame cultures are considered collective societies where people are more likely to choose right behavior by what others expect of them. Rules and laws aren't as effective as deterrents of bad behavior as the risk of bringing shame on one's family, faith, or society. When a person acts in the interest of their community, he is not concerned with the rightness or wrongness of his actions, and he doesn't feel guilty because he acted for the good of his community. In short, it isn't a guilty conscience that torments a citizen of an honor/shame culture of wrongdoing; it's the community who shames him.

Miryam would have had a difficult time in her village and with anyone who knew she bore a baby that was not her husband's. The community served their role in her punishment by pushing her to the outside.

Sanhedrin: The highest court of Jewish law that originated with the seventy elders who assisted Moses. Led by the High Priest, the court met in the Chamber of Hewn Stones within the temple. In the first century, the body held wide powers, adjudicating civil and limited criminal cases according to Jewish law.

Chapter Eleven: "A Wedding Feast"

Ancient Jewish Weddings: Although no wedding date was set, weddings in first-century Israel were elaborate and festive. The coming together of the husband and wife—for they were already married when the woman accepted the cup from her future husband—happened only when the groom's father approved the home the groom built for his new wife. And since the wedding meant seven days of feasting at the father's expense, there were financial considerations for when the wedding took place. Only when these concerns were met did the groom don his wedding clothes and gather his groomsmen. The time had come for him to claim his wife. They then paraded raucously through the village, sounding the *shofar*, in essence announcing to all that this was his wedding day.

Meanwhile, the bride had been watching the progress of her new home and prepared her wedding clothes over the course of a year, for she did not know the exact day of her wedding feast, either. When she heard the horn blasts and the loud cheering of the groom and his men, she finally dressed in her wedding tunic, gathered her bridesmaids, and prepared to greet her groom.

Drums sounded, horns blared, and singers hired for the occasion filled the air with music as the groom drew closer to the bride's house. Once they got within shouting distance, a friend with a booming voice was assigned to call out the bride's name. When the groom arrived at the bride's childhood home, the parents recited the blessing of Rebekah, in essence relinquishing their daughter to her new family.

The bride was carried from her birth home to her new home on the most circuitous route possible—with the groom in the lead—to spread the joy of the occasion to the whole village. Along the way, perhaps in the marketplace, a *huppah* awaited the couple. The four-posted structure with a canopy of cloth was a way to symbolize that while a marriage took place among the mundane activities of life, the relationship was also sheltered and separate.

When they finally arrived at the house of the groom's family, the bride and groom entered the bridal chamber, the little mansion, the room built by the groom. Within those walls the bride and groom could finally speak openly to one another. There, too, the marriage was consummated. The entire wedding party waited for the announcement from the groom that this had been accomplished. The act was announced with exuberance by the friend of the groom.

The bride and groom spent most of the next seven days in the wedding chamber while the wedding party returned each evening to feast in outer rooms and the courtyard. The master of the banquet, as mentioned in John 4, made sure there was plenty of wine for the guests.

Blessing of Rebekah: When Abraham was very old, he called his senior servant to go to the people of his father to find a wife for his son Isaac. The man traveled to the household of Abraham's brother and found Rebekah at the well. After a test to be sure she was the woman God wanted for Isaac, Rebekah traveled back to Hebron to wed Isaac. Before she left her homeland, her family prayed a blessing over her that she would be part of the fulfillment of God's promise for a mighty nation. This blessing has been prayed over countless Jewish brides since that day.

Mattan: Near the end of the betrothal period, the parents gave the bride the *mattan*, a gift funded by the mohar given by the groom. The purpose of the *mattan* was to give the bride something of value that she could use for support in the case of her husband's death, or worse, her abandonment.

Chapter Twelve: "A New Home"

The simplest village homes typically included two rooms. During inclement weather, the women cooked and the family ate in the main room. Otherwise, most domestic activity occurred in the courtyard. The family slept in a loft above the main room. The second room was kept exclusively for guests, for hospitality was and is a way of life for Middle Easterners.

In warmer months, animals were sheltered within the gated courtyard to protect them from thieves. During winter, animals were kept in the house for the extra warmth they provided. The animal keep was a few feet lower than the main level, usually with a door that led to the courtyard. Mangers for the purpose of feeding the animals were hollowed out of the floor of the main level. The animals were let out of the keep each morning to graze in nearby fields.

Each son built a wedding chamber onto his father's home to prepare for marriage. When it was completed, he brought his wife to live with his family. If a family had many sons, the younger sons would have to be creative about how they built onto their father's homes. As a younger son, Yosef gained ground for the home he built for Miryam by chiseling into a rock face. The ruins of a home found in Nazareth, and regarded to be Yeshua's childhood home, was built in such a manner.

Chapter Thirteen: "Rome Demands Its Coin"

Niddah: A woman was considered *niddah*, ceremonially unclean, after the birth of a child and during her menstruation according to Leviticus 12:1-5. Being *niddah* kept a woman from worshipping in the temple. If she gave birth to a son, she was unclean for seven days, with a daughter fourteen days. This is not a state of sin or censure but of ritual uncleanliness. After the prescribed days, a woman entered the *mikveh* to totally immerse herself in pure spring water. This made her acceptable to enter the temple and to resume relations with her husband.

Pilgrim Festivals: Jews were required by *Torah* to make pilgrimages to the temple in Jerusalem three times a year for festivals: *Pesach* (Festival of Passover/Unleavened Bread), *Shavout* (Festival of Pentecost/Weeks), and *Sukkot* (Festival of Tabernacles) in Deuteronomy 16:6-7. It's important to note that while *Torah* only speaks to men in this passage, women had the same religious and spiritual obligations in offering personal sacrifices for thanksgiving and for atonement of sins, and so devout women traveled with the men three times a year.

The Roman Census: Archeological discoveries have proven that regular enrollment of taxpayers was a feature of Roman rule, and that the registration took place every fourteen years. It seems odd to modern readers that Roman officials required travel back to an ancestral home to be counted, but this is exactly what they demanded.

Sukkot: In the fall of the year, this pilgrim feast commemorates the years the Jews spent in the wilderness, experiencing God's deliverance, provision, and protection. Each family builds a three-sided *sukkah*, a booth or tabernacle, with a palm frond roof. The family would eat their evening meal in the *sukkah*, and the children might sleep in it. This most joyous of all the festivals lasted seven days.

Chapter Fifteen: "No Room"

You were probably expecting a harried innkeeper to turn Yosef and Miryam away from an inn bulging with guests, all staying in Bethlehem for the census. Since I've written a narrative that varies from what most accept as Yeshua's birth story, I should explain why.

Several years ago, I came across a book by the late Kenneth E. Bailey, *Jesus Through Middle Eastern Eyes: Cultural Studies in the Gospels*, that challenged my assumptions about how and where Yeshua was born. The seeds of the book you're holding came from what I learned from this worthy scholar, mostly about the supreme importance of hospitality in Middle Eastern culture. But how did that level of hospitality play out in the Christmas story?

First, we must keep in mind that Yosef was returning to the village of his origin, and historical memories are long in the Middle East. He most assuredly had extended family living in Bethlehem, and so a place to stay was assured. If hadn't had family in Bethlehem, he simply would have told potential hosts, "I am Yosef, son of Yaakov, son of Mattan, the son of El-Azar," and most homes in the village would have opened their doors to him and his wife. The couple might have slept on the floor as they do in my story, but they would have been warmly welcomed.

Also, Yosef was a "royal," meaning he was of the King David line. A family would have felt obligated and honored to host him and his wife. Finally, every culture—Middle Eastern or western—extends protection to pregnant women. To turn away a descendent of King David and his pregnant wife would have brought down an odious shame on the whole village of Bethlehem. This is why I gave Yosef an extended family who weren't quite sure what to think about Miryam and her pregnancy of questionable origin, but who were bound by their culture to offer her shelter. This is also why I believe Yeshua was born in a house and not a stable.

I feel obligated, also, to polish the reputation of the nameless innkeeper who we've all believed turned Yosef and Miryam away. To do so, we have to dip into a little Greek, and since I'm not a Greek scholar, I rely on the knowledge of the good Dr. Bailey.

The word translated as "inn" in Luke 2:7 is the Greek word *katalyma* and can very simply be translated as "a place to stay." The word refers to anyplace a traveler might take shelter. The meaning got confused when English translators used "inn," which conjures pictures of a country inn that rents lodging for the night and feeds its guests. Nothing like that was available to Yosef and Miryam. Arabic translators used the word "house" for *katalyma* in this verse for more than a thousand years, and comes closest to its contextual meaning. Luke uses *katalyma* in another place in his Gospel, where the word defines itself:

He replied, "As you enter the city, a man carrying a jar of water will meet you. Follow him to the house that he enters, and say to the owner of the house, 'The Teacher asks: Where is the guest room (katalyma), where I may eat the Passover with my disciples?' Luke 22:11-12.

Luke uses *katalyma* here to refer to a "guest room" or "guest chamber" in a private home. The reference is to the upper room, where Yeshua observed *Pesach* with His disciples. This makes it plausible for a family—like Tamir's and Rut's family—to say to Yosef and Miryam, "Our guest chamber is already in use, but you are welcome to stay with us," rather than, "There is no room in the village inn" as the NIV states. I hope this clarifies that no one—not an innkeeper, at least—was mean to a very pregnant Miryam when she arrived in Bethlehem.

Let me also reiterate that the animals slept inside the house in an animal keep that was two to three feet lower than the main floor. Archeologists have excavated houses from the first century with troughs/mangers hollowed out of the main floor, near the animal keep. One of these mangers would have made a convenient cradle for a baby.

Chapter Seventeen: "A Day's Work"

Heshvan: A huge difference between Western culture and Hebrew culture is the way we measure time. The Jewish calendar is incredibly complex, accounting for the movement of time with both lunar and solar elements. *Heshvan* is the second month of their civil calendar and the eighth month of their religious calendar, usually coinciding with the Gregorian months of October and November. Also, Jewish days begin at the setting of the sun, not at midnight.

Chapter Eighteen: "The Silence is Broken"

Shifrah and Puah: These two midwives saved the day when a new king of Egypt came to power and decided there were too many Israelites dwelling among his people. To solve the problem, he enslaved the people and called Shifrah and Puah to join him in a horrific plot. He commanded the women to kill every male born to the Israelite women. The midwives feared God, so they didn't do as the king wanted. Aware that his plot was failing, he called the midwives back to him. They stood before him—what brave women!—and told him that the Hebrew women were more vigorous than the Egyptian women and gave birth before they arrived, giving them no chance to obey him. For their courage and faithfulness, God rewarded them with families of their own. Without Shifrah and Puah, there would have been no Moses. They're considered heroes of the Jewish faith. You can read their story here: Exodus 1:1-15.

Chapter Twenty: "Purification"

Tahor: This is the state of ritual cleanliness after the prescribed days of quarantine or by act of ritual cleansing, such as immersion in the *mikveh.*

Chapter Twenty-one: "A Day Like No Other"

Brakha: Moses warned the new arrivals to the Promised Land that as their silver and gold multiplied, they would be tempted to forget that all good things came from the Lord's hand. Such forgetfulness could lead to idolatry and pride. To avoid offending the Lord with their pride, the people developed short, specific prayers of thankfulness to offer throughout the day. A devout Jew might wake up and say, "Blessed is he who gives rest to the weary." Later at the breaking of his or her fast, "Blessed is he who gives bread to the hungry."

Ossuary: To conserve space for interred bodies, Jews actually interred their dead twice. The first interment is right after death. The body is prepared by cleansing, the application of spices, and wrapping with a linen shroud before it is laid in a cave-like tomb on a hewn shelf. After a year, the bones are collected and stored in an ossuary—a small, lidded stone box—for the second interment.

Purification: Leviticus 12:1-8 lays out days of quarantine and rituals for purification for new Jewish mothers. It's important to note that the need for purification is not related to sin. Purification rituals are a sort of spiritual hygiene necessary to worship in the temple. A woman is considered ritually "unclean" for a prescribed number of days, thirty-three days after the birth of a son and sixty-six days after the birth of a daughter. At that time, the mother goes to the temple to offer a sacrifice of a young lamb as a burnt offering and a turtledove or pigeon as a purification offering. If she is poor, like Miryam, she is required to bring two turtledoves or two pigeons. The cost of the birds was dropped into a trumpet-shaped collection vase on the temple grounds, and the sacrifices were made collectively.

Ransomed: In Numbers 8:17, Jewish parents were told every firstborn male among the Israelites, both man and beast, belonged to God. Firstborn sons were required to devote their lives to service in the temple. Parents were allowed to "ransom" or "redeem" their sons out of service for the cost of five shekels. Miryam and Yosef show themselves to be devout because of their careful attention to fulfilling the requirements of the Law.

Tallit: The word *"tallit"* is not in the Bible, but the fringe—*tzitzit*—is. God told the Israelites in Numbers 15 to attach blue fringe to each corner of their outer garment, usually woven of heavy wool and shaped like a rectangle. The garment is not the point, the fringe is. The fringe is meant to act as a mnemonic for the commandments.

Chapter Twenty-two: "Wise Men from the East"

Dioptra: This is an astronomical and survey instrument, dating from the 3rd century BC. It was a sighting tube or a rod with a sight at both ends and attached to a tripod sort of stand. They were sometimes fitted with protractors to measure angles. Since the Nabataeans were such accomplished stargazers, I assume they used them.

Nabataea: The Nabataeans were a major power in the Middle East at the time of Christ. Their kingdom covered most of the Sinai Peninsula, and at its height spread across northern Arabia and present-day Jordan to Damascus, Syria. They dominated trade routes from India to the Mediterranean Sea, becoming fabulously wealthy. Their ability to gather and channel water in the desert was the key to their stability as they built dams, cisterns, aqueducts, canals, and piping systems.

I depended on a fascinating book by Dwight Longenecker, *Mystery of the Magi: The Quest to Identify the Three Wise Men*, to craft the Nabataeans as my wise men. If you're curious about why the Magi of these people were most likely the players in Matthew's telling of Yeshua's birth, I can highly recommend this book.

Talent: Used as a standard of measurement in Greece, Rome, and all over the Middle East, the talent is equivalent to 75 pounds.

Chapter Twenty-three: "In Herod's Court"

Nakdimon/Nicodemus: This is a familiar name for Bible readers. Nakdimon went to Yeshua under the cover of darkness to satisfy his curiosity about the itinerate rabbi with extraordinary teaching skills. That conversation is recorded in John 3 and summarizes beautifully God's plan for humankind. After Yeshua's crucifixion, Nakdimon and Yosef of Arimathea claimed Yeshua's body and laid him in a tomb. Many take this act of kindness on Nakdimon's part as an indication that he had become a follower of Yeshua.

Nakdimon was a member of the Pharisees, a group of Jewish leaders who were fastidious about keeping every point of the Law. He was also a member of the Sanhedrin, a ruling body of Jews. The Romans gave Judea a measure of self-rule, and the Sanhedrin ruled on matters concerning Jewish law and religion. Nakdimon was an important man among his peers, so I believe he belonged at the meeting in Herod's court.

Chapter Twenty-four: "Journeys"

Tariq siriyun: The Nabataeans charted routes through the desert that bypassed populated cities and common replenishing spots. Wending through wadis and navigating sandy wastelands allowed them to avoid robbers who preyed on caravans. No one but the Nabataeans knew about the cisterns carved out of rock along these routes. *Tariq siriyun* is Arabic for "secret way," a term I created for the purposes of the story. I believe these hidden sources of water made it possible for the Magi to avoid any of Herod's men who might pursue them.

Glossary of Hebrew Names

Abba	Daddy, Papa
Adonai	description of God or title of respect
Binyamin	Benjamin
Channah	Hannah (Miryam's mother)
Dodah	Aunt
Elisheba	Elizabeth
Gavri'el	Gabriel
Ha'Elyon	God Almighty
HaShem	The Name, used as a substitute for God's name
Hevel	Abel
Ima	Mom, Mama
Kalev	Caleb
Kayafa	Caiaphas
Nakdimon	Nicodemus
Rut	Ruth
Savta	Grandmother
Shim'on	Simon
Yaakov	Jacob
Yeshua	Jesus
Yohanan	John
Yosef	Joseph
Zekharyah	Zechariah

Acknowledgements

I started writing *Out of the Silence* at the beginning of the Covid-19 pandemic of 2020. In those early months, so fraught with uncertainty, the story kept me company in the sweetest way. For several hours each day, I forgot about infection rates and hand sanitizer. Instead, I traveled back in time to the Christmas story. I spent time with Elisheba and Zekharyah, Yosef and Miryam, and a young shepherd and some mysterious Magi. For this gift—for *this* story—I am very grateful, for it is God's story, after all. He made quite an entrance for himself, and it is simply my delight to bring the story to modern readers.

My one and only reader for most of the process was my wonderful husband, Dennis. He worked six days a week during the pandemic as an essential worker but found time and energy to give to the story. He is a careful and observant reader, so the story is better for having his eyes and heart involved. I love you for so many reasons, my love. I only add capable first-reader to a very long list of your attributes. Thanks for making me look better than I deserve.

When Colorado allowed small gatherings in the out of doors this summer, my critique group met in a local park. More eyes made the story even better. My heartfelt gratitude for sharing their amazing skills go to Joyce Anderson, Pamela Larson, Karen McKee, and Lucinda Stein. Because a writer can never have too many friends, I also extend deepest thanks to Sharon Hinck and Rosanne Croft for finding all the embarrassing ways I can muddy up a story. I owe so much to these ladies and the mastery they bring to the craft of writing.

On my last flight before the pandemic slammed into us, I sat beside a couple who gave me just the information and resources I needed to dig deeper into Middle Eastern culture, Kimberly Beine, M.D. and David Beine, Ph.D. Our meeting felt arranged, probably more for me than them. They pointed me toward information I may never have found on my own.

When I needed information about the purification rites of Jewish women, I contacted my dear friend Latayne C. Scott, who referred me to Katie Jane Wadsworth, a most generous and knowledgeable woman. She,

PATTI HILL

in turn, directed me to other resources that help me write about Miryam's purification rituals with some authority. If I got anything wrong, though, that's on me.

You are holding a beautiful book because I have two extremely talented friends who share their skills with me: Rebecca McKenna, the cover designer, and Sharon Souza, the interior designer. Where would I be without these women? Most likely, cranking a mimeograph machine!

My sister, Kathi Keeney, contributed her skilled needlework by reproducing the swaddling cloth Miryam embroiders for Yeshua in the story. I treasure our collaboration on this project and in life. Love you, Sissy!

I thank most heartily my readers, for trusting me to write something worthy of your time. That vote of confidence sweetens my life in the nicest way. A special thanks goes out to all of you who review and tell your friends my books. Such kindness overwhelms me. You are dear.

Bibliography

Amaral, Joe. *Understanding Jesus: Cultural Insights into the Words and Deeds of Christ*. New York, NY: FaithWords, 2011.

Anderson, Christy. "Part 2: Leviticus 18:19 Menstrual Impurity and Keeping the Marriage Bed Holy: What Every Believer Needs to Know but Most Have Never Heard." For It is Written. August 11, 2016. https://foritiswritten.com/blog/part-2-lev-1819-menstrual-impurity-keeping-the-marriage-bed-holy-what-every-believer-needs-to-know-but-most-have-never-heard/?fbclid=IwAR21XZnzsCHH9o2_YNMqQ98C4LqaBu1uJrN9Fqfeh2EM0ILTwJx5KfAh3BA.

Bailey, Kenneth E. *Jesus Through Middle Eastern Eyes: Cultural Studies in the Gospels*. Downers Grove, IL: InterVarsity Press, 2008.

Bible Study Tools. "Circumcision, Temple Service, and Naming of Jesus." https://www.biblestudytools.com/commentaries/the-fourfold-gospel/by-sections/circumcision-temple-service-and-naming-of-jesus.html.

Butler, Trent C. Editor. Entry for 'Synagogue'. Holman Bible Dictionary. 1991. https://www.studylight.org/dictionaries/hbd/s/synagogue.html.

Danby, Herbert. *The Mishnah: Translated from the Hebrew with Introduction and Brief Explanatory Notes*. New York, NY: Oxford University Press Inc., 1933.

Dawn, Tyler. "Metzora in context: Niddah—What the Word Does and Does Not Say." The Ancient Bridge. April 11, 2016. http://theancientbridge.com/2016/04/metzora-in-context-niddah-what-the-word-does-and-does-not-say/

Dye, Dinah. "Torah Gemstones–Ta'zria (She Conceives)–Leviticus 12:1-13:59" Dr. Dinah Dye. April 15, 2013. https://foundationsintorah.com/torah-gemstones-tazria-she-conceives-leviticus-121-1359/

Edersheim, Alfred and Heard, J. *The Life and Times of Jesus the Messiah: Abridged, Illustrated and Including the Scriptures.* Seattle, WA: CreateSpace Independent Publishing Platform, April 8, 2015.

Greenwood, Glenn R. and Scott, Latayne C. *The Shout of the Bridegroom: Understanding Christ's Intimate Love for His Church.* Webb City, MO: Covenant Publishing, 2002.

Hargis, Merilyn. "On the Road: The inns and outs of travel in first-century Palestine." Christianity Today. 1998. https://www.christianitytoday.com/history/issues/issue-59/on-road.html

Hugg, James Ya´akov. "It's About Time: When Was Jesus Born?" Lamb and Lion Ministries. https://christinprophecy.org/articles/when-was-jesus-born/.

Janick, Jules. "Fruits of the Bible." HortScience Volume 42 (August 2007): 1072-1076. https://hort.purdue.edu/newcrop/fruits%20of%20bible.pdf.

The Jewish Agency for Israel. "The Biblical Perspective on Child Development, Part Three." August 28, 2005. http://archive.jewishagency.org/life-cycle/content/24267

Keener, Craig. S. *The IVP Bible Background Commentary.* Second Edition. Downers Grove, IL: InterVarsity Press, 2014.

Longenecker, Dwight. *Mystery of the Magi: The Quest to Identify the Three Wise Men.* Washington, DC: Regenery History, November 6, 2017.

Malina, Bruce J. *The New Testament World: Insights from Cultural Anthropology.* Third Edition. Louisville, Kentucky: Westminster John Knox Press, 2001.

McDowell, Josh and McDowell, PhD, Sean. *Evidence That Demands a Verdict: Life-Changing Truth for a Skeptical World.* Nashville, TN: Thomas Nelson Publishers, 2017.

Mowczko, Marg. "Periods of Purification After Childbirth (Leviticus 12:1-8)." MargMowczko.com. October 18, 2018. https://margmowczko.com/purification-after-giving-birth-leviticus-12/.

Nassau, Scott. "Jewish Practice of Divorce in the Mishnah." The Impact of One Life. https://scottnassau.wordpress.com/.

Olsen, Ted. "The Life and Times of Jesus of Nazareth: Did You Know?" Christianity Today. 1998. https://www.christianitytoday.com/history/issues/issue-59/life-times-of-jesus-of-nazareth-did-you-know.html

Richards, Randolph E. and O'Brien, Brandon J. *Misreading Scripture with Western Eyes: Removing Cultural Blinders to Better Understand the Bible.* Downers Grove, IL: InterVarsity Press, 2012.

Russell, Rusty. "Jerusalem at the time of Christ." Bible History. https://www.bible-history.com/jesus/jesus Jerusalem_at_the_Time_of_Christ.htm

Safrai, Chana. "Jesus' Devout Jewish Parents and Their Child Prodigy." Jerusalem Perspective. Sept. 1, 1993. https://www.jerusalemperspective.com/?s=Jesus%27+Devout+Jewish+Parents

Safrai, Shmuel. "Did Women Go Through a Mikveh (Ritual Immersion Pool) After Childbirth?" Jerusalem Perspective. October 13, 2006. https://www.jerusalemperspective.com/4004/

Safrai, Shmuel. "Pilgrimage in the time of Jesus." Jerusalem Perspective. https://www.jerusalemperspective.com/2392/

Safrai, Shmuel. "The Place of Women in First-century Synagogues." CBE International. January 30, 2002. https://www.cbeinternational.org/resource/article/priscilla-papers-academic-journal/place-women-first-century-synagogues.

Spangler, Ann and Tverberg, Lois. *Sitting at the Feet of Rabbi Jesus: How the Jewishness of Jesus Can Transform Your Faith.* Second Edition. Grand Rapids, MI: Zondervan, 2018.

Spigel, Chad. "First Century Synagogues." Bible Odyssey. https://www.bibleodyssey.org/en/places/related-articles/first-century-synagogues.

Stambaugh, John E. and Balch, David L. *The New Testament in Its Social Environment.* Meeks, Wayne A., ed. Philadelphia, PA: The Westminster Press, 1986.

Stedman, Ray. "The 400 Years Between the Old and New Testaments." Ray Stedman: Authentic Christianity. October 2, 1966. https://www.raystedman.org/bible-overview/adventuring/the-400-years-between-the-old-and-new-testaments

Made in the USA
Monee, IL
28 November 2023

47616839R00132